Edward Kimber, John Adams Library, John Adams

The Peerage of Scotland

a complete view of the several orders of nobility, of that ancient kingdom - their

descents, marriages, issue, and relations

Edward Kimber, John Adams Library, John Adams

The Peerage of Scotland
a complete view of the several orders of nobility, of that ancient kingdom - their descents,
marriages, issue, and relations

ISBN/EAN: 9783337272869

Printed in Europe, USA, Canada, Australia, Japan

Cover: Foto ©Andreas Hilbeck / pixelio.de

More available books at **www.hansebooks.com**

Peerage of SCOTLAND.

A COMPLETE VIEW

Of the feveral ORDERS of NOBILITY, of that ancient KINGDOM; their DESCENTS, MARRIAGES, ISSUE, and RELATIONS; their CREATIONS, ARMORIAL BEARINGS, CRESTS, SUPPORTERS, MOTTOS, CHIEF SEATS, and the High OFFICES they poffefs;

So methodized as to difplay whatever is truly ufeful in this inftructive and amufing Branch of Knowledge.

TOGETHER WITH

A LIST of the SIXTEEN PEERS, from the UNION to 1767.

And an Account of the ATTAINTED PEERS; their Defcents, &c. &c. and the prefent Reprefentatives of thofe unfortunate Families;

Alfo Three ufeful PLATES, teaching the Art of HERALDRY.

By Mr. KIMBER,

Author of the PEERAGE of ENGLAND.

Corrected to April 20, 1767.

LONDON,

Printed for H. WOODFALL; J. FULLER; G. WOODFALL; R. BALDWIN; W. JOHNSTON; B. LAW; T. LONGMAN; T. LOWNDES; J. WILKIE; J. JOHNSON and Co. W. BATHOE; Z. STUART; W. NICOLL; and E. JOHNSON. 1767.

KING GEORGE III.

PRINCE of WALES

KE of YORK

DUKE of GLOUCESTER

G. Lodge sculp.

HERALDRY EXPLAINED.

KING

VISCOUNT

DUKE

MARQUIS

EARL

CINQUEFOILE

NAVAL

TREFOILE

MITRE

A CROWN VALLERY

QUATERFOILE

A CHAPEAU

CELESTIAL CROWN

MURAL

BARON

CROSS RAGULED

CROSS SALTIRE

A CHAPLET

DEGRADED

A CROSS UN3 GRIECES

CROSIER

GUTTE

I. Sedge

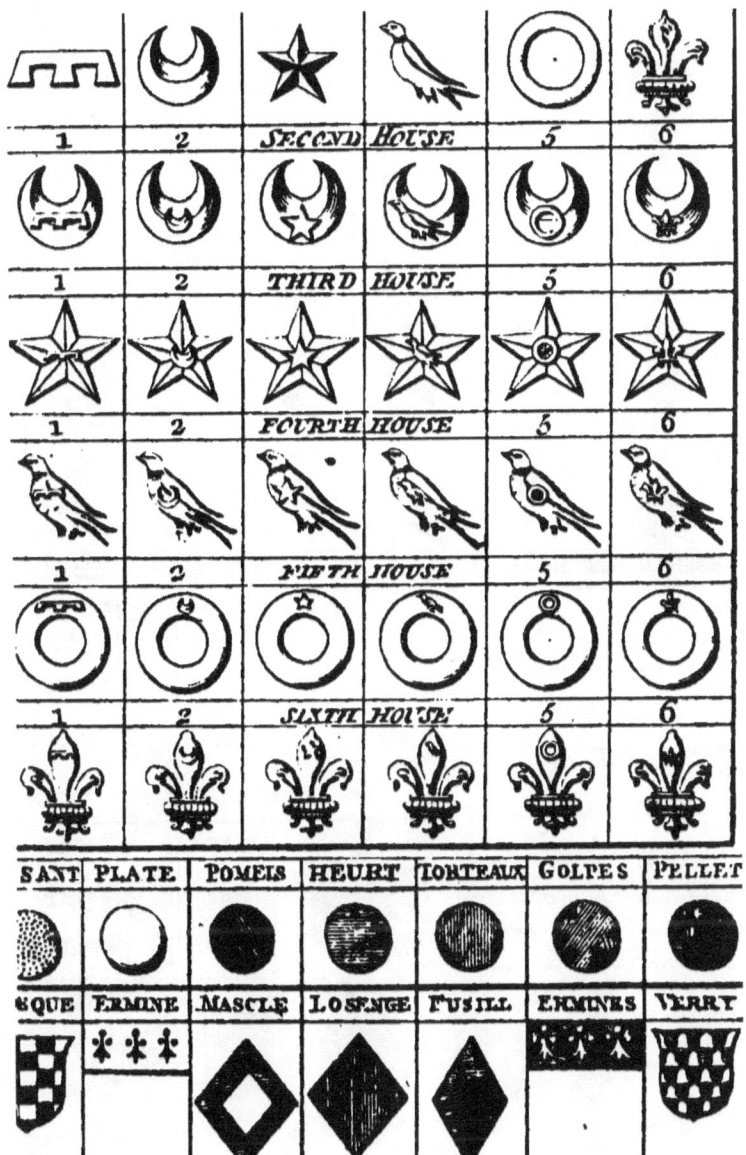

BEND | PALE | CHIEF | A CROSSWAY | PATTEE | A CROSS

PILE | CHEVRON | FESS | FLORY | PATONCE | MOLINE

CANTON | BORDURE | TRESSURE | VOIDED | COUPD | POTENT

PERCHEVRON | FLANCHES | FRET | BOTTONEE | CROS & ITC | CROSLET

A Dexter Chief
B Precise Middle Chief
C Sinister Chief
D Honour Point
E Fesse Point
F Nombril
G Dexter Base
H Exact Middle Base
I Sinister Base

A B C
D
E
F
G H I

QUARTERLY

GOLD · · · OR
WHITE · · · ARGENT
RED · · · GULES
BLUE · · · AZURE
BLACK · · · SABLE
GREEN · · · VERT
PURPLE · · · PURPURE

ESCUTCHEON OF PRETENCE

IMPAIL'D

ESQUIRE

IRONHARTOKEN

A KNIGHT'S

EMBATTLED
RAGULE
INDENTED
DANCETTE

ENGRAILED
INVECTED
WAVY
NEBULEE

J. Lodge sculp.

DUKE of CUMBERLAND

PEERS of SCOTLAND.

IX DUKES.

HAMILTON

THROUGH

BUCCLEUGH

AMO

LENOX

IN LA RO SE UE FLURIE

GORDON

ANIMO·NON·ASTUTIA

J. Lodge sc

6

NE OBLIVIS CARIS

FORWARD
QUEENSBURY

VIX·EA·NOSTRA·VOCO
ARGYLL

FURTH·FORTUNE·AND·FILL·THE·FETTERS
ATHOL

NE·OUBLIE
MONTROSE
III·MARQUIS'S.

PRO·CHRISTO·ET·PATRIA·DULCE·PERICULUM
ROXBURGH

SPARE·NOUGHT
TWEEDALE

SERO·SED·SERIO
LOTHIAN

NUNQUAM·NON·PARATUS
ANNANDALE

J. Lodge sc.

LEAVE BUT & DREAD

CRAUFURD

INDURE FURTH

ERROL

SERVA JUGUM

SUTHERLAND

SANS PEUR

ROTHES

GRIP FAST

MORTON

LOCK SICKER

BUCHAN

IUDGE NOUGHT

GLENCAIRN

OVER FORK OVER

EGLINGTON

GARDE BIEN

J. Lodge sc.

8

CASSILIS

MORAY

HOME

WIGTON

STRATHMORE

ABERCORN

KELLY

HADDINGTON

GALLOWAY

DEO JUVANTE

LAUDERDALE

LOUDON

KINNOUL

DUMFRIES

ELGIN

DALHOUSIE

TRAQUAIR

J. Lodge sc.

FINLATER

LEVEN

DYSERT

SELKIRK

NORTHESK

BALCARRAS

NEWBURGH

ABOYN

J. Lodge s.

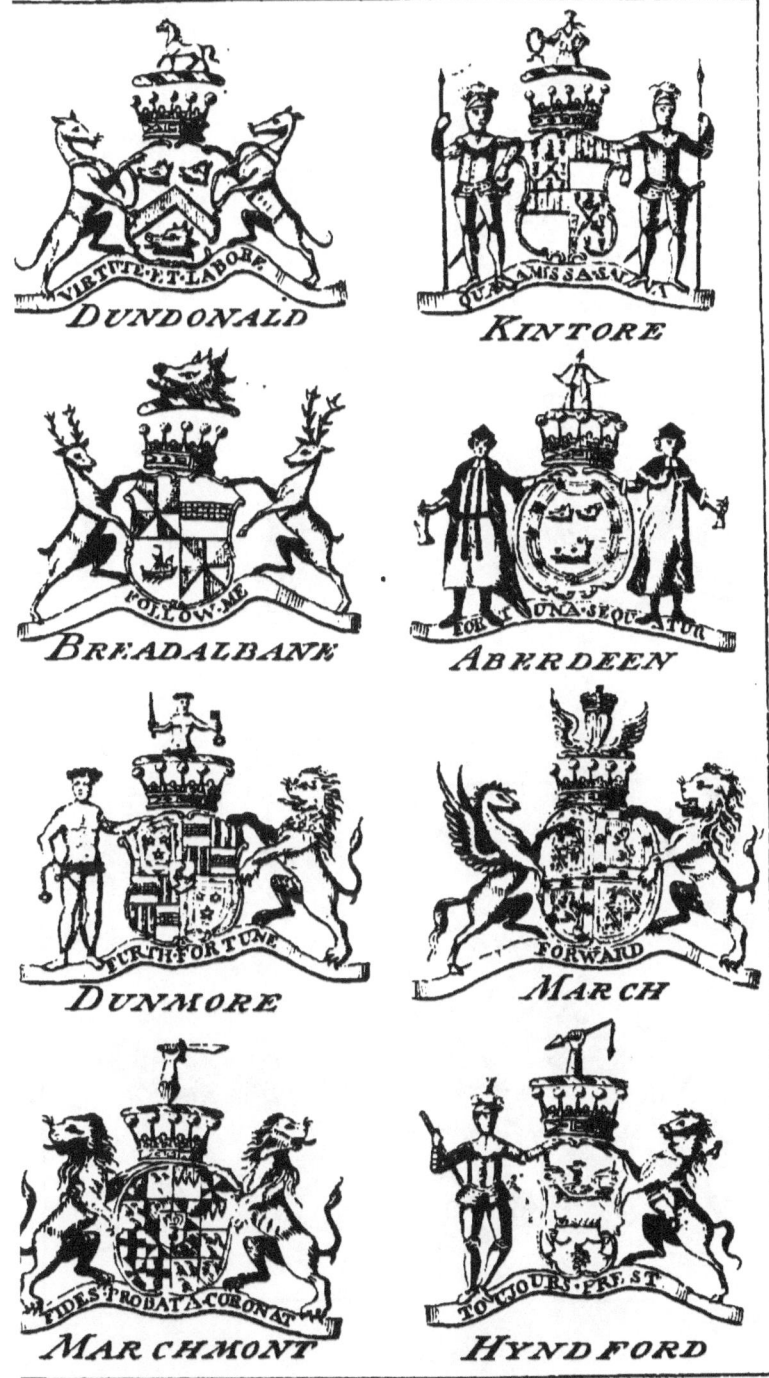

DUNDONALD

KINTORE

BREADALBANE

ABERDEEN

DUNMORE

MARCH

MARCHMONT

HYNDFORD

J. Lodge sc.

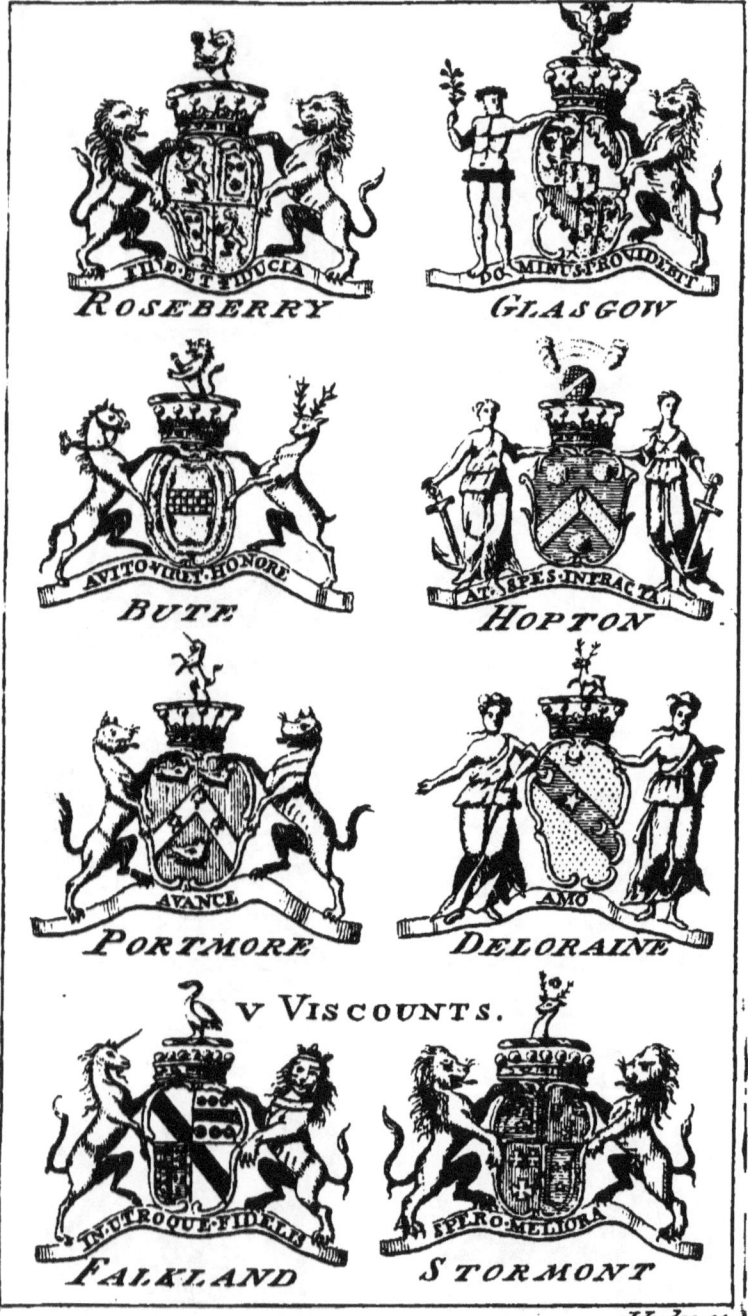

ROSEBERRY

GLASGOW

BUTE

HOPTON

PORTMORE

DELORAINE

v Viscounts.

FALKLAND

STORMONT

J. Lodge sc.

ARBUTHNOT

IRWIN

DUMBLAIN

XXIX BARONS.

FORBES

SALTON

GRAY

CATHCART

SOMERVILLE

J. Lodge sc.

BORTHWICK

MORDINGTON

SEMPILL

ELPHINSTON

TORPICHEN

LINDORES

BLANTYRE

CRANSTOUN

J. Lodge sc.

16

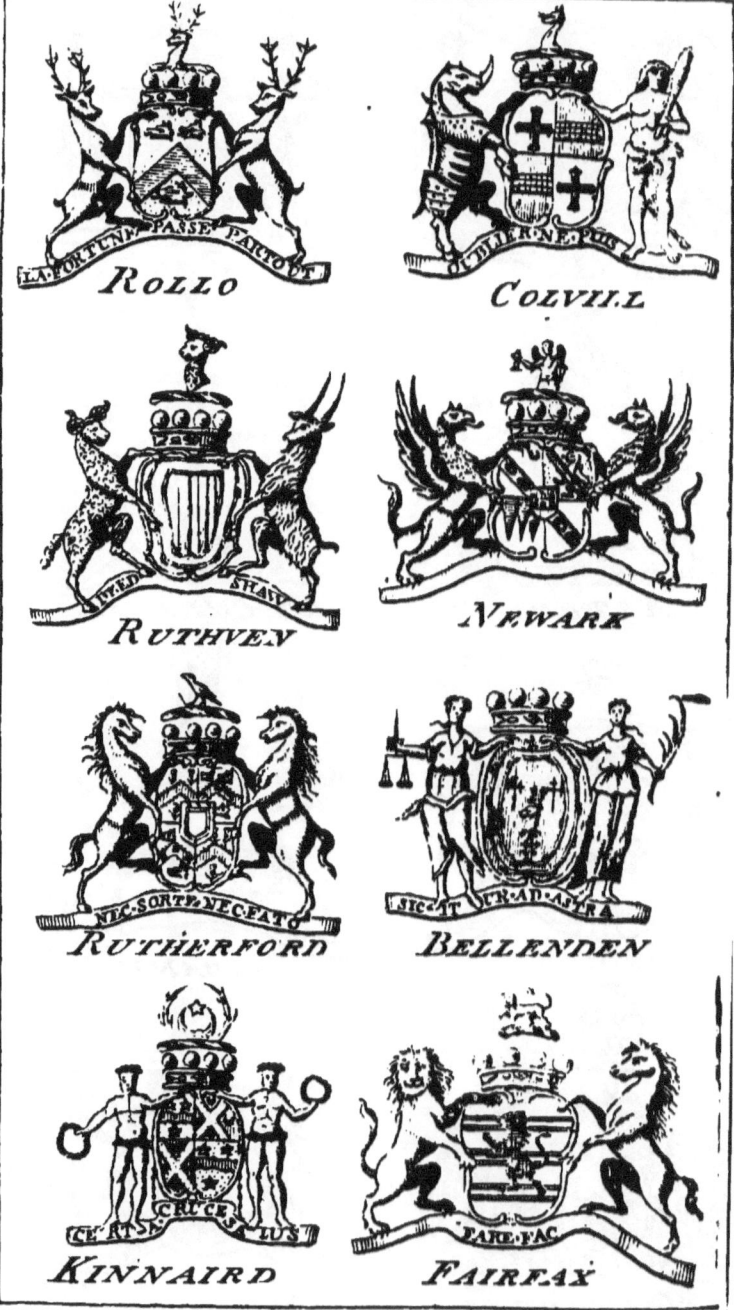

ROLLO   COLVILL

RUTHVEN   NEWARK

RUTHERFORD   BELLENDEN

KINNAIRD   FAIRFAX

DUKES.

DUKE of HAMILTON.

THE moſt high, puiſſant, and moſt noble
Prince JAMES-GEORGE HAMILTON,
Duke of HAMILTON, CHATELHERAULT and
BRANDON, Marquis of Hamilton, Douglas, and
Cliddeſdale, Earl of Arran, Angus, and Lanerk,
Lord Machanſhire, Polmont, and Aberbrothick,
Baron of Dutton, and hereditary keeper of
Holyrood-houſe, was born on Feb. 18, 1755,
and ſucceeded the late Duke, James, his fa-
ther, Jan. 17, 1758.

James, the late Duke, married Elizabeth,
2d daughter of John Gunning, Eſq; by Bridget
his wife, daughter of John, Viſcount Mayo, of
Ireland, by whom he had iſſue, beſide the preſent Duke, Lord Douglas, and Lady Elizabeth.

This illuſtrious family is deſcended of the
Earls of Leiceſter in England, and the firſt on
record was Sir William de Hambleden, or
Hambleton, third ſon of Robert, third Earl of
Leiceſter, deſcended of the Earl of Mellent in
Normandy, who came into England with William the Conqueror. Sir William above, had
his ſirname from the Manor of Hambleton, in
Bucks, and came into Scotland in the reign
of Alexander II. in the year 1215. He married Mary, daughter and heir of Gilbert Earl
of Strathern, by whom he had a ſon Sir Gil-

B   bert,

bert. from whom all the Hamiltons in Scotland are defcended.

Creations.] Summoned to parliament, in 1374, 4 Robert II. Created Earl of Arran, in the county of Bute, Auguft 10, 1503, 15 James IV. Duke of Chatelherault in Poictou in France, 1552, by Henry II. of France ; Marquis of Hamilton, in the county of Lanerk, April 19, 1599 ; Baron of Aberbrothick, June 1606 ; Marquis of Douglas, and Earl of Angus (to which titles his Grace fucceeded upon the death of the late Duke of Douglas) June 17, 1633, and April 18, 1703 ; Earl of the county of Lanerk, Lord Machanfhire and Polmont, March 31, 1639 ; Duke of Hamilton, April 12, 1643 ; and Baron of Dutton in Chefhire, and Duke of Brandon in Suffolk, September 10, 1711, 9 Anne.

Arms.] Quarterly, 1ft and 4th, ruby, three cinquefoils, pierced, ermine, for Hamilton ; 2d and 3d, pearl ; a fhip with its fails furled up, diamond, for the earldom of Arran. The fecond grand quarter is pearl, an human heart imperially crowned, proper, on a chief fapphire, three mullets of the field for Douglas, 3d grand quarter as the 2d, 4th as the 1ft.

Creft.] In a ducal coronet, topaz, an oak fructed and penetrated, tranfverfely, in the main ftem by a frame-faw, proper.

Supporters.] Two antelopes, pearl, their horns, ducal collars, chains and hoofs, topaz.

Motto.] *Through.*

Chief Seats.] At Hamilton in the county of Lanerk, and Kennel in the county of Stirling.

DUKE

DUKE of BUCCLEUGH.

HENRY SCOT, Duke of BUCCLEUGH, Earl of Dalkeith, Baron Scot of Buccleugh, and Efkdale; Baron Scot, of Tindale in Northumberland, and Earl of Doncafter, in Yorkfhire, was born in 1746, fucceeded his father, as Earl of Dalkeith, in 1750, and his grandfather, as Duke of Buccleugh, in 1751. His Grace has two fifters, Ladies Caroline and Frances.

Francis, 2d Earl of Buccleugh had two daughters, Lady Margaret, wife of Walter Scot, of Highchefter, who on marrying the Countefs, was created Earl of Tarras for life; but fhe died without iffue; and Lady Anne, who in 1665, was married to James, the unfortunate Duke of Monmouth, who thereupon took the firname of Scot, and they were created Duke and Duchefs of Buccleugh, to them and their heirs general. He was, as is well known, beheaded on Tower-hill, on July 15, 1685. James Earl of Dalkeith, his 2d fon, left iffue Francis, his fucceffor, who fucceeded his grandmother as Duke of Buccleugh in 1732, and in 1743, was reftored to the titles of Earl of Doncafter, and Baron Scot of Tindale, his grandfather's attainder being reverfed by act of parliament. He married Lady Jane Douglas, daughter of James, Duke of Queenfberry; by whom he had feveral children, one only of whom furvived him, viz. Francis late Earl of Dalkeith, father of the prefent Duke. He married Lady Caroline Campbell, eldeft daughter of John, Duke of Argyle, (who married, 2dly, the Right Honourable Charles

Townf-

Townshend, (brother of the Vifcount Townf-
hend) by whom he had iffue his prefent Grace
and other children, of whom only the before-
mentioned are living.

This family is of great antiquity in Scotland ; Sir Richard Scot, who fwore fealty to
Edward I. of England, as Baron of Laneik-
fhire, married the heirefs of Murdifton in Cliddefdale, and with her obtained that Barony.
Sir Michael his fon, loft his life in the unfortunate battle of Durham, in 1346, from whom
the fucceffive heroes and patriots of the family,
defcended.

Creations.] Lord Scot of Buccleugh, March
16, 1605, Earl of Buccleugh, March 16, 1618,
Baron of Efkdale, Earl of Dalkeith, and Duke
of Buccleugh, April 20, 1673.

Arms.] Quarterly, 1ft and 4th, the royal
arms of Britain, with a battoon finifter, argent ;
2d and 3d, or, on a bend; azure, a ftar of fix
points, between two crefcents of the field, gules.

Creft.] A ftag paffant, proper.

Supporters.] Two maidens, richly attired
in antique habits ; their under robes fapphire,
and the uppermoft emerald, and on their heads
a plume of three feathers, pearl.

Motto.] Amo.

Chief Seats.] At Dalkeith, and Eaft-park
near Edinburgh, at Melrofs in Roxburghfhire,
Hall-place in Berkfhire, and Berkeley-fquare,
London.

DUKE of LENNOX.

See this family under the title of Duke of
Richmond, in my Englifh Peerage.

DUKE

DUKE of GORDON.

ALEXANDER GORDON, Duke of GORDON, Marquis and Earl of Huntley, Earl of Enzie, and Baron Gordon of Strathbogie, succeeded his father Cosmo·George, the late Duke, in 1752. His Grace has two brothers, Lords William and George, and three sisters, Ladies Susan, Anne, and Catherine; an uncle, Lord Adam Gordon, member for Aberdeenshire, and colonel of the 66th regiment of foot; and several aunts, particularly the Countess of Aberdeen, and Mrs. Charteris of Ampsfield. The Duchess his mother, who was Lady Katharine, daughter of William, Earl of Aberdeen, married 2dly, Colonel Morris.

This antient and illustrious family took their firname. from the barony. of Gordon, in the county of Berwick, which was. granted by Malcolm Canmore to a valiant Knight. Richardus de Gordon, that Knight's grandson, flourished in the reigns of Malcolm IV, and William the Lion, in 1160 and 1165. In the reign of Robert Bruce, Sir Adam de Gordon had from that Prince, the Lordship of Strathbogie, in Aberdeenshire, upon which he removed thither from Berwickshire, and gave those lands and lordships the name of Huntley. He was slain at the battle of Halidon Hill, in 1333. His son, Sir Alexander, lost his life at the battle of Durham, in 1346, and his grandson, Sir John, was killed in 1388, at the battle of Otterburn.

Creations.] Lord Gordon of Strathbogie, in the county of Aberdeen, June 16, 1376; Earl

of

of Huntley, in the county of Berwick, in 1449; Marquis of Huntley, April 17, 1599, by James VI. and Duke of Gordon, in the county of Bamff, 1 Nov. 1684, by Charles II.

Arms.] Quarterly, first sapphire, three boars heads erased, topaz, for Gordon; second, topaz, three lions heads erased, ruby, for Badenoch; third topaz, three crescents, within a double treffure ruby, for Seton; fourth sapphire, three cinquefoils, pearl, for Frazer.

Creft.] In a Marquis's coronet topaz, a ftag's head guardant, proper.

Supporters.] On the dexter fide, a greyhound pearl, gorged with a collar ruby, and three buckles topaz. On the finifter, a fenator of the college of Juftice, proper.

Motto.] *Animo non aftutia.* And *Bydand,* i. e. abiding, or lafting.

Chief Seats.] At Strathbogie in the county of Aberdeen, and at Gordon-caftle in Bamff-fhire.

DUKE of QUEENSBERRY.

CHARLES DOUGLAS, Duke of QUEENSBERRY and DOVER, Marquis of Queenfberry, Dumfries, and Beverly, Earl of Queenfberry, Drumlanrig, Sanquhar, and Solway; Vifcount Drumlanrig, Nith, Torthorald, Tibbers, and Rofs; Baron Douglas of Hawick, Kilmount, Middleby, Tibbers, Dornick, and Rippon, and a Lord of the Privy council, fucceeded his father, James, the 2d Duke, in 1711, and in 1719, married Lady Katherine, daughter of Henry Hyde, Earl of Clarendon and Rochefter, by whom he had iffue two fons and a daughter, all

all deceafed. Henry Earl of Drumlanrig, their eldeft fon, married Lady Elizabeth, daughter of John Earl of Hopetoun, but was accidentally fhot by his own piftol on Oct. 20, 1754, aged 34; Charles, Earl of Drumlanrig, the 2d, died in 1756, aged 30, and Lady Catherine, the daughter, died young.

Of this noble family there have been eight Lords, three Earls, and three Dukes. Sir William Douglas, the firft Lord Drumlanrig, fignalized himfelf in the wars againft the Englifh. In the year 1411, he retook the town of Roxburgh, then in their poffeffion. In 1412, he was fent ambaffador to England, to folicit the releafe of King James I. then prifoner in that realm; from whom he obtained a charter, all written with the King's own hand on vellum, confirming to him and his heirs the feveral baronies of Drumlanrig, Hawick in Tiviotdale, and Selkirk, Nov. 30, 1412.

Creations.] Lord Douglas of Hawick and Tibbers, and Vifcount Drumlanrig, April 1, 1628; Earl of Queenfberry, June 13, 1633; Lord Douglas of Kilmount, Middleby, and Dornick, Vifcount Nith, Drumlanrig, Torthorald, and Rofs; Earl of Drumlanrig and Sanquhar, and Marquis of Queenfberry, 11 Feb. 1682; Marquis of Dumfries and Duke of Queenfberry, 5 Feb. 1684; Vifcount Tibbers, and Earl of Solway, in 1707.

For the Englifh Creations, See my Peerage of England.

Arms, Creft, Supporters, Motto, and Chief Seats, See ditto.

DUKE

DUKE of ARGYLL.

JOHN CAMPBELL, Duke, Marquis, and Earl of ARGYLL; Marquis of Kintire and Lorn; Earl of Campbell and Cowal; Viscount Lochow and Glenilla; Lord of Inverara, Mull, Morven, and Tyrie, Lord Lieutenant of Argyllshire, Admiral of the Western Isles, hereditary master of the King's houshold, and hereditable keeper of Dunstaffnage and Carrick, general of the forces, and colonel of the regiment of Scots Greys, governor of Milford Haven and Limerick, a Knight of the Thistle, a Lord of the Privy-council, and one of the sixteen peers for Scotland, was son of John Campbell of Mammore, Esq: 2d son of Archibald ninth Earl of Argyll, and succeeded Archibald, the late Duke, April 15, 1761. In 1720, he married the Honourable Miss Bellenden, daughter of John Lord Bellenden, by whom he has issue, 1. John, Marquis of Lorn, and Baron Sundridge of Coombank in England, a lieutenant general, and colonel of the first regiment of foot, who, in 1759, married the Duchess Dowager of Hamilton, by whom he has three children. 2. Henry, who was killed at La Feldt. 3. Lord William, who in 1763, married Miss Izard, of Charles-Town, South Carolina, is member for Argyllshire, a captain in the navy, and governor of Nova Scotia. 4. Lord Frederick, member for Renfrew, and a barrister at law. 5. Lady Mary, third wife of Charles Bruce, Earl of Aylesbury, and now of the Right Honourable Henry Seymour Conway, by whom she has two daughters.

Camden

Camden derives this family from the Kings of Argyll in the 6th century ; but without re-curring to antient records, every one knows it has produced a long feries of heroes and pa-triots, firm in the caufe of liberty and their country ; and the two laft Dukes, the renowned John, and the great and learned Archibald, are too frefh in our memories to need any encomiums here.

Creations.] Summoned to parliament, as Lord Campbell, in 1445, 8 James II. and by the fame King, in 1457, created Earl of the county of Argyll ; Marquis of the fame, Nov. 15, 1641, 17 Charles I. Duke of Argyll, Marquis of Kintire and Lorn, Earl of Campbell and Cowal, Vif-count Lochow and Glenilla, Lord of Inverara, Mull, Morven, and Tyrie, the 23d of June, 1701, 13 William III.

Arms.] Quarterly, 1ft and 4th, girony, of eight pieces, topaz and diamond, for Campbell. 2d and 3d, pearl, a lymphad, or old-fafhioned fhip, with one maft, clofe fa ls, and oars in action, diamond, with flag and penants flying, ruby, for the lordfhip of Lorn.

Creft.] On a wreath a boar's head, couped, proper, topaz.

Supporters.] Two lions guardant, ruby.

Motto.] *Ne oblivifcaris.* The late Duke John's motto was, *Vix ea noftra voco.*

Note, That behind the arms are two ho-nourable badges in faltire, which his Grace's anceftors have borne a long time, as great maf-ters of the King's houfhold, and Jufticiaries of Scotland. The firft is a battoon topaz, femee of thiftles, emerald, enfigned with an imperial crown, proper ; and thereon the creft of Scot-

land,

land, which is a lion fejant, guardant, ruby,
crowned with the like crown he fits on ; having
in his dexter paw a fword, proper, the pommel
and hilt topaz ; and in the finifter, a fcepter of
the laft.   The other badge is a fword, as that
in the lion's paw.

Chief Seats.] At Inverara in Argyllfhire ;
Campbleton in Kintire, and at Rofeneath in the
county of Dunbarton ; Soho Square, London.

DUKE of ATHOL.

JOHN MURRAY, Duke, Marquis, and Earl
of ATHOL, Marquis and Earl of Tullibardin,
Vifcount Glenalmond, and Lord Murray, one
of the fixteen Peers for Scotland, was the eldeft
fon of Lord George Murray, 4th fon of John
firft Duke of Athol, who was attainted in 1746
for his concern in the rebellion of the preceding year ; but that attainder only operating
againft himfelf, upon the death of his uncle the
late Duke, James, on Jan. 8, 1764, he fucceeded to his honours, and having married his coufin, Lady Charlotte, who upon the deceafe of
her father the late Duke, became Baronefs
Strange, and Lady of the Ifle of Man, by
that marriage, the heirs male and of line of
this illuftrious family are conjoined.   They
have iffue, 1. John Marquis of Tullibardin,
born June 30, 1755 ; Lords James, George,
and William ; Ladies Charlotte, Emilia, and
Rachael.   His Grace has one fifter, Amelia,
wife of the late mafter of Sinclair, two bro-
-thers, James and George, and three uncles ;
Lord John Murray, colonel of the Highland
regiment, and a lieutenant general ; Lords Edward

ward and Frederick, a captain in the navy;
alfo an aunt, Lady Defkford.

The late Duke married Mrs. Jane Lanoy,
widow of James Lanoy, of Hammerfmith, in
Middlefex, Efq; and fifter of Sir John Frederick, of Weftminfter, Bart. by whom he had a
fon in 1735, who died in the fame year, and
two daughters; Lady Jane, wife of John Earl
of Crawford, who died without iffue, and the
prefent Duchefs.

His Grace became an Englifh peer by the
title of Lord Strange; as alfo Lord of the Ifle
of Man, on the deceafe of James Stanley, the
tenth Earl of Derby, who died, without iffue,
on the 1ft of February, 1735-6; which digni-
ties he derived from his grandmother, Amelia
Sophia, daughter of James Earl of Derby, beheaded in 1651.

This noble family of Murray is of antient
fettlement in the county of Perth, and are defcended from Sir Malcolm Murray; whofe fon
Sir William Murray, in the year 1282, marrying Adda Moravia, daughter of Malyfs, fenef-
chal of Strathern, thereby became poffeffed of
the barony of Tullibairdin, as appears by a
charter dated in that year.

Creations.] Lord Murray of Tullibairdin,
15 April, 1604, 3 James VI. Earl and Marquis
of Athol, 17 Feb. 1675, 28 Charles II. Vifcount Glenalmond and Earl of Tullibairdin,
27 July, 1697, 9 William III. Marquis of Tullibairdin and Duke of Athol, 30 April, 1703,
2 Anne.

Arms.] Quarterly, firft fapphire, three mullets pearl, within a double treffure flowered and
counterflowered, with fleurs-de-lis, topaz, for

Murray.

Murray. 2d quarter is quarterly, 1ſt and 4th, topaz, a feſſe cheque, pearl and ſapphire, for Stewart. 2d and 3d, pally of ſix, topaz, and diamond, for the title of Athol. In the 3d, ruby, three legs armed proper, corjoined in the center at the upper part of the thighs, flexed in a triangle, garniſhed and ſpurred topaz, for Lord of the Iſle of Man. The 4th as the 1ſt.

Creſt.] On a wreath a demi ſavage, wreathed about the head and waiſt, emerald, holding in his right hand a dagger proper, the pommel and hilt topaz, and in his left a key of the latter.

Supporters.] On the dexter ſide a lion ruby, gorged with a collar ſapphire, and thereon three mullets pearl, being the ſupporter of Tulli-bairdin. On the ſiniſter, a ſavage wreathed about the head and waiſt, as the creſt, his feet in fetters of iron, and the chain over his right arm.

Motto.] *Furth fortune, and fill the fetters.*

Chief Seats.] At Dunkell, near the river Tay; at Blair-caſtle in Athol; at the caſtle of Tullibairdin, in Perthſhire; at Caſtleton in the Iſle of Man; and Groſvenor-ſquare, London.

DUKE of MONTROSE.

WILLIAM GRAHAM, Duke, Marquis, and Earl of MONTROSE, Marquis and Baron of Graham, Dundaff, Kincarn, Mindoc, and Ki-naber, Chancellor of the Univerſity of Glaſgow, and Governor of the royal bank of Scotland, was third ſon of James, fourth Marquis, and firſt Duke of Montroſe; and his two elder bro-thers, James Marquis of Graham, and David,

(who

(who was created an Englifh peer, by the title of Earl and Baron Graham, which fee in my Englifh Peerage) dying before their father, on the demife of his father, the faid late Duke, in 1741, he fucceeded him as Duke of Montrofe, &c. and in 1742, married Lady Lucy, daughter of John Duke of Rutland, by whom he has one fon and heir, born Feb. 8, 1755, ———, Marquis of Graham, and a daughter, Lady Lucy, born in July, 1751.

According to the Scots writers, this great and noble family is defcended from the renowned Greme, who, in the year 404, was general of King Fergus IId's army; and in 420, made a breach upon the trench or wall, which the emperor Severus had built between the rivers Forth and Clyde, as the utmoft bounds of the Roman empire, to keep out the Scots from molefting them in their poffeffions; and the faid trench has ever fince been called Greme's Dyke; and during the minority of Eugene II. the fon of Fergus II. he was governor of Scotland, and married a lady of the royal houfe of Denmark. In the year 1125, William de Greme, or Grame, was one of the witneffes to the foundation of the abbey of Holyrood-houfe, by King David I. and Sir David Graham, obtaining from William the Lion, a grant of feveral lands near Glafgow, and in the county of Kincardin, was therein fucceeded by Sir David his fon, who had feveral other grants of lands in Stirlingfhire, &c.

See more of this family in my Englifh Peerage, under the title *Earl Graham.*

Creations.] Earl of Montrofe, March 5, 1504, 5 James IV. Marquis, May 16, 1644;

20 Charles I. Marquis of Graham and Duke of Montrofe, April 4, 1707, 6 Anne. For the Englifh creations, See my Englifh Peerage, as above.

Arms.] Quarterly, 1ft and 4th, topaz, on a chief diamond, three efcallop-fhells of the firft, for the name of Graham. 2d and 3d, pearl, three rofes ruby, barbed and feeded proper, for the title of Montrofe.

Creft.] On a wreath an eagle topaz, talloning a ftork proper.

Supporters.] Two ftorks of the latter.

Motto.] *Ne oublié.*

Chief Seats.] At Glafgow, in the county of Lanerk ; at Kincarn, in the county of Perth ; at Myndock-caftle, in the county of Lennox ; and Upper Grofvenor-ftreet, London.

DUKE of ROXBURGH.

JOHN KER, Duke of ROXBURGH, Marquis of Beaumont and Cefsford, Earl of Roxburgh and Kelfo, Vifcount Broxmouth, Baron Ker, of Roxburgh, Cefsford and Caverton, and Earl and Baron Ker, of Wakefield in Yorkfhire, fucceeded his father Robert, the late Duke, on Aug. 20, 1755. His Grace has a brother Lord Robert, born in 1745, and a fifter, Lady Effex.

Of this antient family, which is faid to come from Normandy, was Ker of Ker-hall, in the county of Lancafter, from whom defcended two brothers, Ralph and Robert, in the county of Roxburgh, who made the two branches of Cefsford and Ferniherft, about the time of King David II. in 1340 ; and Robert, having obtained from the King the lands of Oultoburn,

lying

lying near the water of Beaumont, was anceſtor to the houſe of Ceſsford, of whom we are treating. The other branch of Ferniherſt is the Marquis of Lothian.

Creations.] Lord Ker of Ceſsford in 1603 ; Earl of Roxburgh and Kelſo, Sept. 19, 1616, by James VI. and Marquis of Beaumont and Ceſsford, and Duke of Roxburgh, April 27, 1707.

Arms.] Quarterly, 1ſt and 4th, emerald, a chevron between three unicorns heads, eraſed pearl, horned and maned topaz ; as many mullets diamond, for the name Ker. 2d and 3d, ruby, three macles topaz, for Weepont, as being deſcended from that family.

Creſt.] On a wreath an unicorn's head, as thoſe in the coat.

Supporters.] Two ſavages wreathed about the waiſt with laurel, each holding a battoon over his ſhoulder, all proper.

Motto.] *Pro Chriſto & Patria dulce periculum.*

Chief Seats.] At Floor, in Roxburghſhire ; at the Friers in the ſame county ; at Broxmouth, in the county of Haddington ; and at Bray in the county of Bucks. Hanover-ſquare London.

MARQUISSES.

MARQUIS of TWEEDALE.

THE moſt Honourable GEORGE HAY, Marquis and Earl of TWEEDALE, Viſcount Peebles, and Lord Yeſter, ſucceeded his father, John, the late Marquis, on Dec. 9, 1762. His Lordſhip is unmarried, and has two ſiſters, Ladies Grace and Catherine.

William de la Haya, anceſtor of this noble family, ſettled in Lothian, about the reigns of David I. and Malcolm IV. In the reign of William the Lion 1200, John, the ſon of William Hay, marrying the heir of Robert de Lyne, with her had the barony of Lockhart; and from him deſcended Sir Gilbert Hay, who was highly favoured by King Robert Bruce, and marrying Mary, daughter and coheir of Simon Fraſer, Lord of Oliver-caſtle, with her obtained a fair eſtate, in the county of Tweedale, and thereupon the family has continued to quarter the arms of Fraſer.

Creations.] Earl of Tweedale, in the county of Peebles, Dec. 1, 1646, 22 Charles I. and Marquis Dec. 26, 1694, 7 William III.

Arms.] Quarterly, 1ſt and 4th, ſapphire, three cinquefoils pearl, for Fraſer; 2d and 3d, ruby, three bars ermine, for Gifford of Yeſter, and over all, by way of ſurtout, pearl, three eſcutcheons ruby, being the paternal coat of Hay.

Creſt.]

Crest.] On a wreath a Stag's head, erased, horned topaz.

Supporters.] Two bucks proper, attired and unguled topaz, each having a collar sapphire, charged with three cinquefoils, as in the coat.

Motto.] *Spare nought.*

Chief Seats.] At Pinkie, in Mid-Lothian; at Yester, in East-Lothian; and in Grosvenor-street, London.

MARQUIS of LOTHIAN.

WILLIAM-HENRY KER, Marquis and Earl of LOTHIAN, Earl of Ancram, Baron Ker of Newbottle and Jedburgh, and Knight of the antient order-of the Thistle, succeeded his father William, the last Marquis, on March 1, 1721-2, and married first, Margaret, daughter of Sir Thomas Nicholson, Bart. (who died Sept. 27, 1759) and by her had issue, 1. William, Earl of Ancram, colonel of a regiment of dragoons, and a lieutenant-general. He married Lady Louisa, only daughter of Robert, Earl of Holdernesse, by whom he has a son, William, Lord Newbottle, born in 1737, who married in 1762, Miss Fortescue, niece of the Earl of Mornington, of the kingdom of Ireland, by whom he has a son, William, master of Newbottle; also two daughters, Lady Louisa, wife of Lord George Lennox, and Lady Wilhelmina Carolina. 2. Lord Robert, a captain in the army, slain at Culloden, April 16, 1746.

He married 2dly Jane, daughter of his cousin, Lord Charles Ker, of Cramond.

This

This family has the fame original with the Dukes of Roxburgh.

Creations.] Baron of Newbottle Oct. 15, 1587, Baron of Jedburgh, Feb. 1621, Earl of Lothian, 10 July 1606; and Earl of Ancram, all by James VI. Marquis of Lothian, June 23, 1701, by William III.

Arms.] Quarterly, 1st and 4th fapphire, the fun in its fplendour, as a coat of augmentation for Lothian; 2d and 3d ruby; on a chevron pearl, three mullets of the field for the name of Ker.

· *Creft.*] On a wreath, the fun, as in the coat.

Supporters.] On the dexter fide, an angel apparelled, fapphire, the hair and wings, topaz; on the finifter, a unicorn, pearl, horned, mained, and unguled, topaz.

Motto.] *Sero fed ferio.*

Chief Seats.] At Newbottle, in Edinburgh-fhire, and Monteviot Lodge, in the fhire of Roxburgh.

MARQUIS of ANNANDALE.

GEORGE JOHNSTON, Marquis and Earl of ANNANDALE, Vifcount Annan, and Lord John-fton, of Lockwood, Lochmaban and Moffat, in Annandale, and hereditary Keeper of Loch-maban, fucceeded his brother, James, the late Marquis, in 1745; but is a lunatic; fo declared by commiffioners, in the fame year.

The Johnftons are an antient and warlike family, and derive their firname from the barony of Johnfton in Annandale.

Creations.] Lord Johnfton, June 20, 1633; Earl of Hartfield, in 1643, by King Charles I. Earl of Annandale, in the county of Dumfries,

in

in 1661, by King Charles II. and Marquis of Annandale, June 24, 1701, by King William III.

Arms.] Quarterly, 1ft and 4th, pearl, a faltire diamond, on a chief ruby three cufhions topaz. 2d and 3d, topaz, an anchor in pale ruby.

Creft.] On a wreath a fpur, erect topaz, winged pearl.

Supporters.] On the dexter fide a lion pearl, armed and langued fapphire, and imperially crowned topaz. On the finifter, a horfe pearl, furnifhed ruby.

Motto.] *Nunquam non paratus.*

Chief Seat.] At Lockwood, in Annandale.

EARLS

E A R L S.

EARL of CRAWFORD and LINDSAY.

THE right Honourable·GEORGE LIND-SAY CRAWFORD, Earl of CRAWFORD and LINDSAY, Vifcount and Baron Garnock, Baron Crawford and Spinzy, fucceeded his father Patrick, Vifcount Garnock, in 1737, and his coufin John Lindfay, the brave Earl of Crawford, as 18th Earl of Crawford and fifth Earl of Lindfay, in 1749, as being defcended of Patrick, fecond fon of John, firft Earl of Lindfay, and 14th Earl of Crawford. He married on Dec. 26, 1755, Jane, Daughter of Robert Hamilton, of Bourtree Hill, Efq; by whom he has three fons and two daughters : George, Lord Lindfay, born on Feb. 4, 1758, Robert and Bute; Ladies Jane and Mary.

Of the antient and honourable family of Lindfay, which came firft to Scotland with Edgar Atheling, and Margaret his fifter, Queen to King Malcolm Canmore, there were two principal branches, the one of Crawford, and the other of Byres, in the county of Haddington. In the reign of David I. about the year 1140, William de Lindfay was a perfon of great note, as was David his fucceffor, who lived in the time of William the Lion, about 1200; and he marrying the daughter of John de Crawford, with her got the barony of that name,

name, in which he was fucceeded by his fon David, who lived in the time of Alexander II. and had two fons, David his fucceffor, and John, who was chamberlain of Scotland to Alexander III.

Creations.] Earl of Crawford in the county of Lanerk, 1399, by Robert III. Baron of Spinzy, in 1590, by James VI. Earl of Lindfay, in the county aforefaid, by Charles I. in 1633; Baron and Vifcount Garnock, April 10, 1703, by Queen Anne.

Arms.] Quarterly, 1ft and 4th, ruby, a feffe cheque pearl and fapphire. 2d and 3d, topaz, a lion rampant ruby, fuppreffed with a ribband diamond.

Creft.] On a wreath an oftrich proper, holding in its beak a key topaz.

Supporters.] Two lions fejant ruby.

Motto.] *Indure furth.*

Arms of the Vifcount Garnock.] Quarterly, 1ft and 4th, ruby, a feffe ermine; 2d and 3d, fapphire, a chevron between three croffes patee topaz.

Creft.] On a wreath an ermine couchant proper.

Supporters.] Two greyhounds of the laft.

Motto.] *Sine labe nota.*

Chief Seats.] At Struthers, in the county of Fife; at Kilbirny, in Airfhire.

EARL of ERROL.

JAMES HAY, Earl of ERROL, Baron Hay, of Stanes, and hereditary high Conftable of Scotland, was the eldeft fon of William, late Earl of Kilmarnock, (beheaded for high treafon, in 1746) and then called Lord Boyd, by

his

his wife Lady Anne, daughter of James, Earl
of Linlithgow and Callendar, by his wife the
Lady Margaret, youngeſt ſiſter of Charles, 14th
Earl of Errol, and ſucceeded his mother, the
Counteſs of Errol, in 1747, when he took the
firname of Hay, and at the coronation of the
preſent King, officiated as Lord high Conſtable of Scotland. He married Rebecca, daughter
of Alexander Lockhart, Eſq; by whom he had
one daughter, Lady Mary Hay. Her Ladyſhip dying in 1764, he married, 2dly, Miſs Carr,
daughter of William Carr, of Etal, in Northumberland, Eſq; by whom he has one daughter,
Lady Charlotte. His Lordſhip has two brothers, Charles and William.

William de Haya, anceſtor of this family,
had a grant of the lands of Errol, from William
the Lion, and others of the family were heard
of in the reigns of William and Alexander II.

Creations.] Baron Hay, of Slanes, and Earl
of Errol, in the county of Perth, March 17,
1452, by James II.

Arms.] Pearl, three eſcutcheons, ruby.

Creſt.] On a wreath, a falcon, proper.

Supporters.] Two men in country habits,
each holding an ox yoak over his ſhoulder.

Motto.] *Serva jugum.*

Chief Seats.] At Dalgety and Slanes, in
Aberdeenſhire.

COUNTESS of SUTHERLAND.

ELIZABETH SUTHERLAND, Counteſs of Su-
THERLAND, and Baroneſs of Strathnaver in the
county of Sutherland, became ſo on the death
of William her father, the late Earl, on June
16, 1766, and is in her infancy. That nobleman

man and his amiable confort, were remarkable
patterns of conjugal felicity, and fhe died about
a fortnight before him, worn out with anxiety
and watching in attending her Lord in his laſt
illneſs.   His Lordſhip was a lieutenant colonel,
aid-de-camp to his Majeſty, and one of the
ſixteen peers for Scotland.   Her Ladyſhip, to
whom he was married in April 1761, was Mary,
eldeſt daughter of William Maxwell, of Reſton,
Eſq; by whom he had alſo another daughter,
whoſe death is ſaid to have occaſioned thoſe
cruel regrets which cauſed the Earl's illneſs,
and ended in the deaths of the illuſtrious pair,

According to the traditional account of ſome
Scotch writers, this family in the peerage is
older than any in North Britain, if not in all Europe; for in the reign of Corbred II. and the
year of Chriſt 76, a colony called Catti, coming from Germany to Scotland, and there dividing themſelves into two parts, from thoſe in
the North the country was called Caithneſs,
and from thoſe in the South, Sutherland: and
were Thanes thereof, before the title of Earl
was uſed in the kingdom.   Allan, who was
Thane of Sutherland, gave a very ſignal defeat
to part of the Daniſh army, who had invaded
his country, and afterwards was treacherouſly
murdered by the uſurper Macbeth, for adhering to his rightful ſovereign Malcolm Canmore,
the ſon of King Duncan.

Creations.] Earl of Sutherland and Baron of
Strathnaver, in 1057, by King Malcolm Canmore.

Arms.] Ruby, three mullets topaz, within
a border of the latter, charged with a double
treſſure, flowered and counterflowered, with
fleurs de lis of the firſt.

Creſt.]

Crest.] On a wreath, a cat fejant proper.

Supporters.] Two favages wreathed about their heads and waifts, with laurel, each holding a battoon over his fhoulder, all proper.

Motto.] *Sans peur.*

Chief Seat.] At Dunrobin, Dornock Caftle and the ifland of Brora, in the county of Sutherland.

EARL of ROTHES.

JOHN LESLEY, Earl of ROTHES, Lord Lefley and Bambreigh, knight of the antient order of the Thiftle, general of his Majefty's forces, colonel of the third regiment of foot guards, governor of Duncannon fort, general and commander in chief of the forces in Ireland, and one of the fixteen peers for Scotland, fucceeded his father, John, 8th Earl of Rothes, in 1763, and in 1740, married Mifs Hannah Howard, daughter and coheir of Matthew Howard, of Thorpe, in Norfolk, Efq; (who died in April 1761) by whom he had iffue two fons, John Lord Lefley, born in October 1744, and Charles-Howard Lefley, who died in the 15th year of his age, in 1762; alfo two daughters, Lady Jane Elizabeth, born in 1741, and Lady Mary, in 1750. His Lordfhip married, fecondly, in July, 1763, Mifs Lloyd, daughter of the Countefs of Haddington's firft marriage, by whom he has alfo iffue.

John, the late Earl, married Lady Jane, fecond daughter of John Hay, Marquis of Tweedale, by whom he had iffue 8 fons and four daughters, Ladies Jane, Mary, Margaret and Anne. The fons were, 1. John, the pre-

icnt

ſent Earl. 2. Charles, a Colonel in the Dutch
ſervice. 3. Thomas, Chamberlain of Strathern
and Fife, and barrack maſter-general of Scotland. 4. James, an advocate, who died in
1761. 5. David, who died young. 6. William,
major commandant of invalids, in Ireland. 7.
Francis, who died young, and, 8. Andrew,
equerry to the Princeſs Dowager of Wales.

The origin of this noble family is Hungarian,
taking their name from the caſtle of Leſley in
that country; but are ſince diſperſed into many
other nations; ſo that there are few countries
in Europe, wherein ſome of them have not
raiſed their characters, and borne conſiderable
offices and honours; and the family is now ſo
increaſed in number and honour, that beſides
the Earl of whom we are ſpeaking, there are
the Earl of Leven, the Lord Lindores, and the
Lord Newark; though it muſt be remembered,
that this family of Rothes is paternally of the
name of Hamilton.

There are at preſent ſeveral Counts of the
family in Germany, beſides many families in
Scotland, France, Sweden, Muſcovy, and Po-
land; and one of this name governed the kingdom of Hungary, as the Emperor's viceroy;
he having ſome time before been married to
that Emperor's daughter.

The firſt of this name in Britain was Bár-
tholdus Leſley, one of the firſt rank of nobility
in Hungary, who, in the year 1068, attended
Margaret, ſiſter of Edgar Atheling, the wife
of King Malcolm Canmore, into Scotland,
where his ſervices to that Princeſs were thought
ſo conſiderable, that King Malcolm gave him
his ſiſter to wife; and beſides many large poſ-

C   ſeſſions,

feffions, which are ftill in the family, made
him governor of Edinburgh-caftle ; after which
he was created Lord Lefley, and Earl of Rofs.

Creations.] Earl of Rothes, in the county
of Elgin, in 1457, the 19th of James II.

Arms.] Quarterly, 1ft and 4th, pearl; on
a bend fapphire, three buckles topaz, for Lefley. 2d and 3d, topaz, a lion rampant ruby,
fuppreffed by a ribband diamond, for Abernethy.

Creft.] On a wreath, a demi-gryphon proper.

Supporters.] Two gryphons, party per fefs,
pearl and ruby.

Motto.] *Grip faft.*

Chief Seats.] At Lefley, in the county of
Fife. Great Brook-ftreet, London.

EARL of MORTON.

JAMES DOUGLAS, Earl of MORTON, and
Lord Aberdour, in Fife ; hereditary fteward,
and juftice general of the Oikney Iflands,
Knight of the antient order of the Thiftle,
Lord Regifter of Scotland, prefident of the
Royal Society, one of the fixteen Peers for
Scotland, and a commiffioner for forfeited
eftates, fucceeded the laft Earl, George, his
father, in January 1738. His Lordfhip married, firft, Agatha, daughter of James Hali-
burton, of Pitcur, by whom he had iffue five
fons and two daughters, of whom there are
living Sholto-Charles, Lord Aberdour, commiffioner of the Police, who married Catherine, daughter of John Hamilton, Efq; by
whom he has a fon ; James and George, and
Lady Mary. He married, 2dly, Bridget,
daughter

daughter of Sir John Heathcote, of Normanton, Bart. by whom he has a son, John, born in July, 1756, and a daughter, Lady Bridget, born in April, 1758.

The first of this collateral branch of the great and noble family of Douglas, was Sir James Douglas of Loudon, who was succeeded by his son Sir William, the Laird of Liddesdale, who, for his bravery, was called the Flower of Chivalry: but he dying without issue, his brother Sir John Douglas became heir, and was captain of the castle of Lochleven in Fife, the property of which was 300 years in the family; and herein was imprisoned Mary Queen of Scots, who from thence made her escape into England, by means of one Mr. George Douglas. In the reign of this unfortunate Queen, James, the fourth Earl of Morton, was one of the privy council, and by her Majesty sent ambassador into England, and made lord high chancellor of Scotland. But, in the same reign, the Earl of Bothwell having a design to murder Henry Lord Darnly, the Queen's husband, in order to marry the Queen, and craving the Earl of Morton's assistance therein, the Earl, who abhorred such a detestable enterprize, retired from court into the country, during which time that scandalous and bloody tragedy was acted; whereupon the Earl of Morton was one of the nobility who entered into an association to preserve the infant Prince, whose life was thought to be in danger by such an union; and on the 29th of July. 1567, which was the day of his coronation, took the oath to the young King. In this new turn of affairs, the Earl of Morton's share was very considerable; and he was

soon

foon after declared high chancellor of Scotland, then high admiral, fheriff of the county of Edinburgh, and, on Nov. 24. 1572, Regent of the kingdom during the King's minority: but being difagreeable to the other party, who had the young King in their hands, they at length brought about his ruin; for by accufing him as acceffary to the murder of the King's father, he was thereupon fent prifoner to Dunbarton caftle; from whence, on the 1ft of June, 1581, he was brought to his trial at Edinburgh, where he was found guilty by his peers of being a party in the faid murder, by not revealing it when the Earl of Bothwell propofed it to him, and was fentenced to be hanged and quartered; but, by the favour of the King, he was the next day beheaded at the Market-crofs of Edinburgh; and what is remarkable, the execution was performed by an engine of his own inventing for that ufe, called the Maiden, he being the firft who fuffered by it. Upon the death and forfeiture of the Regent, the title of Earl of Morton was foon after fettled, by act of parliament, on the Earl's nephew, Archibald Douglas.

Creation.] Earl of Morton, in the county of Edinburgh, the 14th of March, 1456, the 20th of James II.

Arms.] Quarterly, 1ft and 4th, pearl, a man's heart, enfigned with an imperial crown, all proper. On a chief, fapphire, three mullets of the field, being his paternal coat. 2d and 3d, pearl, three piles iffuing from the chief, ruby, the exteriors charged with a mullet, topaz, for Douglas, of Dalkeith, and Lochleven.

Creft.]

- *Crest.*] On a wreath a wild boar, sticking between two stems of oak, a chain and lock holding them together.

Supporters.] Two savages, wreathed about their hands and waists with oak leaves, each holding a battoon in his hand, the great end to the ground, all proper.

Motto.] *Lock sicker*, or securely.

- *Chief Seats*] At Aberdour in the county of Fife; Dalmahoy and Belfield, in the Lothians. Lower Brook-street, London.

EARL of BUCHAN.

HENRY-DAVID ERSKINE, Earl of BUCHAN, and baron Cardrofs, of Menteith, in the county of Perth, succeeded his father, David, the late Earl, Oct. 14, 1745, and in March, 1738, married Anne, daughter of Sir James Stewart, of Goodtres, Bart. by whom he has issue three sons and two daughters, viz. Stewart, Lord Cardrofs, born in March 1740, late Secretary to the embassy to Spain ; Henry and Thomas ; Ladies Agnes and Isabella.

David, the late Earl, married Frances, daughter and at length sole heir, of Henry Fairfax, of Hurst, in Berkshire, Esq; only son of Henry, second son of Thomas, Lord Fairfax, of Ireland, by whom he had nine sons and seven daughters, of whom, of the former, only the present Lord survived him, and of the latter all but two died in infancy, viz. Lady Catherine, wife of William Frafer, of Fraferfield, son of Alexander Lord Salton, and Lady Frances, of the brave and pious colonel Gardner, slain at the battle of Preston-pans.

Th's

This Earl was of the privy counc'l to King William and Queen Anne; and upon the accession of King George I. was made one of the commissioners of trade, lord lieutenant of the shires of Stirling and Clackmannan, and elected one of the sixteen peers to the first parliament after his Majesty's arrival, and to the two succeeding parliaments.

This noble family is descended from the Earls of Mar; for John Stewart, son of John Earl of Buchan, had a son John, who being killed in his father's life-time, at the battle of Musselburgh, in 1547, left by Beatrix his wife, daughter of Sir William Ogilvy of Bayne, a daughter, Christian; who, in 1551, succeeded her grandfather in the earldom, and she marrying Robert Douglas, brother of William the sixth Earl of Morton, he, in her right, became Earl of Buchan; and by her had a son, James, who succeeded. This James married Margaret, daughter of Walter Ogilvy Lord Deskford, ancestor of the Earl of Finlater, and had an only daughter, Mary; who marrying Sir James Erskine, eldest son of John Earl of Mar, high treasurer of Scotland, by his second wife Lady Mary Stewart, daughter of Esme Duke of Lennox, upon that marriage the right of succession to the earldom of Buchan, which before had been to the heirs of either sex, was, by patent under the great seal of Scotland, limited to the said Sr James Erskine her husband, and his lawful heirs male.

Creation.] Earl of Buchan in 1469, by James III.

Arms.] Quarterly, first sapphire, three garbs topaz, for the earldom of Buchan, 2d grand quarter,

quarter, 1ft and 4th fapphire, a bend between
fix crofs croflets, fitchy, topaz for Mar. 2d
and 3d pearl, a pale diamond for Erfkine. 3d
grand quarter, 1ft and 4th topaz, a feffe cheque pearl and fapphire for Stewart, 2d and 3d
Buchan ; 4th pearl, three lions gemel, ruby ;
furmounted of a lion rampant, diamond for
Fairfax ; and over all, by way of furtout, an
efcutcheon ruby, charged with an eagle difplayed, topaz, looking towards the fun in his
fplendor, placed in the dexter chief point, for
Cardrofs.

Creft.] On a wreath a dexter arm, couped
below the fhoulder, and erect, grafping a battoon, or rugged club, both proper.

Supporters.] Two oftriches of the latter.

Motto.] *Judge nought.*

Chief Seats.] At Uphall, in Weft-Lothian,
and Cardrofs in Perthfhire.

EARL of GLENCAIRN.

WILLIAM CUNNINGHAM, Earl of GLEN-
CAIRN, and Baron Kilmaurs, a lieutenant-colonel in the army, fucceeded William, the late
Earl, his father, in 1733, and in 1744, married
Mifs Macguire, by whom he has iffue four fons
and two daughters ; William Lord Kilmaurs,
born in June 1748 ; James, in June 1749 ; John,
in May 1750: Alexander, in June 1754 ; Ladies
Henrietta and Elizabeth. His Lordfhip has feveral brothers and fifters.

This antient family, according to Sir George
Mackenzie, took their firname from the lands
of Coningham, in the north divifion of the
county of Air ; and being, by office, maiter of

the

the King's stables and horses, took for their armorial figure the instrument whereby hay is thrown up to horses, which, in blazon, is called a shake fork.

In the year 1162, lived Robert de Coningham ; who then marrying the daughter of Sir Humphrey de Barc'ay, by her was father of Sir Robert, direct anceftor of this noble family.

Creation.] Earl of Glencairn, in the county of Dumfries, May 28, 1488, 21 James III.

Arms.] Pearl, a shake fork, diamond.

Crest.] On a wreath an unicorn's head, couped, pearl, horned and maned, topaz.

Supporters.] Two rabbits sejant, proper.

Motto.] *Over fork over.*

Chief Seats.] At Kilmaurs in Cunningham ; and at Finlaylton in the county of Renfrew, near the river Clyde.

EARL of EGLINGTON.

ALEXANDER MONTGOMERY, Earl of Eglington, Lord Montgomery, a Lord of his Majefty's bedchamber, and one of the sixteen Peers for Scotland, fucceeded his father, Alexander, the late Earl, in the year 1729, and is unmarried.

Alexander, his father, married, first, Margaret daughter of William Lord Cochran, fon and heir of William Earl of Dundonald, by whom he had two fons, who died young, and four daughters ; Lady Katherine, wife of James Stewart, Earl of Galloway ; Lady Eupheme, of George Lockhart, of Carnwath, Efq; Lady Grace, of Robert Dalziel, Earl of Carnwath ; and Lady Jane, of Sir Alexander Maxwell, of

Mon-

Monreith. He married, fecondly, Lady Anne, daughter of George Gordon, the firft Earl of Aberdeen, by whom he had one daughter, Lady Mary, wife of Sir David Cunningham, of Milcraig. He married, thirdly, Sufanna daughter of Sir Archibald Kennedy, of Culzean, Bart. by whom he had three fons ; James Lord Montgomery, who died before him ; Alexander, now Earl, and the Honourable Archibald Montgomery, colonel of an Highland regiment of foot, which acted with bravery in the late war in America, and governor of Dunbarton caftle. Alfo feven daughters ; Lady Elizabeth, wife of Sir John Cunningham, of Caprington, Bart. Lady Helen, of the Honourable Francis Stewart, fon of the Earl of Moray ; Lady Sufan, of John Renton of Lamerton, Efq; Lady Margaret, of Sir Alexander Macdonald, Bart. Lady Frances ; Lady Chriftian, wife of James Murray of Abercairney, Efq; and Lady Grace, of —— Boyne, Efq.

Of this noble family, which is originally French, was Roger de Montgomery, a relation of William Duke of Normandy, whom he accompanied into England in 1066 ; and commanding the firft body of his army at the memorable battle of Haftings, where King Harold was flain, for that fignal fervice the Duke beftowed on him very large gifts, as the territory and honour of Arundel, with the earldom of Salifbury. He married Mabel, daughter of William de Talvaife, and had a fon, Philip, who, in the reign of King Henry I. coming to Scotland, got a fair inheritance in the fhire of Renfrew, and from him defcended Sir Robert Montgomery of Eglefham, in that county, who, in 1388, being at the battle of Otterburn, in Northumberland, took prisoner with his own hands Henry Lord Percy, named Hotspur, who, after killing James Earl of Douglas, and mortally wounding the Earl of Murray, still pressed on too boldly among his foes. For his ransom he obliged him to build the castle of Punnoon, in the lordship of Egglesham.

Creation.] Earl of Eglington, and Lord Montgomery in 1503, 15 James IV.

Arms.] Quarterly, 1st and 4th, sapphire, three fleurs de lis topaz for Montgomery. 2d and 3d, ruby, three annulets topaz, stoned sapphire for Eglington; all within a border topaz, charged with a double tressure, flowered and counter flowered, ruby.

Crest.] On a wreath a maid, or the picture of Hope, dressed in antient rich apparel, holding in her dexter hand a man's head, and in her sinister an anchor.

Supporters.] Two wyverns emerald, vomiting fire, being the crest of the Earl of Winton.

Motto.] *Garde bien.*

Chief Seats.] At Eglington, and at Ardrossan in Airshire. Piccadilly, London.

EARL of CASSILIS.

THOMAS KENNEDY, Earl of CASSILIS, and Lord Kennedy, bailiff of Carrick, was lineally descended of Sir Thomas Kennedy, of Culzean, second son of Gilbert, third Earl of Cassilis, and succeeded John, the eighth Earl of Cassilis, in August 1759, after a contest with the Earl of March, which was decided in his favour.

The

The firſt of this name and family is ſaid to be one Kenneth, an Iriſhman, or a Scotch highlander, from whom this noble family took the name of Kennedy. And in the reign of King William the Lion, 1183, lived Henry Kennedy, who affiſted Gilbert Lord Galloway, in his wars. In the reign of King David II. lived Sir John Kennedy, who from that King got ſeveral lands, and added to his paternal inheritance of Dunnure the barony of Caſſilis, which he obtained by Mary his wife, the daughter of Sir John Montgomery.

Creation.] Earl of Caſſilis, in the county of Air, in 1509, 21 James IV.

Arms.] Pearl, a chevron ruby, between three croſs croſlets fitchy, diamond; all within a double treſſure flowered and counter-flowered, with fleurs de lis of the ſecond.

Creſt.] On a wreath a delphin, naiant ſapphire.

Supporters.] Two ſwans proper.

Motto.] *Aviſe la Fin.*

Chief Seat.] At Caſſilis in Airſhire, in the diviſion of Carrick.

EARL of CAITHNESS.

ALEXANDER, the late Earl of CAITHNESS, who died in 1766, married Lady Margaret Primroſe, daughter of Archibald, Earl of Roſeberry, by whom he had iſſue a daughter, Lady Dorothea, born in 1739, and married to James Viſcount Macduff, now Earl of Fife, of the kingdom of Ireland, who, I preſume, may claim the title.

This

This family is defcended from William Sinclair, Earl of Orkney, by Ægidia, daughter of William Douglas, Lord of Nilthifdale, and the princefs Ægidia, daughter of king Robert II. who in the reign of James II. got a grant of the earldom of Caithnefs, from whom it defcended to his eldeft fon, by the fecond venter, William, fecond Earl of Caithnefs.

Creation.] Earl of Caithnefs, April 29, 1556, 14 Mary.

Arms.] Quarterly, firft fapphire, a fhip at anchor, within a double treffure topaz, her oars erect, in faltire, for Orkney; 2d and 3d topaz, a lion rampant, ruby, for Far; 4th fapphire, a fhip under fail, topaz, for Caithnefs; and over all a crofs ingrailed, dividing the four quarters, diamond, for Sinclair.

Creft.] On a wreath, a cock, proper.

Supporters.] Two griphons, of the latter, armed and beaked, topaz.

Motto.] *Commit thy work to God.*

Chief Seats.] At Caftles Sinclair and Thurfo, in the county of Caithnefs.

EARL of MURRAY.

JAMES STEWART, Earl of MURRAY, and Lord Down, of Down, in Menteith, one of the fixteen Peers for Scotland, and a Knight of the antient order of the Thiftle, fucceeded his father, Francis, the late Earl, in 1739, and married firft, Grace, Countefs Dowager of Aboyne, daughter of George Lockhart, of Carnwath, Efq; by whom he had iffue, Francis, lord Down, who in June 1763, married Mifs Gray, eldeft daughter of the Lord Gray, and

Lady

Lady Euphemia. And 2dly, Lady Margaret, daughter of David, Earl of Wemyfs, by whom he has two fons, James and David.

Francis the laft Earl, married Jane, daughter of John, 4th Lord Balmerino, by whom he had five fons; James, the prefent Earl; John, a colonel in the Dutch fervice; Francis, who married Lady Helen, daughter of Alexander, ninth Earl of Eglington, was a colonel in the army, and died in Germany; Archibald, captain in the navy, and Henry, major of Dragoons, who died in Germany: alfo two daughters, Lady Anne, wife of John Stewart, of Blair-Hall, Efq; and Lady Amelia of Sir Peter Halket, Bart. colonel of a regiment of foot, flain in general Braddock's unfortunate expedition in North America, July 9, 1755.

James Stewart, natural fon of King James IV. by Jane, daughter of John Lord Kennedy, was created an Earl by the faid King, and marrying Lady Margaret, daughter of Collin Campbell, the third Earl of Argyll, by her had a daughter Mary, who was married to John Stewart, mafter of Buchan; but having no male iffue, the earldom reverted to the crown, and by Queen Mary was, Feb. 10, 1561, beftowed on James Stewart, prior of St. Andrew, natural fon of the faid King, by Margaret, daughter of John Lord Erfkine; and by the faid Queen was made one of the privy council. He was alfo made Lord Lieutenant of the borders towards England; and after fhe was obliged to refign the government, in favour of her fon King James VI. he was chofen regent during the King's minority; but on June 23, 1570, as he was riding through

through the street of Lithgow, he was shot from a window, with a musquet-ball into the belly, of which wound he died the same evening. The assassin was one James Hamilton, of Bothwel, incited thereto by the Romish party.

Creations.] Earl of the county of Murray, Feb. 10, 1561, 20 Marv.

Arms.] Quarterly, 1st and 4th, topaz, a lion rampant within a double treffure, (being the arms of Scotland) all within a border compone, pearl and sapphire, for Stewart. 2d, topaz, a fesse cheque pearl and sapphire, for Stewart of Down. 3d, topaz, three escutcheons pendent by the corners, within a double treffure ruby, for Randolph earl of Murray.

Crest.] On a wreath a pelican in her nest, feeding her young.

Supporters.] Two greyhounds proper.

Motto.] *Salus per Christium redemptorem.*

Chief Seats.] At Dunibrifil, on the coast of Fife; at Castle-Stewart, in the county of Invernefs; at the castle of Tarnaway, in the county of Nairn; and in Albemarle-Street, London.

EARL of HOME.

ALEXANDER HOME, Earl of HOME, and baron of Dunglafs, succeeded his brother, William, the late earl, on April 28, 1761, and married Primrose, daughter of Charles, ninth Lord Elphingston, by whom he had a son, William, Lord Dunglafs; and a daughter, Lady Elizabeth. He married secondly, Marian, daughter of James Home, of Ayton, Efq;

Alex-

. Alexander, Earl of Home, father of the prefent Earl, was general of the Mint in Scotland, and was fome·time one of the fixteen peers for that kingdom. He married Lady Anne Ker, daughter of William, fecond Marquis of Lothian, by whom he had fix fons and two daughters, of whom only William Lord Dunglas, and Alexander the prefent Earl furvived him.

William, his eldeft fon, the late Earl, was one of the fixteen peers, a lieutenant-general of the forces, colonel of a regiment of foot, and governor of Gibraltar, when he died. He married Mrs. Laws, by whom he had no iffue.

This noble family took their furname from the caftle of Home, in Berwickfhire, and are derived from William, a fon of Patrick Home, Earl of Dunbar, who was fprung from the Saxon Kings of England, and the Princes and Earls of Northumberland. The Homes of Wedderburn, Tyninghame, Ninewells, Spot, Ayton, Faftcaftle, Coldingknows, are collateral branches of th's family.

Creations.] Earl of Home, and Baron of Dunglafs, in the county of Berwick, March 4, 1604, by James VI.

Arms.] Quarterly, 1ft and 4th, emerald, a lion rampant pearl, armed and langued, ruby, for Home. 2d and 3d, pearl, three popinjays emerald, beaked and membered ruby for Pepdies, of Dunglafs ; and over all, by way of furtout, an efcutcheon topaz, charged with an orle fapphire, for Landel.

Creft.] On a cap of dignity a lion's head, erafed, ruby.

Supporters.] Two lions, as thofe in the arms.
Motto.]

· *Motto.*] *True to the end.*
Chief Seats.] At Home-Caftle, and Hirfel,
in the county of Berw.ck.

EARL of WIGTON.

CHARLES-ROSS FLEMING, Earl of WIG-
TON and Lord Fleming, upon the death of
Charles the feventh Earl, without iffue, claimed
the title, which by the Lords of Seffion was
determined in his favour in 1748, and in 1752,
he voted as fuch, at the election of a fixteenth
peer; but I believe his claim has been fet afide
fince by the Houfe of Lords. If fo, the prefent Lady Elphingfton and her iffue, are the
reprefentatives of the family, her Ladyfhip
being 2d daughter of John the fixth Earl, as I
believe the eldeft, Lady Primrofe, had no iffue.
   This family is derived from a perfon of
great diftinction, who in the reign of David,
about the year 1140, tranfplanted himfelf from
Flanders into that realm, and took his furname
Fleming from the country of his origin. We
find feveral of this name in the reigns of Malcolm IV. William I. Alexander II. and III.
and Sir Robert Fleming being one of thofe pa-
triots, who, in 1209, ftood up for the intereft
of King Robert I. and the independence of
Scotland, and never leaving his rightful fove-
reign, till he had fet the crown upon his head,
his Majefty, in recompence for that fignal fervice, and his other merits, rewarded him with
the baronies of Lenzie, and Cumbernald, in
the county of Stirling, and with feveral other
idonations.

Crea-

| No c

Creations.] Lord Fleming, by King James II. and Earl of Wigton, March 19, 1605, 38 James VI.

Arms.] Quarterly, 1ft and 4th, pearl, a chevron with a double treffure, flowered and counterflowered, with fleurs de lis, ruby, for Fleming. 2d and 3d, fapphire, three cinque-foils pearl, for Frafer.

Creft.] On a wreath a goat's head erafed, pearl armed topaz.

Supporters.] Two ftags proper, attired and unguled topaz, each gorged with a collar fapphire, charged with three cinquefoils, pearl.

Motto.] *Let the deed fhaw.*

Chief Seats.] At Cumbernald, in the county of Stirling ; and at Boighall, in Cliddefdale.

EARL of STRATHMORE.

JOHN LYON, Earl of STRATHMORE, Lord Glamis and Kinghorn, fucceeded his father, Thomas, the late Earl, in the year 1755, and on February 14, 1767, married Elizabeth, daughter and heir of the late George Bowes, of Gibfide, in the county of Durham, Efq; a Lady of an immenfe fortune.

Thomas, the late Earl, married Jane, daughter and coheir of James Nicholfon, of the county of Durham, Efq; by whom he had iffue the prefent Earl, James and Thomas, Ladies Sufan, Anne, Mary and ——.

This noble family is defcended of that of Leonne, in France, which is derived from the noble houfe of Leoni, at Rome, a branch whereof came from France into England with William the Conqueror, and from thence, in 1098,

1098, Sir Roger de Leonne, came to Scotland with King Edgar, son of Malcolm Canmore. Ths Sir Roger, for the good services he had done against Dona'd Bane, the usurper, had a grant of considerable lands in Perthshire, which from him received the name of Glen-lyon. Afterwards John de Lyon obtained a grant from King David II. of the baronies of Forteviot and Fergundeny, in the said county, with Drumgawan, and others in the shire of Aberdeen.

John Lyon, son of the said John, was commonly called the White Lyon, from his complexion. He was secretary to King Robert II. who, in the year 1379, granted him the Thanedom of Glamis in Forfarshire, preferred him to be great chamberlain of Scotland, advanced him to the degree of a lord in parliament, by the title of Lord Glamis; and gave him in marriage the Lady Anne, his third and youngest daughter. with many baronies and grants of lands; after which he was made governor of Edinburgh-castle, and lord chancellor of Scotland.

Of this noble family there have been ten lords, and the present is the ninth Earl.

Creations.] Lord Glamis, in the county of Forfar; and Kinghorn, in the county of Fife, by Robert II. and Earl of Kinghorn, July 10, 1606, 39 James VI. which title was changed to Strathmore, in Angus, soon after the restoration of Charles II.

Arms.] Pearl, a lion rampant sapphire, armed and langued ruby, within a double tressure, flowered and counter-flowered with fleurs de lis of the latter.

Crest.]

Creſt.] On a wreath, a Lady to the girdle, holding in her right hand the royal Thiſtle, incloſed with a circle of laurel, proper, in honour of the family's marriage, with a daughter of King Robert II.

Supporters.] On the dexter ſide an unicorn pearl, armed, maned, and unguled topaz; on the ſiniſter a lion ruby.

Motto.] *In te domine ſperavi.*

Chief Seats.] At Glamis, in the county of Forfar; and at Caſtle-Lyon, in the county of Perth.

EARL of ABERCORN.

JAMES HAMILTON, Earl and Baron of ABERCORN, and Baron of Paiſley, Viſcount and Baron of Strabane, in Ireland, and Baronet, one of the ſixteen Peers for Scotland, and a privy counſellor in Ireland, ſucceeded his father, James, the late Earl, Jan. 13, 1743-4.

James, the late Earl, was a privy counſellor, both of Great Britain, and Ireland, and married Anne, daughter of colonel John Plumer, of Blakeſware, in Hertfordſhire, and by her, who died March 16, 1754, had iſſue ſix ſons and one daughter, Lady Anne, wife of Sir Henry Mackworth, Bart. The ſons were, James, the preſent Earl; John, the brave and humane commander of the Lancaſter Man of War, drowned unfortunately, going from his ſhip, at Portſmouth, and married the relict of Richard Elliot, of Port Elliot, in Cornwall, Eſq; William, who died young; George, a clergyman; Plumer, who died young; and

William,

William, lieutenant of the Victory man of war, and loft with Sir John Balchen, in the year 1744.

The defcent of this noble family is from that of the Duke of Hamilton; for James, the fourth Earl of Hamilton, and fecond Earl of Arran, marrying Lady Margaret Douglas, daughter of James, the third Earl of Morton, by her had four fons, James, Earl of Arran and Duke of Chatelherault; John, firft Marquis of Hamilton; Claud, and David; whereof Claud was progenitor of the Lord I am now fpeaking of; and, in confideration of his merit and loyalty to Mary Queen of Scots, James VI. created him Lord Pafley.

Creations.] Baron of Pafley, in the county of Renfrew, in 1591; Baron of Abercorn, in the county of Lanerk, in 1604; Earl of the fame place; Baron of Hamilton, Mountcaftle, and Kilpatrick, July 10, 1606; Baron of Strabane, in the county of Tyrone, May 8, 1618, all by King James VI. of Scotland, and Ift of England; and created Vifcount of Strabane, and Baron of Mountcaftle, in the county of Tyrone, Dec. 2, 1701, the 13th of William III. The title of baronet was given by Charles I.

Arms.] Quarterly, 1ft and 4th, ruby, three cinquefoils pierced ermine for Hamilton. 2d and 3d, pearl, a fhip with its fails furled up, diamond, for the earldom of Arran.

Creft.] In a ducal coronet topaz, an oak fructed and penetrated tranfverfely in the main ftem, by a frame-faw, proper, the frame topaz.

Supporters.] Two antelopes pearl, their horns, ducal collars, chains, and hoofs, topaz.

Motto.]

Motto.] *Sola nobilitat virtus.*

Chief Seats.] At Stephen's-green, in the city of Dublin, at Paiſley, in the county of Renfrew, in Scotland; and at Witham, in the county of Eſſex, in England, Groſvenor-ſquare, London.

EARL of KELLY.

ALEXANDER ERSKINE, Earl of KELLY, Viſcount Fenton and Baron of Dirleton, ſucceeded his father Alexander the late Earl, in March 1756, and is unmarried.

Alexander the late Earl married firſt Miſs Murray, daughter of William Murray, of Abercairny, Eſq; by whom he had no iſſue: his ſecond Lady was daughter of Dr. Archibald Pitcairn, by whom he had three ſons and three daughters: Alexander, the preſent Earl, born in 1732; Archibald and Andrew, officers in the army; Lady Betty, wife of Walter Macfarlane, of that Ilk; Lady Anne, of Sir Robert Anſtruther, Bart. and Lady Janet. His Lordſhip was attainted in 1746, but ſurrendering in due time avoided the penalties of the act.

This noble family is deſcended from Sir Thomas Erſkine, ſon of Sir Alexander, brother of John the 5th Earl of Mar, who being educated with King James VI. became a great favourite with that Prince, and being one of thoſe that reſcued him from being murdered by the ſons of the Earl of Gowrie, in reward of that ſervice, had a grant of the Lordſhip of Dirleton; was made captain of the Engliſh guards, groom of the ſtole; created Viſcount
.Fenton,

Fenton, and Earl of Kelly; and in 1615, made a Knight of the moft noble order of the Garter.

Creations.] Baron of Dirleton, in the county of Hadington, 1603; Vifcount Fenton, in 1606; and Earl of Kelly, in the county of Fife, March 12, 1619, all by King James VI.

Arms.] Quarterly, 1ft and 4th, ruby, an imperial crown within a double treflure, flowered and counter-flowered, with fleurs de lis, topaz. 2d and 3d, pearl, a pale diamond, for Erfkine.

Creft.] On a wreath a demi-lion guardant, ruby.

Supporters.] Two gryphons topaz, charged on their breafts with a crefcent diamond.

Motto.] *Decori Decus addit Avito.*

Chief Seat.] At the caftle of Kelly, in the county of Fife.

EARL of HADDINGTON.

THOMAS HAMILTON, Earl of HADDINGTON, and Baron of Binny, fucceeded the late Earl, his grandfather, in 1735, and in 1750 married Mary, daughter of Rowland Holt, of Redgrave-hall, in Suffolk, Efq; nephew of the great Lord Chief Juftice Holt; by whom he has iffue two fons, Charles Lord Binny, born July 5, 1753, and Thomas.

Thomas the late Earl, reprefented the peerage of Scotland in three parliaments, and was a Knight of the antient order of the Thiftle, governor of Edinburgh-caftle, and a Lord of the Privy Council to George II. He married Lady Helen, fifter of Charles, Earl of Hopetoun, and had iffue two fons, Charles Lord Binny,

9   and

and John; and two daughters, Lady Margaret, and Lady Chriftian, wife of Sir James Dalrymple, of Hailes, Bart. Charles Lord Binny, was a commiffioner of trade in Scotland, and dying in 1732, left iffue by his wife Rachael, daughter of George Baillie, of Jervifwood, Thomas the prefent Earl; George who has taken the name of Baillie, as reprefentative of his grandfather; Charles-James, a captain of dragoons; Grifel, wife of Philip Earl Stanhope, and Rachael.

The immediate anceftor of this noble Lord, was Sir Thomas Hamilton, of Byres, defcended from John Hamilton, of Innerwick, fecond fon of Sir Walter Hamilton, anceftor of the firft Duke of Hamilton, and his fon, Sir Thomas Hamilton, of Prieftfield, marrying Elizabeth, daughter of James Heriot, of Trabrowne, by her had a fon, Sir Thomas, who being bred to the law, was by King James VI. made one of the Senators of the College of Juftice, Secretary of State, Lord-Advocate and Regifter, Baron of Binny, and Earl of Melrofs in the county of Roxburgh; but he afterwards, by his Majefty's approbation, changed the latter title to Haddington.

Creations.] Baron of Binny, Nov. 30, 1613, and Earl of Haddington, in Eaft Lothian, March 20, 1619, by James VI.

Arms.] Quarterly, 1ft and 4th, ruby, on a chevron between three cinquefoils pearl, two muchetors, and a buckle, fapphire, all within a border topaz, charged with eight thiftles emerald, for Hamilton of Innerwick. 2d and 3d, pearl a feffe wavey, between three rofes ruby,

ruby, barbed and feeded proper, as a coat of augmentation for Melrofs.

Creſt.] On a wreath two dexter hands con-joined, iſſuing out of clouds proper, and hold-ing between them a branch of laurel.

Supporters.] Two talbots pearl, each gorged with a plain collar, ruby.

Motto.] Præſto & perſto.

Chief Seat.] At Tyningham, in Eaſt Lo-thian, near Haddington.

EARL of GALLOWAY.

ALEXANDER STEWART, Earl of GALLO-WAY, and Gairlies, a Lord of the Police, ſuc-ceeded his father, James, the late Earl, in 1747, and married, firſt, Lady Anne, daughter of William Earl Marſhal, by whom he had iſſue two ſons and a daughter. The ſons died young, and the daughter, Lady Mary, was wife of Ken-neth Lord Fortroſe, eldeſt ſon of the late Earl of Seaforth. He married, ſecondly, Lady Kathe-rine, daughter of John Earl of Dundonald, by whom he had iſſue four ſons and ſix daughters; John Lord Gairlies, member for Morpeth; George, an officer in the army, killed at Ticon-deroga; William, who died young; and Keith, captain in the navy; Lady Catherine, wife of James Murray, of Broughton, Eſq; member for the Shire of Wigton; Lady Suſanna; Lady Margaret, wife of Charles Earl of Aboyne; Ladies Euphemia and Henrietta, and Lady Char-lotte, wife of William Earl of Dunmore.

James, the late Earl, married Lady Kathe-rine, daughter of Alexander Earl of Eglington, by whom he had iſſue Alexander the preſent Earl;

Earl; James, lieutenant colonel of the third regiment of foot guards, twice member for Wigtonshire, and twice for the Burghs of Wigton, &c. William, a captain of dragoons, member for Wigton, &c. in the ninth parliament of Great Britain, and George; Lady Margaret, wife, first of James Earl of Southesk, and, 2dly, of John Lord Sinclair; Lady Euphemia, of Alexander Murray, of Broughton, Esq; Ladies Anne and Catharine, deceased.

Alexander Stewart, founder of Paisley, having a son Alexander, he, for his good services against the Danes, at the battle of Largis in Coningham, and attempting to recover the Isle of Man to the crown of Scotland, had a grant from King Alexander III. in 1263, of the lands of Gairlies and Glasserton; and therein was succeeded by Walter, his son and heir, who, after the death of Alexander III. joining Sir William Wallace, against the English, was slain at the famous battle of Falkirk against King Edward I. in person, in 1298. Alexander his son succeeded, who, immediately after the battle of Bannockburn, was knighted, and obtained a charter from King Robert I. of the lands of Dalswinton in Nithisdale. From this ancestor descended the Lord Blantyre, as well as the noble Lord I am speaking of.

Creations.] Baron of Gairlies, in the county of Wigton, April 2, 1607: and Earl of the county or province of Galloway, on Sept. 19, 1623, by James VI.

Arms.] Topaz, a fesse cheque pearl and sapphire, surmounted of a bend ingrailed ruby, within a double tressure, flowered and counterflowered with fleurs de l s of the last.

D   *Crest.*]

Creſt.] On a wreath, a pelican feeding her young in the neſt, all proper.

Supporters.] On the dexter ſide a ſavage, wreathed with laurel about the temples and middle, holding a battoon over his ſhoulder, all proper; and on the ſiniſter, a lion rampant ruby.

Motto.] *Vireſcit vulnere virtus.*

Chief Seats.] At Gairlies, Glaniſh, Glaſſerton, and Clary, all in Wigtonſhire.

EARL of LAUDERDALE.

JAMES MAITLAND, Earl of LAUDERDALE, Viſcount Maitland, baron of Thirleſtan, Muſſelburgh and Bolton, ſucceeded his father, Charles the late Earl, in 1744, and married Mary, daughter and coheir of Sir Thomas Lombe, alderman of London, by whom he had iſſue Valdave-Charles, who died an infant; James Lord Maitland, born in June 1759; James; John; Lady Hannah, deceaſed; Ladies Elizabeth, Mary-Julian, and Hannah-Charlotte.

Charles, the late Earl, married Lady Elizabeth, daughter of James Ogilvie, Earl of Finlater and Seafield, by whom he had iſſue eight ſons and three daughters, viz. James, the preſent Earl; Charles, who married Miſs Barclay of Towie; George, a dignified clergyman in Ireland; Richard, a lieutenant colonel in the army; Alexander, colonel in the guards, and uſher to the Princeſs Dowager of Wales, who married Miſs Maden, daughter of colonel Maden; Frederick, a captain in the navy; Patrick, captain of a ſhip in the ſervice of the Eaſt-India company; John, a captain in the army; Lady Eliza-

Elizabeth, wife of James Ogilvie of Rothmay, Efq; Lady Margaret, who died unmarried; and Lady Janet, wife of Thomas Dundas of Fingafk, Efq.

Of this family, whofe name of old was written De Mautland, was Richard de Mautland of Thirleftan, who gave divers lands to the abbey of Dryburgh; all which was confirmed by his fon William, whofe heir, Sir Robert, was alfo a great benefactor to the faid abbey. In the reign of David II. this Sir Robert Maitland, fucceffor to Thomas, obtained a grant from Sir John Gifford, Lord of Yetter, of the lands of Leithington, in Eaft Lothian.

John, the fecond Earl of Lauderdale, being taken prifoner at the battle of Worcefter, 1651, and committed to the Tower of London, for his loyalty to King Charles II. there underwent a fevere confinement for the fpace of nine years, till the reftoration of the King, when he was releafed; and then, as a recompence for his fufferings, he was made Secretary of State, Prefident of the Council, one of the extraordinary Lords of Seffion, firft Commiffioner of the Treafury, one of the gentlemen of his Majefty's Bed-chamber, and High-Commiffioner to the Parliament; and on May 2, 1672, was created Marquis of March, and Duke of Lauderdale; and on the 3d of June following, was likewife inftalled at Windfor, a Knight of the moft noble order of the Garter. He was alfo created by that King a peer of England, by the title of Baron Peterfham, and Earl of Guildford; and made one of the Privy Council for the kingdoms of England, Scotland, and Ireland; but dying without heirs male, Aug. 24, 1682,

his

his Englifh titles, and the dignity of Marquis
and Duke became extinct; but that of Earl defcended to his brother Charles.

Creations.] Baron of Thirleftan, in the
county of Berwick, in 1590; and Vifcount
Maitland, and Earl of Lauderdale, in the county aforefaid, March 24, 1623, by James VI.

Arms.] Topaz, a lion rampant dechauffé,
within a double treffure, flowered and counterflowered, with fleurs de lis ruby.

Creft.] On a wreath a lion fejant, guardant,
ruby, crowned by a ducal crown, holding in his
dexter paw a drawn fword, pommelled and
hilted, topaz; and in the finifter, a fleur de lis
fapphire; which royal creft was allowed to
John Duke of Lauderdale, by King Charles II.

Supporters.] Two eagles proper.

Motto.] *Confilio & animis.*

Chief Seats.] At Lauder-Forth, near Lauder,
in the county of Berwick; alfo at Halton, in
the county of Edinburgh, or Mid-Lothian.

EARL of LOUDOUN.

John Campbell, Earl and Baron of Loudoun, and Lord Mauchlane, one of the fixteen
Peers for Scotland, governor of Edinburgh
caftle, a lieutenant-general, colonel of the 30th
regiment of foot, and F. R. S. fucceeded Hugh,
the late Earl his father, in 1732.

Hugh, the late Earl, was Secretary of State
in 1704, an extraordinary Lord of Seffion,
Knight of the ancient order of the Thiftle, and
one of the fixteen Peers to the firft feven parliaments of Great Britain. He was a commiffioner for the Union, of the Privy Council to
King

King George I. and in 1722, High Commissioner to the general affembly of the Church of Scotland. He married Lady Margaret Dalrymp'e, daughter of John Earl of Stair, by whom he had the prefent Earl, and two daughers; Lady Betty, and Lady Margaret, wife of John Campbell, of Shawfield, Efq.

This family have long flourifhed in the county of Air; and, like many other great families, have taken their firname from the lordfhip of Loudon, in the fhire of Air. Of this family was James Loudon, whofe daughter and heir being married to Sir Reginald Crawford, in the county of Lanerk, fhe brought him the barony of Loudon, with many other lands; and by him had Hugh, their heir, from whom defcended Sir Reginald, whofe only daughter Sufanna, being married to Sir Donald Campbell, of Redcaftle, in Angus, he, in her right, became Lord Loudon, and was confirmed therein by King Robert I.

Creations.] Baron of Loudon, in Coningham, in the county of Air, in 1604, by James VI. and Earl of the fame place May 12, 1633, 9 Charles I.

Arms.] Gyrony of eight pieces, ruby and ermine, being the field of Crawfurd of Loudon, who bore gules a feffe ermine.

Creft.] On a wreath an eagle difplayed, with two heads ruby, in a flame proper, looking towards a fun, with the dexter head.

Supporters.] On the dexter fide, a chevalier in armour, plumed on the head, with three feathers ruby, and holding a fpear in his right hand. On the finifter a lady nobly dreffed,

plumed

plumed on the head with three feathers pearl, and holding in her left hand a letter of challenge. *Motto.*] *I bide my time.*

Chief Seats.] At London-castle, in Coningham, in the county of Air; and in Privy Garden, London.

EARL of KINNOUL.

THOMAS HAY, Earl of KINNOUL, Viscount Dupplin, and Baron of Kinfauns, and Baron Hay, of Pedwardin in England, succeeded his father, George-Henry, the late Earl, in 1758, and in June, 1741, married Constantia, daughter of John Kirle Ernle, of Whitham in Wiltshire, Esq; (who died June 29, 1753, without surviving issue.) His Lordship is a Lord of the Privy Council, Recorder of Cambridge, and Chancellor of the University of St. Andrews.

George-Henry, the late Earl, was created a Peer of Great Britain by Queen Anne, when Viscount Dupplin. In 1709, he married Lady Abigail Harley, youngest daughter of Robert Earl of Oxford, and by her, who died on July 15, 1750, had issue four sons and six daughters, viz. Ladies Margaret, Elizabeth, Anne, Abigail, and Henrietta, married on July 30, 1754, to Robert Roper, of Trimden, in the county of Durham, L. L. D. and Lady Mary, to Dr. John Hume, bishop of Salisbury. The sons were, 1. Thomas, the present Earl. 2. Robert, who took the name and arms of Drummond, as heir of intail to his great grandfather William Viscount Strathallan, and is Archbishop of York, and a Lord of the Privy Council. He married Henrietta, daughter of Peter Auriol, merchant.

merchant in London, and has iffue fix fons and
one daughter. 3. John, rector of Epworth in
Lincolnfhire, who died unmarried in 1751. 4.
Henry·Edward, conful-general in Portugal,
aad now plenipotentiary at that court, who
married Mary, daughter of Peter Flower, merchant in London, by whom he has three fons
and three·daughters.

George Hay, the firft Earl of Kinnoul, was
a collateral branch of the noble family of Errol,
and fon of Peter Hay of Melginch ; and being
well brought up, was, after his return from his
travels, introduced at the court of King James I.
of England ; and, in a very fhort time, raifed
to be one of the gentlemen of his Majefty's
bed-chamber, and had a gift of the priory of
the charter-houfe at Perth. He was, by the
faid King, preferred to the office of clerk-
regifter in 1616 ; and, in 1622, made Lord-
Chancellor of Scotland ; in which poft he was
continued by Charles I. who was pleafed to
advance him to the degrees of Vifcount Dupplin, and Earl of Kinnoul.

Creations.] Lord Hay, of Kinfauns, and
Vifcount Dupplin, May 4, 1627 ; Earl of Kinnoul, May 25, 1633. For the Englifh honours,
fee Lord Hay, in my Englifh Peerage.

Arms.] Quarterly, 1ft and 4th, fapphire, a n
unicorn rampant pearl, armed, maned, and unguled topaz, within a border of the laft, charged with eight half thiftles emerald, and as
many half rofes ruby, joined together by way
of party per pale, given to the family, when
created Earl, as a coat of augmentation, the
unicorn and border being part of the royal at-
chievement, and the thiftles and rofes con-

j ined,

joined, reprefenting the unicorn of the two kingdoms, in the perfon of James VI. 2d and 3d pearl, three efcutcheons ruby, for the name of Hay.

Creft.] On a wreath, a countryman couped at the knees, vefted in grey, his waiftcoat ruby, and bonnet fapphire, bearing on his fhoulder an ox-yoke, proper.

Supporters.] Two countrymen habited as the creft, the dexter holding over his fhoulder the coulter of a plough, and the finifter the paddle, both proper.

Motto.] *Renovate animos.*

Chief Seats.] At Dupplin, and Balhufy, in Perthfhire; at Brodefworth, in Yorkfhire; and Scotland-yard, London.

EARL of DUMFRIES and STAIR.

WILLIAM CRICHTON, Earl of DUMFRIES and STAIR, Vifcount Air, and Baron Crichton of Crichton, in Mid-Lothian; Vifcount and Baron Stair, Baron Dalrymple and Stranrawer, and Knight of the antient order of the Thiftle, fucceeded his mother Penelope, late Countefs of Dumfries, in 1742, and his brother James, late Earl of Stair, in 1761. He married firft, Lady Anne Gordon, daughter of William late Earl of Aberdeen, and fifter of the prefent Earl (who died April 15, 1755) and by her had iffue a fon, William Lord Crichton, who died in the tenth year of his age; and his Lordfhip married, fecondly, Anne daughter of William Duff, of Crombie, Efq;

Penelope,

Penelope, the late Countess, married colonel William Dalrymple, son of John, Earl of Stair, and brother of the late Earl, and by him had issue six sons, and two daughters, viz. William, now Earl of Dumfries and Stair ; John, captain of dragoons, who died unmarried ; James, who succeeded his uncle, the renowned John Earl of Stair, in 1747, but died without issue ; Charles, Hugh and George ; Lady Betty, wife of John Macdowal, of Freugh, Esq; and Lady Penelope.

The family of Crichton, Earls of Dumfries, were a branch of the family of Crichton of Lothian, who, in the time of King Malcolm III. came from Hungary, of which was Sir William Crichton, who, in the reign of King Robert I. marrying Isabel de Rofs, daughter and coheir to Rofs of Sanquhar, with her had half that barony ; and from that match descended Sir Robert Crighton, who was father of Robert, the first Lord Crighton, or Crichton.

Creations.] Viscount Air in the county of Air, 1622, by James VI. and Earl of Dumfries, June 10, 1633, by Charles I. Earl and Viscount of Stair, Lord Glenluce and Stranrawer, April 1, 1690, 1 William III.

Arms.] Quarterly, 1st and 4th, topaz, on a faltire sapphire, nine lozenges of the first, for Dalrymple. 2d and 3d, topaz, a chevron cheque pearl and diamond, between three water-budgets of the last, for Rofs ; and over all, by way of furtout, an efcutcheon pearl, charged with a lion rampant sapphire, for Crighton.

Crest.] On a wreath, a dragon's head couped emerald, spouting fire.

Supporters.

Supporters.] Two lions sapphire, each crowned with an earl's coronet, topaz.

Motto.] *God send grace.*

Chief Seat.] At Sanquhar, in the county of Dumfries.

EARL of STIRLING.

WILLIAM ALEXANDER, Earl of STIRLING, Viscount Stirling, Lord Alexander, and Baronet, succeeded Henry the fifth Earl, who died without issue; as being son of James, second son of David, son of Alexander, son of John, second son of Andrew, fourth Baron of Menstrie, uncle of Alexander, first Earl of Stirling. He married Sarah daughter of Philip Livingston, Esq; by whom he has issue two daughters; Lady Mary, wife of John, son and heir of Alexander Robertson, of Stralochy, and Lady Catharine.

This family was a branch of that of Macdonald: Alexander Macdona'd, a younger son of the Lord of the Isles, obtaining from the family of Argyll the lands of Menstrie, in the county of Clacmannan, where he fixed his residence, his descendants took the surname of Alexander.

Creations.] Baronet of Nova-Scotia, May 21, 1625, Baron Alexander and Viscount Stirling, in 1626, and Earl of Stirling, June 14, 1633, all by Charles I.

Arms.] Quarterly, 1st and 4th, party per pale, pearl and diamond, a chevron, and in base a crescent, all counterchanged; 2d and 3d, topaz, a ship with the sails furled up diamond, between three cross croslets, fitchée, ruby,

ruby, and over all, in furtout, the badge of a
Baronet of New Scotland, which is pearl, on a
faltire fapphire, the royal arms of Scotland, enfigned on the top with an imperial crown,
proper.

Creſt.] On a wreath, a bear ſejant erect,
proper.

Supporters.] On the dexter ſide, an Indian,
with long hair, and a dart in his right hand,
having a plain circle or rim of gold on his
head, beautified with a plume of ſeven feathers, topaz and fapphire; and round his waiſt
a like circle and feathers. On the ſiniſter a
mermaid, with her comb and mirror, all proper.

Motto.] *Per Mare, per Terras.*
Chief Reſidence.] At New-York.

EARL of ELGIN and KIN-CARDIN.

CHARLES BRUCE, Earl of ELGIN and KIN-
CARDIN, Baron Bruce of Kinlofs and Torry,
ſucceeded his father William, the late Earl of
Kincardin, in 1740, and Charles late Earl of
Aylefbury and Elgin, &c. in the laſt title, upon
his deceaſe, in 1746-7. He married the only
daughter and heir of Thomas White, Eſq;
banker in London, by whom he has iſſue a
ſon ——, Lord Bruce, and two daughters,
Ladies Martha and Janet.

William, the late Earl of Kincardin, married Janet, daughter and heir of James Ro-
berton, advocate, and one of the princ'pal
clerks of feſſion, by whom he had iſſue, Charles,
the preſent Earl; James, a clergyman, and

Thomas,

Thomas, an officer in the army: alfo two daughters, Ladies Rachael and Chriftian.

Sir George Bruce of Carnock, was the immediate anceftor of this noble family, who was third fen of Sir Edward Bruce, of Blair hall, and younger brother of Edward, Lord Bruce of Kinlofs, who was knighted by James VI. and appointed a commiffioner to treat of an union with England, in 1604.

Creations.] Baron Bruce, of Kinlofs, July 8, 1604, and Earl of Elgin June 21, 1611, by James VI. Earl of Kincardin and Lord Bruce of Torry, Dec. 26, 1647, (fee Lord Bruce in my Englifh Peerage.)

Arms.] Topaz, a faltire and chief ruby, on a canton pearl, a lion rampant, fapphire, being the original arms of Bruce, of Skelton ; and the field topaz, faltire and chief ruby, were the arms of Robert I. they altering the field, from pearl, as he bore it, to topaz.

Creft.] On a wreath, a lion paffant, fapphire.

Supporters.] Two favages regardant. proper, wreathed about their temples and waifts with laurel.

Motto.] *Fuimus.*

Chief Seats.] At Broomhale, near Dunfermline ; and Dairfie, near Coupar, in Fiffhire.

EARL of DALHOUSIE.

GEORGE RAMSAY, Earl of DALHOUSIE, and Lord Ramfay, fucceeded his brother Charles, the late Earl, in January, 1764.

William, the fixth Earl, married Jane, daughter of George Lord Rofs, by whom he had iffue three fons and two daughters, whereof

the

the eldest George Lord Ramſay, married Jane, daughter of the Right Honourable Henry Maul, of Kelly, by whom he had two ſons, Charles the late, and George the preſent Earl, and two daughters, Ladies Anne and Jane.

Of this family, which is ſaid to be originally from Germany, was Simon de Ramſay of Dalhouſie, in the county of Edinburgh, who lived in the time of David I. about the year 1140; and from whom deſcended Sir William Ramſay of the ſame place, who was one of thoſe barons that, in 1320, wrote to the Pope, aſſerting the independency of their country. To him ſucceeded Sir Alexander Ramſay of Dalhouſie, who, in 1332, was made conſtable of the caſtle of Roxburgh, which he had taken from the Engliſh, by getting over the walls with ſcaling-ladders.

Creations.] Lord Ramſay, Aug. 25, 1618, by James VI. and Earl of the caſtle of Dalhouſie, in Mid-Lothian, June 19, 1633, by Charles I.

Arms.] Pearl, an eagle diſplayed diamond, beaked and membered ruby.

Creſt.] On a wreath, an unicorn's head couped, pearl, horned, and maned, topaz.

Supporters.] Two gryphons, proper.

Motto.] *Ora et labora.*

Chief Seat. At Dalhouſie, near Dalkieth, in the county of Edinburgh.

EARL of TRAQUAIR.

JOHN STEWART, Earl of TRAQUAIR, Baron of Traquair, and Lord Linton, ſucceeded his brother Charles, the laſt Earl, in 1764.

Charles

Charles the late Earl, married Terefa, daughter of Sir Baldwin Conyers, of Hornden, in the county of Durham, Bart. His Lordfhip was committed to the Tower in 1745 for a fuppofed treafonable correfpondence, but was bailed thereout in 1747.

Charles, the late and prefent Earl's father, married Lady Mary Maxwell, daughter of Robert, fourth Earl of Nithifdale, by whom he had iffue, Charles, the late Earl; John, the prefent Earl, who married Chriftian, daughter of Sir Philip Anftruther, of Anftrutherfield; Ladies Lucy, Anne, Mary, wife of John Lord Drummond, eldeft fon of James, fourth Earl of Perth; Lady Catherine, of William Lord Maxwell, fon and heir of Robert Earl of Nithifdale; Ladies Barbara and Margaret.

The paternal anceftor of this noble family was James Stewart, Earl of Buchan, whofe father was Sir James Stewart, commonly called the Black Knight of Lorn; and his mother Jane, daughter of John Beaufort, Duke of Somerfet, in England, and widow of King James I. fo that the faid James Earl of Buchan, being uterine brother to King James II. was by King James III. conftituted Lord-Chamberlain of Scotland, and obtaining from him the lands and barony of Traquair, then in the crown, and marrying to his fecond wife, Margaret, a daughter of the family of Murray of Philpfhaugh, by her had a fon James, upon whom he beftowed the faid barony.

Creations.] Baron Linton, and Earl of Traquair, in the county of Peebles, June 22, 1633, by Charles I.

Arms.]

Arms.] Quarterly, 1ft. topaz, a feffe cheque pearl and fapphire for Stewart. 2d, fapphire, three garbs topaz for Buchan. 3d, diamond, a mullet pearl. 4th, pearl an orle
ruby, and three martlets in chief diamond, for
the name of Rutherfoord.

Creft.] On a wreath, a garb topaz, furmounted of a crow proper.

Supporters.] Two bears of the latter.

Motto.] *Judge nought.*

Chief Seat.] At Traquair, in the county of
Peebles.

EARL of FINLATER and SEAFIELD.

JAMES OGILVIE, Earl of FINLATER and
SEAFIELD, Vifcount Redhaven, and Baron
Defkford. Sheriff of the county of Banff, fucceeded in 1764, James, the late Earl, his father, who married, firft, Lady Elizabeth Hay,
daughter of Thomas Earl of Kinnoul, by whom
he had iffue a fon, James, Lord Defkford, (the
prefent Earl) a commiffioner of forfeited
eftates, &c. who married Lady Mary, daughter of John Duke of Athol, by whom he has
iffue James, mafter of Defkford; John Ogilvie, Efq; (who died in 1764) and two daughters, Lady Margaret, wife of Sir Ludovic
Grant of that Ilk, Bart member for the fhire
of Elgin; and Lady Anne, of John Earl of
Hopetoun, who is deceafed. His Lordfhip
married fecondly, Lady Sophia, daughter of
Charles, Earl of Hopetoun, who died in April
1762.

James,

James, the late Earl's father, married Anne, daughter of Sir William Dunbar, of Durn, Bart. by whom he had issue two sons and two daughters; James, late Earl, and George, an advocate, who died without issue : Lady Elizabeth wife of Charles Maitland Earl of Lauderdale, and Lady Janet, first of Hugh Forbes, Esq; son and heir of Sir William Forbes, of Craigyvar, Bart. and secondly of William Duff, of Braco, afterwards Earl of Fife of Ireland.

Walter Ogilvy, of Lintreithan, Lord-Treasurer of Scotland, marrying Isabel de Dorward, heirefs of Lintreithan, by her had John, his successor, and Sir Walter Ogilvy of Auchleven, the progenitor of this noble family, who, marrying Margaret, only daughter and heir to Sir John Sinclair of Deskford and Finlater, in the county of Banff, with her had those baronies. He had two sons, Sir James, his heir, and Sir Walter, ancestor of the Lord Banff.

Creations.] Baron of Deskford, Oct. 4, 1616, by James VI. Earl of Finlater, Feb. 20, 1637, by King Charles I. both in the county of Banff; Viscount Redhaven, June 28, 1698, by King William III. and Earl of Seafield, in the county of Fife, June 24, 1701, by the same King.

Arms.] Quarterly, 1st and 4th, pearl, a lion passant guardant, ruby, crowned with an imperial crown proper, for Ogilvie. 2d and 3d, pearl, a cross ingrailed diamond, for Sinclair.

Crest.] On a wreath, a lion rampant ruby, holding between his paws, a plumb rule erect, proper.

Sup-

Supporters.] Two lions guardant, ruby.
Motto.] *Tout jour.*
Chief Seats.] At Cullen, in Bamffshire; at
Deskford in the same county; and St. James's-
Place, London.

EARL of LEVEN.

DAVID LESLEY, Earl of LEVEN, and Melvil, Baron Melvil and Balgony, succeeded his
father Alexander, the late Earl, Sept. 2, 1754,
and married Wilhelmina, daughter of William
Nisbet, of Dirleton, Esq; by whom he has issue
three sons and three daughters; Alexander,
Lord Balgony; William and David: Ladies
Jane, Mary-Elizabeth, and Charlotte.

Alexander, the late Earl, was commissioner
to the general assembly of the church of Scotland for thirteen years, from 1741 to 1753 in-
clusive, and one of the sixteen peers to the
parliaments of 1747 and 1754, and an ordinary
Lord of Session. He married first, Mary,
daughter of colonel John Erskine, of Carnock,
by whom he had issue, David, the present
Earl; and secondly Elizabeth, daughter of
David Moneypenny, of Pitmilly, by whom he
had colonel Alexander Lesley: Lady Anne,
wife of George Earl of Northesk; Lady Elizabeth, and Lady Mary, wife of Dr. James
Walker, of Innerdivot.

In the time of King Robert I. Andrew de
Lesley, one of the progenitors of the Earl of
Rothes, marrying Elizabeth, daughter of James
Lord Douglas, by her had a son George, on
whom he bestowed the lands of Balquahan, in
the county of Aberdeen; and he marrying a

daughter

daughter of the family of Keith of Inverugy, had a fon, George Lefley, of Balgony, whofe younger fon, Sir Alexander Lefley, ferving under Guftavus Adolphus, King of Sweden, was promoted by the faid King to be lieutenant-general of his armies. In 1638 returning to his own country, he commanded the Scotch army, and was in 1641, created Earl of Leven. His fon James who died before him, married the Lady Margaret, daughter of John Lefley, the fixth Earl of Rothes, by whom he had Alexander, who fucceeded his grandfather; and a daughter Katherine, who was married to George Earl of Melvil. Alexander, the fecond Earl, dying without iffue male, the eftate and honour devolved fuccefsively upon his two daughters Margaret and Katherine, who both dying without iffue, the eftate and title, by intail, came to David, the fecond Earl of Melvil, and the third Earl of Leven, though the latter takes place of the former.

Of the noble family of Melvil, which is faid to be Hungarian, and came to Scotland foon after the Norman fettlement in England, there have been three Lords, and one Earl, before they fucceeded to the earldom of Leven.

Creations.] Lord Melvil, April 30, 1616, by James IV. Earl of Leven, and Lord Balgony, in Fifefhire, Nov. 15, 1641, by Charles I. and Earl of Melvil, by William III.

Arms.] Quarterly, 1ft and 4th, fapphire, a thiftle proper, enfigned with an imperial crown of the laft, as a coat of augmentation. 2d and 3d, pearl, on a bend fapphire, three buckles topaz, for Lefley.

Creft.]

Creſt.] On a wreath, a chevalier in compleat armour, holding in his right hand a dagger erect proper, the pommel and hilt topaz.

Supporters.] Two chevaliers as the creſt, each holding in his exterior hand the banner of Scotland.

Motto.] Pro rege, & patria.

Chief Seats.] At Balgony and Melvil in Fifeſhire.

EARL of DYSART.

LIONEL TALMASH, Earl of DYSART, and Lord Huntingtour, and Knight of the antient order of the Thiſtle, ſucceeded the late Earl, Lionel, his grandfather, in 1726; and in 1713, married Lady Grace, eldeſt daughter of John Earl Granville, and by her (who died July 23, 1755) had iſſue a daughter, who died young; Lady Harriot, who died in 1733: Lady Grace born in 1736, and another daughter born in 1745; alſo ſix ſons, of whom Lord Huntingtour, the eldeſt, married on Oct. 3, 1760, the youngeſt natural daughter of the Right Honourable Sir Edward Walpole, by whom he has iſſue.

Lionel, the late and firſt Earl, and fourth Baronet, married Grace, one of the two daughters and coheirs of Sir Thomas Wilbraham, of Woodhey, in the county of Cheſter, Bart. by whom he had one ſon Lionel, Lord Huntingtour, and four daughters, Ladies Mary and Grace, who died unmarried; Lady Elizabeth, wife of Sir Robert Cotton, of Cumbermere in Cheſhire, Bart. and Lady Katherine, of John Marquis of Caernarvon, heir apparent of James
Duke

Duke of Chandos, and died in January 1754. Lionel Lord Huntingtour deceased before his father in 1712, leaving one son, the present Earl.

Of this noble family, whose extraction is English, there was in the twenty-fifth of Edward I. one Hugh de Talmash, who held, of the crown, the manor of Bentley, in the county of Suffolk, and, in the twenty-ninth, had summons among the Knights of that county, to attend the King at Berwick for an expedition into Scotland.

Sir Lionel Talmash, the third Baronet of Bentley in Suffolk, married the Lady Elizabeth, eldest of the two daughters and coheirs of William Murray, Earl of Dysart, in Scotland, a cadet of the illustrious house of Tullibardin, which Lady procuring letters patent in the third of Charles II. whereby the honour was granted to herself and her heirs, he, by her, who afterwards married John Maitland, Duke of Lauderdale, had Sir Lionel Talmash, the late Earl of Dysart; Thomas, the brave general in the reign of King William III. and another son, William: also two daughters, Lady Elizabeth, married to Archibald Duke of Argyll; and Lady Katherine, married first to James Stewart Lord Down, son of the Earl of Murray, and secondly, to John, the nineteenth Earl of Sutherland.

Creations.] Lord Huntingtour, in the county of Perth, and Earl of Dysart, in the county of Fife, by Charles I. 1646.

Arms.] Pearl, a fret diamond.

Crest.] On a wreath, a nag's head couped pearl, between two wings erect topaz.

Sup-

Supporters.] Two antelopes proper, attired, and ung led topaz.

Motto.] *Confido conquiefco.*

Chief Seats.] At Ham, in the county of
Surry; at Harrington, in the county of Nor-
thampton; at Helmingham, in the county of
Suffolk; and at Woodhey, in the county of
Chefter.

EARL of SELKIRK.

DUNBAR DOUGLAS, Earl of Selkirk, and
Lord Dair, fucceeded to thofe honours, upon
the death of John the third Earl, and Earl of
Ruglen, his great uncle. He was fon of Bafil
Hamilton, of Baldon Efq; by Ifabella, daughter of colonel Alexander Mackenzie, fon of
Kenneth, third Earl of Seaforth. His Lordfhip's father had alfo a fon Bafil, who died
young, and two daughters, Mary, wife of Ronald Macdonald of Clanronald, and Elizabeth
who died young.

His Lordfhip's grandfather, Lord Bafil Hamilton, youngeft fon of Wiliam Duke of Hamilton, by his wife Mary, daughter and heir
of Sir David Dunbar, of Baldoon, had iffue
Bafil abovementioned, father of the prefent
Earl, and two daughters, Mary, wife of John
Murray, of Philiphaugh, Efq; and Catharine,
of Thomas, Earl of Dundonald.

This noble family are defcended from the
Duke of Hamilton's family, who were paternally Douglas's.

Charles Hamilton, the firft Earl, third fon
of William Duke of Hamilton, was gentleman
of the bed-chamber to the Kings William III.
George

George I. and II. and sheriff of Lanerkshire, and one of the sixteen peers in the 4th, 6th, 7th, and 8th parliaments of Great Britain, and dying unmarried was succeeded by his next brother,

John Hamilton, Earl of Ruglen, who by his first wife Lady Anne, daughter of John, 7th Earl of Caffilis, had William Lord Dair, who died before his father; Lady Anne, wife of William Douglas, Earl of March, and Lady Susanna, of John ninth Earl of Caffilis.

Creations.] Earl of Selkirk, in the county of Selkirk, Aug. 14, 1646, Charles I.

Arms.] Quarterly, 1st and 4th argent, an heart gules, ensigned with an imperial crown, or, on a chief azure, three mullets of the first, for Douglas; 2d gules, three cinquefoils, ermine, for Hamilton; 3d gules, a lion rampant, argent, within a border of the 2d, charged with ten roses of the first, for Dunbar, of Baldoon.

Crest.] A salamander in flames.

Supporters.] On the dexter, a savage wreathed about the loins with laurel; and on the sinister, an antelope, both proper.

Motto.] *Jamais arriere.*

Chief Seats.] At Crawford, in the county of Lanerk; at Baldoon, in Galloway, and at St. Mary's Isle in the stewarty of Kircudbright.

EARL of NORTHESK.

GEORGE CARNEGIE Earl of NORTHESK, and Lord Rosehill; Vice-Admiral of the White, succeeded his brother, David the fifth Earl, in 1741, and married Lady Anne Lesley, daughter of the Earl of Leven, by whom he has issue,

iſſue, David, Lord Roſehill, born in May, 1749; Lady Elizabeth, married in 1766, to the Honourable James Hope, ſecond ſon of the Earl of Hopetoun, and Lady Margaret.

David, fourth Earl of Northeſk, was a Lord of Queen Anne's privy council, ſheriff of Forfar, and one of the ſixteen peers in the 2d, 3d and 4th, parliaments of Great Britain. He married Lady Margaret, daughter of James Lord Bruntiſland, and Margaret Counteſs of Wemyſs, and by her, who died in March, 1763, had two ſons, David the late Earl, who died unmarried, and George the preſent Earl. Alſo five daughters: Lady Margaret, wife of George Lord Balgony, eldeſt ſon of David, firſt Earl of Leven and Melvil; Lady Betty, of James Lord Balmerino; Lady-Anne, of Sir Alexander Hope, of Carſe, Bart. Lady Chriſtian and Lady Mary. This Earl died in 1749.

The immediate anceſtor of this family was Sir David Carnegie, of Colluthie, the tenth generation of the family of Southeſk (of whom under the attainted peers) his ſecond ſon John, had a ſon Sir John, who was created Lord Lour and Earl of Ethie, which titles by the approbation of King Charles I. he changed to that of Earl of Northeſk and Lord Roſehill.

Creations.] Lord Roſehill, April 20, 1639; and Earl of Northeſk, in the county of Forfar, Nov. 1, 1647, by King Charles I.

Arms.] Quarterly, 1ſt and 4th, topaz, an eagle diſplayed ſapphire, armed and membered, ruby, for Carnegie. 2d and 3d, pearl, a pale ruby, for Northeſk.

Creſt.] On a wreath, a demi leopard proper.

Supporters.] Two leopards reguardant proper.

Motto.]

Motto.] *Tache fans tache.* ...

Chief Seat.] At Ethie, in the county of
Forfar. ...

EARL of BALCARRAS.

JAMES LINDSAY, Earl of BALCARRAS, and
Lord Lindfay, of Cumbernauld, fucceeded his
brother Alexander the late Earl, in 1746, and
in 1749, married Anne, daughter of Sir Robert Dalrymple, fon of Sir Hugh Dalrymple,
Lord prefident of the feffion, by whom he has
iffue fix fons and two daughters, viz. Alexander, Lord Cumbernauld; Robert, Colin,
James, William and Charles; Ladies Anne and
Margaret.

Colin, the third Earl of Balcarras, a privy
counfellor to Charles and James II. married
four wives, and by the fecond, Lady Jane,
daughter of David Earl of Northefk, had iffue
a daughter, Lady Anne, Wife of Alexander,
Earl of Kelly. By his third Lady Jane Ker,
daughter of William fecond Earl of Roxburgh,
he had a daughter, Lady Margaret, wife of
John fixth Earl of Wigton, and a fon, Colin
Lord Cumbernauld, who died unmarried. By
his fourth wife, Lady Margaret, daughter of
James, Earl of Loudoun, he had two fons,
Alexander, the late Earl, who died with
iffue, and James the prefent Earl, and two
daughters, Lady Eleanor, wife of James Frafer
of Loonnay, third fon of William, Lord Car-
ton, and Lady Elizabeth who died unmarried.
This Earl deceafed in 1722.

The firft of this branch of the family of
Lindfay was John, the fecond fon of Sir David

Lindfay

Lindſay of Edzal, in Angus, who was by King James VI. made one of the ſenators of the college of juſtice, and a commiſſioner of the treaſury. David, his ſon, was created Lord Lindſay, and Alexander, the ſon of Lord David, was created Earl of Balcarras, in the county of Fife.

Creations.] Lord Lindſay, June 7, 1633, by Charles I. Earl of Balcarras, in 1551, by Charles II.

Arms.] Quarterly, 1ſt and 4th, ruby, a feſs cheque pearl and ſapphire for Lindſay. 2d and 3d, topaz, a lion rampant ruby, debruiſed with a ribband diamond, for Abernethy, all within a border of the third, ſemee of ſtars topaz.

Creſt.] On a wreath, a tent proper, ſemee of ſtars, as the arms.

Supporters.] Two lions ſejant, guardant ruby, each having a collar ſapphire, charged with three ſtars, as the creſt.

Motto.] *Aſtra, Caſtra, Numen, Lumen.*

Chief Seat.] At Balcarras in Fifeſhire.

EARL of ABOYNE.

CHARLES GORDON, Earl of ABOYNE, and Baron Gordon of Glenlivet, ſucceeded his father John, the late Earl, in 1732, and married Lady Margaret, daughter of Alexander, Earl of Galloway, by whom he has iſſue, a ſon George, Lord Glenlivet, and Ladies Catherine and Margaret.

John, the late Earl, married Grace, daughter of George Lockhart, of Carnwath, Eſq; and by her, who after his deceaſe married James

E

Earl

Earl of Murray, had iffue three fons, Charles the prefent Earl, George and Lockhart.

Charles, the fecond Earl, by his wife Lady Elizabeth, daughter of Patrick, Earl of Strathmore, had a fon John, the late Earl, and three daughters; Lady Helen, wife of George Kinnaird, Efq; and mother of Charles Lord Kinnaird; Lady Elizabeth, who died unmarried; and Lady Grace, wife of James Grant, of Knockando, Efq;

Charles, the third and youngeft fon of George, the fecond Marquis of Huntley, having highly manifefted his loyalty to King Charles I. in time of the civil wars, as alfo to King Charles II. during the ufurpation, was, in recompence of thofe fervices, raifed to the dignity of Earl of Aboyne, by Charles II. and dying in 1680, left by his wife, Lady Elizabeth Lyon, daughter of John Earl of Strathmore, three fons, Charles, fecond Earl above, George and John; and a daughter Lady Elizabeth, married to John, fon and heir of George Earl of Cromartie.

Creations.] Earl of Aboyne in Aberdeenfhire, Sept. 10, 1660, 12 Charles II.

Arms.] Sapphire, a chevron between three boars heads erafed, topaz, for Gordon, with a double treffure flowered with fleurs de lis within, and adorned with crefcents without, of the laft, for Seton.

Creft.] On a wreath a demi-lion ruby, armed and langued fapphire.

Supporters.] Three chevaliers in complete armour each holding an halbert proper.

Motto.] *Stant cætera tigno.*

Chief Seat.] At Aboyne, in the county of Aberdeen.

EARL

EARL of DUNDONALD.

THOMAS COCHRAN, Earl of DUNDONALD and Lord Cochran, fucceeded William 7th and late Earl of Dundonald, who was killed at the taking of Cape Breton, in July 1758, as being fon of William, fon of Sir John Cochran, of Ochiltree, fecond fon of William firft Earl of Dundonald. His Lordfhip was many years a commiffioner of the excife in Scotland, and married firft, Elizabeth, daughter of John Ker, of Morrifton, Efq; by whom he had a fon William that died young, and a daughter Lady Grifel. By his fecond wife, Jane, daughter of Archibald Stewart, of Torrence, Efq; he has iffue fix fons and one daughter, viz. Archibald, Lord Cochran ; Charles, John, James, Bafil, Alexander. and Lady Betty.

This family, which originally took its firname from the barony of Cochran, in the county of Renfrew, is of great antiquity; and though none of them arrived to the dignity of peerage till the reign of Charles I. yet they were Barons of fome diftinction for many centuries before, and had large poffeffions in thofe parts : but the paternal name now is Blair; for Elizabeth, the heirefs of the Cochran family, marrying Alexander, a younger fon of John Blair of that Ilk, the faid Alexander, by the marriage-articles, changed his name to Cochran, and had feven fons, four of whom were officers in the fervice of King Charles I. and the eldeft fon dying without iffue, was fucceeded by his brother Sir William, who was created Baron

of

of Cochran in Renfrew; and Earl of Dundonald, near Irwin, in the county of Air.

Creations.] Lord Cochran, Dec. 17, 1647, by Charles I. Earl of Dundonald, May 12, 1669, by Charles II.

Arms.] Pearl, a chevron ruby between three boars heads erazed, sapphire.

Crest.] On a wreath a horse passant, pearl.

Supporters.] Two greyhounds of the last, coloured and leished, topaz.

Motto.] *Virtute & labore.*

Chief Seat.] At Culross in Fifeshire; and the castle of Dundonald, in Airshire.

EARL of KINTORE.

Upon the decease of WILLIAM KEITH, fourth Earl of KINTORE, without issue, in 1761, his honours lay dormant; but his estate devolved upon George, late Earl Marshal, as heir of entail, who being attainted and forfeited for the rebellion in 1715, in the year 1759, received a pardon, from King George II. and was thereby enabled to succeed to the said estate, and is governor of Neufchatel for the King of Prussia.

This noble family was descended from that of the Earl-Marshal; for William, the sixth Earl-Marshal, marrying Lady Mary Erskine, daughter of John Earl of Mar, had first, William his successor; secondly, George, who succeeded his brother William; and thirdly, Sir John Keith, who, being instrumental in preserving the regalia of the kingdom from falling into the hands of the English, during the usurpation of Oliver Cromwell, was, after the reftoration, created Knight-Marfhal, and Eul of Kintore, by Charles II. June 26, 167 , and made one of his privy-council and treafurer-depute.

Creations.] *Ut fupra.*

Arms.] Quarterly, 1ft and 4th, ruby, a fcepter and fword in faltire. with an imperial crown in chief topaz, al within an orb of eight thiftles of the fecond, as a coat of augmentation. 2d and 3d, pearl, on a chief ruby, three pallets topaz, for Keith.

Creft.] On a wreath, an aged Lady from the middle upwards, richly attired, holding in her right hand a garland of laurel.

Supporters.] Two chevaliers in armour, each holding a pike in a centinel's pofture, proper.

Motto.] *Quæ amiffa falva.*

Chief Seat.] At Keith hall, near Inverury, in the county of Aberdeen.

EARL of BREADALBINE.

JOHN CAMPBELL, Earl of BREADALBINE, Vifcount Glenorchy, Lord Campbell and Baronet, one of the fixteen peers for Scotland, Knight of the moft honourable order of the Bath, and LL.D. fucceeded his father, John, the late Earl, in February 1752; paffed through the higheft offices in the late reign, and in the prefent was keeper of the privy feal in Scotland, which he refigned in 1766. In 1721, he married Lady Amabel Grey, eldeft daughter of Henry Duke of Kent, and by her, who died at Copenhagen (where his Lordfhip was then ambaffador and minifter plenipotentiary) on March 2, 1726-7, had one fon, Henry, and one

one daughter, (both born in Denmark.) The
son died young, but the daughter, Lady
Jemima, is wife of Philip Earl of Hardwick,
and Marchioness Grey (which titles see in my
English Peerage.) He married, secondly, in
1730, Arabella, grand-daughter and heir of
Sir Thomas Perfhal, of Great Sugnal, in Staffordshire, Bart. and had issue by her, George,
who died in his infancy, and John, Lord Glenorchy, who married Wilhelmina, 2d daughter
of William Maxwell, of Prefton, Esq; fifter of
the late amiable Countess of Sutherland, and
aunt of the present.

John, the late Earl, married Henrietta,
daughter of Sir Edward Villiers, and fifter of
Edward, the first Earl of Jerfey, by whom he
had the present Lord, and two daughters, Ladies
Charlotte, and Henrietta, who was Lady of
the bed-chamber to the Princesses Amelia and
Carolina.

This antient and noble family is defcended,
in a regular fucceffion, from Duncan, the first
Lord Campbell, anceftor of the family of
Argyll. John, the first Earl of Breadalbine,
in confideration of his perfonal merit, and the
loyalty of his anceftors, was, from a Baronet,
created Lord Campbell, Vifcount Glenorchy,
and Earl of Breadalbine, in the county of
Perth. He married, first, the Lady Mary,
daughter of Henry Rich, Earl of Holland, and
had two fons, Duncan, who died before his
father without iffue, and John, the late Earl.
He married, secondly, Mary Countess Dowager
of Caithness, daughter of Archibald Marquis of
Argyll, by whom he had a fon Colin, who
died

died young, and Lady Mary, wife of Archibald Cockburn, of Langton, Efq.

Creations.] Baronet of Nova Scotia, May 29, 1625, by Charles I. Lord Campbell, Vifcount Glenorchy, and Earl of Breadalbine, Jan. 28, 1677, by Charles II.

Arms.] Quarterly, 1ft and 4th, Gyrony of eight pieces topaz and diamond, for Campbell. 2d, topaz, a feffe cheque pearl and fapphire, for Stewart. 3d pearl, a galley diamond, her oars in action, and fails furled clofe, for the Lordfhip of Lorn.

Creft.] On a wreath a boar's head erafed proper.

Supporters.] Two ftags of the latter, attired and unguled topaz.

Motto.] *Follow me!*

Chief Seats.] At Kelchurn-caftle and Glenorchie in the county of Argyll; at Finlarrig and Taymouth in Breadalbine; at Great Sugnal, in Staffordfhire; and Cleaveland Court, London.

EARL of ABERDEEN.

GEORGE GORDON, Earl of ABERDEEN, and Lord Haddo, fucceeded his father. William, the late Earl, in 1745, and was one of the fixteen Peers in the two laft parliaments. He married Catherine, daughter of Sir Ofwald Hanfon, of Wakefield in Yorkfhire, by whom he has iffue, George Lord Haddo; William; Ladies Catharine, Anne, Sufanna, and Mary.

William, the late Earl, fucceeded George his father, the firft Earl, in 1720, and married Lady Mary, daughter of David Earl of Leven

E 4   and

and Melvil, by whom he had a daughter, Lady Anne, wife of William Earl of Dumfries, and died in 1755. He married, 2dly, Lady Susan, eldest daughter of John Duke of Athol, by whom he had issue George, the present Earl, and Lady Catharine, wife, first, of Cosmo Duke of Gordon, and mother of the present Duke, and, 2d, of colonel Staats Long Morris. He married, 3dly, Lady Anne, third daughter of Alexander Duke of Gordon, by whom he had four sons and one daughter, viz. William, captain of dragoons; Cosmo, an officer in the guards; Alexander, an Advocate; and Charles: Lady Henrietta, wife of Robert Gordon, of Haugh-head, Esq;

Of this antient family, who sprung from the noble house of Gordon three hundred years ago, and for many centuries were possessed of a large estate in the county of Aberdeen, was Patrick Gordon of Haddo, from whom descended Sir John Gordon, who, in 1642, was created a Baronet; but two years after, for his adherence to King Charles I. and holding out his castle of Haddo against the parliament-army, was taken prisoner, condemned, and executed at Edinburgh. His son George was created an Earl, made one of the judges of session, president of the council, and afterwards Chancellor of Scotland.

Creations.] Earl of Aberdeen and Baron Haddo, Nov. 30, 1682, by Charles II.

Arms.] Sapphire, three boars heads couped with n a double tressure of thistles, roses, and fleurs de lis, flowered and counterflowered topaz.

Crest

Crest.] On a wreath two naked arms, holding a bow to let fly an arrow.

Supporters.] On the dexter side a senator of
the college of juftice; and on the finifter a
minifter of ftate, in his robes, both proper.

Motto.] *Fortuna fequatur.*

Chief Seats.] At Haddo-houfe and Kelly, in
Aberdeenfhire; and Hill-ftreet, London.

EARL of DUNMORE.

JOHN MURRAY, Earl of DUNMORE, Vifcount Fincaftle, and Baron Murray of Blair,
Mouilli, and Tillimet, one of the fixteen Peers
for Scotland, fucceeded his father, William,
the late Earl, in 1756, and in 1759, married.
Lady Charlotte, daughter of Alexander Earl
of Galloway, by whom he has iffue a fon,
George Lord Fincaftle, and two daughters,
Ladies Catharine and Augufta.

William, the late and fourth Earl, married
Catherine, daughter of William Lord Nairn,
by whom he had iffue, John, the prefent Earl;
Charles; William, an officer in the army;
Lady Margaret; Lady Catharine, wife of John
Drummond of Logiealmond, Efq; Ladies Jane
and Elizabeth. His brother,

John, third Earl, was colonel of the third
regiment of foot guards, general of foot, a
Lord of the bedchamber, and governor of Ply-
mouth. His brother,

James, fecond Earl, died without iffue; and
their father, Lord Charles Murray, the firft
Earl, was fecond fon of John Marquis of Athol,
and brother of John the firft Duke of Athol,
and of the Privy Council to Queen Anne. He
married

E 5

married Catherine, daughter of Robert Watts of Herefordſhire, Eſq; by whom he had iſſue five ſons and three daughters, viz. James, John, and William, ſucceſſively Earls of Dunmore, as above recited; Robert, a brigad'er general, and colonel of a regiment, who died in 1738; Thomas, colonel of a regiment of foot; Lady Henrietta, wife of Patrick Lord Kinnaird; Lady Anne, of John Cochran, Earl of Dundonald; and Lady Katherine, of John Lord Nairn.

Creations.] Earl of Dunmore, in Perthſhire, Viſcount, Baron, &c. Aug. 16, 1686, by James VII. 2d of England.

Arms.] Quarterly, firſt, ſapphire, three ſtars pearl, within a double treſſure with fleurs de lis topaz, for Murray. 2d, quarterly, firſt and fourth topaz, a feſſe cheque pearl and ſapphire, for Stewart. 2d and 3d, pally of ſix, topaz and diamond, for Athol. 3d, grand quarter as the 2d, the 4th as the firſt; and over all, as a ſurtout, an eſcutcheon ruby, charged with three legs in triangle, conjoined in feſſe at the upper part of the thigh, and garniſhed proper, for the Iſle of Man, as related to the Earls of Derby.

Creſt.] On a wreath, a demi-ſavage, wreathed about the middle with laurel, holding in his right hand a ſword erect, proper, the pommel and hilt topaz, and in the left a key of the latter.

Supporters.] On the dexter, a ſavage wreathed as the creſt, his feet in fetters, and a chain over his right arm. On the ſiniſter, a lion ruby, with a collar ſapphire, charged with three ſtars pearl.

Motto.] *Furth Fortune.*

Chief

Chief Seats.] At Dunmore-park, in Stirlingfhire, and Fincaftle, of Athol, in the county of
Perth.

COUNTESS of ORKNEY.

MARY O-BRIEN, Countefs of the Iflands of
ORKNEY, Vifcountefs Kirkwall, and Baronefs
Dechmont, fucceeded her mother, the late
Countefs, in 1756, and in 1753, married cap-
tain Obrien of the guards, by whom fhe has
iffue,

George, firft Earl of Orkney, was a gallant
officer, and fifth fon of William, firft Duke of
Hamilton of the Douglas family; diftin-
guifhed himfelf greatly in the wars of King
William and Queen Anne, and after rifing
gradually through the feveral military ftations,
was, at h's death, field marfhal of the forces,
&c. &c. &c. He married Elizabeth, eldeft
daughter of Sir Edward Villiers, and fifter of
Edward Earl of Jerfey, by whom he had iffue,
1. Lady Anne, (the late Countefs) wife of
William Obrien, Earl of Inchiquin, by whom
fhe had two daughters, Lady Mary, the prefent Countefs, and Lady Anne. 2. Lady Frances, wife of Thomas Lumley Saunderfon, late
Earl of Scarborough. 3. Lady Harriot, of John
Earl of Cork and Orrery, and died Aug. 28,
1732. This Earl died Jan. 29, 1736-7.

Creations.] Earl of Orkney, Vifcount Kirkwall, and Baron Dechmont, Jan. 3, 1695-6, by
King William III.

Arms.] Quarterly, 1ft fapphire, a fhip at
anchor within a double treffure, with fleurs de
lis topaz, for Orkney. 2d and 3d, the quar-

tered arms of Hamilton ; and in the duch, the
arms of Douglas.

Creſt.] In a ducal coronet topaz an oak fructed, as in the arms of Hamilton.

Supporters.] On the dexter ſide an antelope
pearl, his horns, ducal collar, chain, and hoofs,
topaz. On the ſiniſter a ſtag proper, attired,
collared, chained, and hoofed as the dexter.

Motto.] *Thorough.*

Chief Seats.] At Cliefden and Taplow-court
in the county of Buckingham.

EARL of MARCH and RUG-LEN.

JAMES DOUGLAS, Earl of MARCH and RUG-
LEN, Baron Douglas of Niedpath, Lymn and
Manerhead, a Lord of the King's bedchamber,
a Knight of the Thiſtle, and one of the ſix-
teen Peers for Scotland, ſucceeded his father
William, the late and ſecond Earl : which

William, ſecond Earl, was the eldeſt ſon and
ſucceſſor of William, firſt Earl of March,
ſecond ſon of William Duke of Queenſberry,
who died in 1705. The ſaid William, the ſecond Earl, married Lady Anne, Counteſs of
Ruglen, as heir general of her father John,
Earl of Selkirk and Ruglen (ſee that title) by
whom he had iſſue the preſent Earl: His Lady
ſurviving him married Anthony Sawyer, Eſq;
Pay-maſter of the forces in Scotland.

Creations.] Earl of March, &c. April 20,
1697, by William III. Earl of Ruglen, April
15, 1697, by William III.

Arms.] Quarterly, 1ſt and 4th, the whole
arms of the Duke of Queenſberry ; ſecond and
third,

third, ruby, a lion rampant, pearl, within a border of the laft, charged wi h eight cinque-foils of the firft; for the title of March.

Creft.] On a wreath a man's heart, ruby, enfigned with an imperial crown proper, between two wings erect, topaz.

Supporters.] On the dexter-fide a Pegafus, pearl, the fame with Queenfberry. On the finifter a lion, as in the arms.

Motto.] *Forward.*.

Chief Seats.] At Niedpath-Caftle, in the county of Tweeddale or Peeblefhire; at Barnton, in Mid-Lothian; Seymour-place, London.

EARL of MARCHMONT.

HUGH HUME, Earl of MARCHMONT, Vifcount Blaffonbury, Lord Polwarth of Polwarth, Redbraes and Greenlaw, in Berwickfhire, and, Baronet, a Privy Counfellor, one of the fixteen Peers for Scotland, and keeper of the Great Seal there, F. R. S. fucceeded his father, Alexander, the late Earl; in 1740, and married Mifs Anne Weftern, by whom he had a fon, who died young, and three daughters; Lady Anne wife of John Patterfon, Efq; eldeft fon of Sir John Patterfon, of Eccles, Bart. Lady Margaret, of lieutenant-colonel Stewart, and died in 1765, without iffue; and Lady Diana, wife of Walter Scott, of Harden, Efq; and a fon, Patrick, who died young. Her Ladyfhip deceafing in 1747, he married, fecondly, Mifs Elizabeth Crompton, of London, by whom he has iffue a fon, Alexander, Lord Polwarth, born in July, 1750.

Alexander,

Alexander, the late Earl, held many great poſts under the government, and married Margaret, daughter and heir of Sir George Campbell, of Cefnock, by whom he had iſſue four ſons and four daughters, viz. George and Patrick, who died in 1724; Hugh the preſent Earl; and Alexander Hume Campbell, who was a Privy Counſellor, and member for Berwickſhire in four parliaments, and Lord Regiſter of Scotland: he died in July, 1760, and by his wife, Miſs Paris, left no iſſue. The daughters were Lady Anne, wife of Sir William Purves, Bart. Lady Grifel, who died unmarried; Lady Jane, wife of James Nimmo, Eſq; and Lady Margaret, who died unmarried.

John Hume, in 1444 married Katherine Hume, daughter of Sir Thomas Hume of that Ilk, and in the ſame year, obtained a charter from King James II. of the barony of Polwarth to himſelf and Katharine his wife, and to their heirs; and leaving only two daughters, Mary, married to George Hume of Wedderburn, in Berwickſhire; and Margaret, to Sir Patrick the ſon of Sir David Hume, Laird of Wedderburn, who was younger ſon of Sir Thomas Hume of that Ilk before-mentioned, the ſaid Sir Patrick obtained with her the barony of Polwarth; and for his military ſervices to King James II. his ſon Patrick had many lands beſtowed on him by King James III. and IV. and, in 1499, was made comptroller of Scotland.

: Sir Patrick Hume, grandfather of the preſent Earl, attended King William into England, in 1688; and being inſtrumental in bringing about the Revolution, he was made one of

of the Privy Council, and created Lord Polwarth, Dec. 26, 1690, by William and Mary.
He was likew'se appointed fheriff of the county
of Berwick, high commiffioner to the parliament, one of the extraordinary Lords of Seffion, Lord Chancellor of Scotland, a commiffioner of the Treafury and Admiralty; and
created Earl of Marchmont, April 23, 1697,
by King William III.

Creations.] *Ut fupra.*

Arms.] Quarterly, firft grand quarter counter-quartered, firft and fourth emerald, a lion
rampant, pearl, for Hume; fecond and th'rd
pearl, three fwallows of the firft, for Pepdie;
fecond pearl, three piles iffuing from the chief
ingrailed, ruby, for Polwarth; th'rd pearl, a
crofs ingrailed, diamond, for Sinclair; the
fourth grand quarter as the firft; and over all,
as a furtout, an efcutcheon pearl, charged with
an orange enfigned with an imperial crown, all
proper, as a coat of augmentation, given by
King William III.

Creft.] On a wreath a man's heart, out of
which iffues a dexter arm erect, grafping a fci-
mitar, all proper.

Supporters.] Two lions reguardant pearl,
armed and langued, ruby.

Motto.] *Fides probata coronat.*

Chief Seats.] In the town of Berwick upon
Tweed; at Redbraes, in the county of Berwick;
and in Curzon ftreet, May-Fair, London.

EARL

EARL of HYNDFORD.

JOHN CARMICHAEL, Earl of HYNDFORD, Lord Carmichael and Baronet, a Lord of the Privy Council, commiffioner of the Police, and vice-admiral of Scotland, alfo one of the fix-teen Peers, and a Knight of the antient order of the Thiftle, fucceeded his father, James, the late and fecond Earl, on Aug. 16, 1737. He married Elizabeth, eldeft daughter of that brave admiral Sir Cloudefley Shovel, and widow of Robert Lord Romney, but by her had no iffue ; and married fecondly, Jane, daughter of Benjamin Vigor, of Fulham, in Middlefex, Efq; This noble Lord has been twice high commiffioner to the general affembly of the church of Scotland, envoy extraordinary to the courts of Pruffia and Ruffia, and a Lord of the King's bedchamber.

James, the late Earl, was a Lord of the Police, colonel of a regiment of dragoons, and a brigadier-general. He married Lady Elizabeth, daughter of John, Earl of Lauderdale, by whom he had iffue five fons and fix daughters, viz. John, the prefent Earl; William, late Bifhop of Meath, in Ireland; James, member in three parliaments for the burghs of Selkirk, &c. Archibald, a captain of foot, and Charles, in the fervice of the Eaft India company, which laft four died without iffue: Lady Margaret, wife of Sir John Anftruther, of that Ilk; Lady Mary, of Charles O Hara, Efq; Lady Anne, of —— Dufcina, Efq; Ladies Elizabeth, Rachael and Grace, who died young.

John,

John, the second Lord Carmichael, and first Earl of Hyndford, the father of the late Lord, being one of the Scots Peers who joined most early in the revolution, was, by King William, in recompence of his services, made a commissioner of the Privy Seal, colonel of a regiment of dragoons, one of the Privy Council, high commissioner to the general assembly, one of the Secretaries of State, and was created an Earl by King William III.

Of this antient family, which is said to assume their sirname from the lands of Carmichael, in the county of Lanerk, where they still have their chief seat, was Sir John Carmichael, who accompanied Archibald Earl of Douglas to the assistance of Charles VI. of France against the English; and signalizing his valour at the battle of Baugey, in April 1421, and breaking his spear, when the French and Scots got the victory, had thereupon added to his paternal arms, a dexter hand, an armed arm holding a broken spear, which is now the crest of the family.

Creations.] Baronet by Charles I. Baron of Carmichael, in the county of Lanerk, Dec. 27, 1647, Earl of Hyndford, June 25, 1701, by William III.

Arms.] Pearl, a fess wreathy, sapphire and ruby.

Crest.] On a wreath, an armed arm erect, holding a broken spear.

Supporters.] On the dexter side a chevalier in compleat armour, plumed on the head with three feathers pearl, and holding in his right hand, a battoon royal. On the sinister, a horse of the latter, furnished ruby.

Motto.]

Motto.] *Toujours preſte.*

Chief Seats.] At Carmichael in the county, of Lanerk; at Wefter Hall, in the ſame county; and in Groveſnor-ſquare, London.

EARL of ROSEBERRY.

NEIL PRIMROSE, Earl of ROSEBERRY, Viſcount Primrofe and Roſeberry, Lord Dalmenie, and Baronet, ſucceeded his father, James, the late Earl, in 1755, and in 1764, married ——, only daughter and heir of Sir —— ——, Bart.

James, the ſaid late and ſecond Earl of Roſeberry, married Mary, fiſter of the preſent Duke of Argyll, and by her had a ſon Archibald, Lord Dalmenie, who died in Aug. 1755, and John Lord Dalmenie, who alſo died before his father; James, who died young, and Neil the preſent Earl; alſo two daughters, Lady Mary, who died young, and Lady Dorothea, wife of Adam Inglis, Eſq; eldeſt ſon of Sir John Inglis, of Cramond, Bart.

Archibald, firſt Earl, and father of James the late Earl, was one of the commiſſioners for the treaty of Union, and one of the ſixteen Peers to the four firſt parliaments of Great Britain. He married Dorothy, daughter and heir of Everingham Creſſy, of Birkin, in Yorkſhire, Eſq; by whom he had iſſue, James, the late Earl; Richard, John, Lady Mary, wife of Sir Archibald Primroſe, of Dunipace; Lady Margaret, of Alexander Earl of Caithneſs; and Ladies Dorothy and Elizabeth, who died young.

Of this family, who took their name from the lands and barony of Primroſe, in the county of of Fife, was James Primrofe, who, being bred to the law, was, by King James VI. in 1602, made clerk of the council, which poft he held near forty years. From him defcended Archibald Primrofe, who was alfo appointed clerk of the council, by King Charles I. as his father and grandfather had been; and, by Charles the fecond, was created a Baronet. At the time of the reftoration, he was, for his loyalty and merit, made one of the judges in the court of feffion, and Lord Regifter. He married, to his firft wife, Elizabeth, daughter of Sir James Keith, fon of George, the fourth Earl Marfhal; by whom he had Sir William Primrofe, of Carington, who was father of James the firft Vifcount Primrofe; and by his fecond wife, Agnes, daughter of Sir William Grey of Pittendrum, had a fon Sir Archibald, and a daughter Grifel, who was married to Francis the ninth Lord Semple.

James, above-mentioned, was created Vifcount Rofeberry, in Mid Lothian, by Queen Anne, and his male iffue ceafing, in Hugh his fon, the third Vifcount, was fucceeded by Sir Archibald Primrofe of Dalmenie, only fon of the fecond marriage of Sir Archibald Primrofe above-mentioned, who was, as obferved, firft Earl of Rofeberry.

Creations.] Baronet, by Charles II. Vifcount Rofeberry, April 1, 1700, Earl, April 10, 1703.

Arms.] Quarterly, 1ft and 4th, topaz, a lion rampant, emerald; fecond and third emerald, three primrofes in a double treffure counterflory, topaz, for the name of Primrofe.

Creft.] On a wreath a demi lion ruby, holding in his dexter paw a primrofe, as in the arms.

Sup-

Supporters.] Two lions emerald.
Motto.] *Fide & Fiducia.*
Chief Seats.] At Barnbougle and Dalmenie,
in the county of Linlthgow, and at Roseberry,
in the county of Edinburgh.

EARL of GLASGOW.

DAVID BOYLE, Earl of GLASGOW, Viscount
Kelburn, and Lord Boyle of Stewarton, succeeded his father John, the late Earl, in 1740,
and in June 1755, married Elizabeth, daughter
of George Lord Rofs; by whom he has issue
John, Lord Boyle, born March 26, 1756, and
two daughters, Ladies Betty and Jane.

John, the late Earl, married Helen, daughter
of William Morrifon, of Prefton-Grange, Efq;
by whom he had two fons and fix daughters:
John, now Earl; Patrick, who married Mifs
More, of Caldwell, without iffue ; Ladies Janet,
Margaret, Jane, Marian, deceafed ; Catherine
and Helen.

This family is of great antiquity, and had
large poffeffions in Airfhire. In the reign of
Alexander III. Richard Boyle, of Kelburn,
had a fon and heir, Richard, who, in 1296,
was one of the Barons of Scotland, that fwore
allegiance to King Edward I. of England ;
and from him defcended Hugo de Boyle, who
in 1399 gave his lands to the monks of Paifley,
for the welfare of his foul. From the faid
Hugo defcended John Boyle of Kelburn, who
loft his life at the battle of Bannockburn with
King James III. 1488 ; and his fon John fucceeding, obtained from James V. a grant of
divers lands in the ifle of Cumra, near Bute.

From

From this John defcended another John, who was a zealous loyalift in the fervice of Queen Mary; and his fon John was banifhed his country ten years, for his adherence to Charles I. This John left an only daughter Grifel, who, being an heirefs, was married to David Boyle of Halkhead, Efq; her coufin; and the faid David dying in 1672, left a fon John, who, marrying Mary, daughter of Sir William Stewart, of Allington, in the county of Lanerk, had two fons, David and William.

David his heir, being returned member in the convention of eftates for the county of Bute, which declared the Prince of Orange King of Scotland, was made one of his Majefty's council, and created a Baron, Jan. 13, 1699, by William III. and was created Vifcount and Earl, April 10, 1703, by Queen Anne. He was at the fame time made deputy-treafurer, one of the Privy Council, Lord Regifter, and one of the commiffioners for concluding the Union, in which year he had the honour to reprefent her Majefty's perfon in the general affembly.. He married firft Margaret, fifter of John Crawford, Vifcount Garnock, by whom he had three fons, viz. John, the late Earl; Patrick, for many years one of the Lords of Seffion; and Charles.

By his fecond wife, who was Jane, daughter and fole heir of William Muir of Rowallan, in Coningham, he had two daughters, Lady Jane, married to major-general Sir James Campbell, brother of Hugh, Earl of Loudon; by whom he had a fon, who took the name of Muir, as reprefenting his mother who was an heirefs; Lady Anne.

Crea-

Creations.] *Ut supra.*

Arms.] Quarterly, 1ft and 4th topaz, an imperial eagle, ruby, for Glafgow ; fecond and third party per bend, crenelle pearl and ruby, for Boyle of England ; and over all, by way of furtout, an efcutcheon of the fi ft, charged with three ftags horns of the fecond, for Boyle of Kelburn.

Creft.] On a wreath an eagle with two heads party per pale, crenelle, topaz, and ruby.

Supporters.] On the dexter fide a favage proper, wreathed about the temples and middle with laurel, a branch of which he holds in his right hand. On the finifter, a lion, party per pale, crenelle, pearl and ruby.

Motto.] *Dominus providebit.*

Chief Seats.] At Kelburn and Rowallan, in Airfhire.

EARL of BUTE.

JOHN STUART, Earl of BUTE, Baron Mount Stewart, Knight of the moft noble order of the Garter, of the ancient order of the Thiftle, and Baronet ; a Lord of the Privy Council, a governor of the Charterhoufe, ranger of Richmond park, chancellor of the Univerfity of Aberdeen, and one of the fixteen peers for Scotland, fucceeded James, the late Earl, his father, in 1722, and married Mary, only daughter of the Honourable Edward Wortley Montague, by the Lady Mary Pierpont, daughter of Evelyn, firft Duke of Kingfton, (who died in Auguft 1762) by which Lady, (who upon the death of her father in 1761, fucceeded to a very large eftate, and was created Baronefs

Mount

Mount Stewart, which fee in my Englifh Peerage) he has iffue five fons ; John Lord Mount Stewart, member for Boffiney in Cornwall, who married, Nov. 12, 1766, Mifs Windfor, eldeft of the daughters and coheirs of the late Vifcount Windfor ; James, who on the deceafe of his mother will fucceed to his grandfather's vaft eftate, taking the firname of Wortley Montague ; Frederick, Charles, and William ; and fix daughters, Lady Mary. wife of Sir James Lowther, Bart. Lady Jane ; Lady Anne, wife of Hugh Earl Percy, fon and heir of Hugh Duke of Northumberland ; Ladies Augufta, Caroline, and Louifa.

James, the late Earl, fucceeded his father James in 1710, was a gentleman of the bedchamber to King George I. one of the commiffioners of trade in Scotland, and one of the fixteen peers for North Britain in the two parliaments of George I. He married Lady Anne, daughter of Archibald Duke of Argyle, and by her, who died Jan. 28, 1723, had two fons, viz. John, the prefent Earl ; James, chofen reprefentative in parliament for Argyllfhire, in Jan. 1741-2 ; for the fhire of Bute in 1747 ; and for the burghs of Air, &c. in 1754, inherits the name and fortune of his great grandfather, Sir George Mackenzie of Rofehaugh. In 1747, he married Lady Betty Campbell, fecond daughter and coheir of John late Duke of Argyle, by whom he has iffue. He is Lord Privy Seal for Scotland, member for Rofsfhire, and a Privy Counfellor. And four daughters : Lady Mary, wife of Sir Robert Menzie, of Weeme, Bart. Lady Anne, of James Ruthven, Lord Ruthven ; Lady Jane, of William Courtenay, Efq; and

9   **Lady**

Lady Grace, of John Campbell, of Stonefield, Efq;

Sir James Stewart, the father of the late Earl, was one of the Privy Council to Queen Anne, by whom he was created a Baron and Earl. He married Agnes, daughter of Sir George Mackenzie, of Rofehaugh, Lord Advocate to James VII. and had iffue, James, the late Earl, and a daughter, Lady Margaret, married to John Crawford, Vifcount Garnock. By his fecond wife, who was Chriftian, daughter of William Douglas of Kincavil, he had a fon John, who died without iffue.

This noble family is defcended from Sir John Stewart, a fon of King Robert II. who, by his father's grant, had a fair poffeffion in the ifland of Bute, with the heritable jurifdiction of that county, wherein he was confirmed by the charter of Robert III. his brother.

Creations.] Baronet by Charles I. 28 March, 1627. Baron Mount Stewart, in the ifle of Bute, and Earl of Bute, April 14, 1703, by Queen Anne.

Arms.] Topaz, a feffe cheque, pearl, and fapphire, with a double treffure counterflory, with fleurs de lis, ruby.

Creft.] On a wreath, a demi-lion, ruby.

Supporters.] On the dexter fide, a horfe, pearl; on the finifter, a ftag, proper.

Motto.] *Avito viret honore.*

Chief Seats.] At Mount Stewart, in the ifle of Bute; Montague-houfe, Yorkfhire; Luton-hoe, Bedfordfhire, and Kew, in Surry; South Audley-ftreet, London.

JOHN HOPE, Earl of HOPETON, and Lord Hope, F. R. S. succeeded his father Charles, the late Earl, in 1741, and married Lady Anne Ogilvie, eldest daughter of James Earl of Finlater and Seafield, and by her, who died in Feb. 1759, he had issue Charles Lord Hope ; James, who married Lady Betty, sister of the Earl of Northesk ; John, who died in September 1759 ; Henry ; Lady Betty, late Countess of Drumlanrig, (see Duke of Queensberry) who died in April 1756 ; Ladies Henrietta and Sophia. His Lordship, secondly, married Jane daughter of Robert Oliphant, of Rossie, Esq; by whom he has one son and two daughters. He is a commissioner of forfeited estates.

Charles Hope, Esq; father of the present Earl, being Knight for the county of Linlithgow, was one of the Privy Council to Queen Anne, who created him an Earl. He was one of the sixteen peers for Scotland, from 1722, till his death. In 1738, he was invested with the order of the Thistle ; and married Lady Henrietta Johnston, daughter of William marquis of Annandale, and by her, who died in 1750, had two sons and six daughters, viz. John, the present Earl of Hopeton ; Charles, elected Knight of the shire for Linlithgow, in April 1743, which he has represented ever since. In 1744, he was made commissary-general of the musters in Scotland, and governor of Blackness Castle, and is F. R. S. He takes the name of Weir, by marrying the heiress of Sir William Weir of Blackwood, Bart. by whom he had

two fons and one daughter ; but that Lady
dying, he married, 2dly, in March 1746, Lady
Anne, daughter of Hen y late Earl of Darling-
ton, by whom he has two fons ; Lady Sophia,
fecond wife of James Earl of Finlater and Seafield ; Lady Henrietta, of Francis Lord Napier ;
Lady Margaret, of John Dundas of Du ding-
fton, Efq; Lady Helen, of James Watfon of
Saughton, Efq; Lady Charlotte, of Thomas
Lord Erfkine ; and Lady Chriftian, of Thomas
Graham of Balgowan, Efq;

This noble family is defcended from Henry
Hope, a native of Holland, who, about two
centuries ago, came over and fettled in Scot-
land, and was an eminent merchant at Edin-
burgh, who by his wife Jacquet de Tott, a
French Lady, had iffue Sir Thomas Hope, of
Craigie-hall, Lord Advocate to James and
Charles I.

Creations.] Earl of Hopeton, &c. in the
county of Stirling. April 15, 1703, 2 Anne.

Arms.] Sapphire on a chevron, topaz, between three befants, a bay leaf, emerald.

Creft.] On a wreath a globe fplit on the top,
and above it a rainbow with a cloud at each
end, all proper.

Supporters.] Two women in loofe garments,
the hair of their heads hanging down, each
holding an anchor in the outer hand.

Motto.] *At fpes nonfracta.*

Chief Seats.] At Abercorn, now Hopeton-
houfe, in Weft Lothian, or county of Linlithgow ; and at Byres, in Eaft-Lothian.

E A R L

EARL of PORTMORE.

CHARLES COLLIER, Earl and Baron of PORT-MORE, Vifcount Milfington, and Knight of the antient order of the Thiftle, fucceeded his father, David, the late Earl, in 1729, and in 1732, married Juliana, Duchefs Dowager of Leeds, and daughter of Roger Hele of Devonfhire, Efq; by whom he has iffue Lady Catharine, born in 1733, and in 1750, married to Nathaniel Curzon, Efq; now Lord Scarfdale ; a daughter born in 1735 ; a fon, Lord Milfington, who died Jan. 16, 1756, and other children.

His Lordfhip, while a commoner, and the fecond fon of a peer, was, in 1727, elected member of parliament for Andover in Hampfhire ; and, in 1734, and 1741, elected one of the fixteen Peers for Scotland.

On Feb. 26, 1676, Alexander Robertfon, alias Colyear, or Collier, of the province of Holland, being created a baronet, Sir David his fon, who, in 1691, helped to reduce Ireland, was created Lord Portmore. In the firft of Queen Anne he was promoted to the rank of major-general ; and April 16, 1703, created an Earl. In 1710 he was made commander in chief of her Majefty's forces in Portugal, in the room of the Earl of Gallway. In 1711, he was made a general of foot ; and, in 1712, commanded part of the army in Flanders under the Duke of Ormond. The fame year, he was made one of the Queen's Privy Council, and a Knight of the Thiftle. In Auguft 1713, he was appointed governor of Gibraltar ; and in October, that year, chofen one of the fixteen

F 2

Peers for Scotland. He married Katharine, daughter of Sir Charles Sidley of Great-Chart, in the county of Kent, Bart. who, by King James VII. was created Countefs of Dorchefter for life; and by her had two fons, viz. David Lord Millington, who married Bridget, daughter of John Noel, third fon of Baptift Noel, the fecond Vifcount Campden, by whom he had feveral children; but he and his children died before the Earl his father; and Charles, the prefent Earl.

Creations.] Baron of Portmore, June 1, 1699, by William III. Vifcount Millington, and Earl of Portmore, April 16, 1703, by Queen Anne.

Arms.] Ruby, on a chevron between three wolves heads couped pearl, three trees emerald, fructed of the firft.

Creft.] On a wreath, an unicorn rampant pearl, horned and unguled topaz.

Supporters.] Two wolves pearl.

Motto.] *Avance.*

Chief Seat.] At Weybridge in the county of Surry.

EARL of DELORAINE.

HENRY SCOT, Earl of DELORAINE, Vifcount Hermitage, and Baron Scot of Goldieland, fucceeded his father Henry, the late Earl, in 1739-40, and is unmarried.

Henry, the late Earl, fucceeded his brother Francis, the fecond Earl of Deloraine, in 1739, being then a captain in the navy. He married Elizabeth, daughter of John Fenwick, of Charles-Town, in South Carolina, Efq; by whom he
had

had iffue two fons, Henry, now Earl, born in Jan. 1736, and John, in Oct. 1738.

Lord Henry Scot, third fon of the unfortunate James Duke of Monmouth, born in 1676, (fee Duke of Buccleugh) was, by Queen Anne, dignified with the above titles. He was one of the fixteen Peers for Scotland in the fifth, fixth, and feventh parliaments of Great Britain. In 1715, he was appointed colonel of the fecond troop of grenadier guards; and, in 1723, elected a knight of the moft honourable order of the Bath: after which he was colonel of a regiment of foot, a major-general, and a gentleman of his Majefty's bedchamber, in which appointments he died in Dec. 1730. He married Anne, daughter and heir of William Duncomb of Battlefden, in Bedfordfhire, Efq; by whom he had two fons, and one daughter, viz. Francis and Henry, above-mentioned, fucceffively Earls of Deloraine; and Lady Anne, who died in infancy.

Creations.] Earl, Baron, and Vifcount, March 29, 1706. 5 Anne.

Arms.] Topaz, on a bend fapphire, a ftar between two crefcents of the field, a crefcent for difference.

Creft.] On a wreath, a ftag trippant proper.

Supporters.] Two maidens richly attired in antique habits, their under robe emerald, the middle one fapphire, and the uppermoft ruby, and each plumed on her head with feathers.

Motto.] *Amo.*

Chief Seat.] At Battlefden, in Bedfordfhire, &c.

VIS.

VISCOUNTS.

VISCOUNT FALKLAND.

THE Right Honourable Lucius Charles Carey, Baron Carey, and Viscount Falkland, fucceeded his father Lucius-Henry, the late Vifcount, in ——, and married, in April 1734, Jane, daughter and heir of Richard Butler, Efq; an eminent conveyancer, widow of Lord Villiers, fon of the Vifcount Grandifon, of Ireland ; by whom he had iffue ——, mafter of Falkland ; Lucius Ferdinand, late governor of Goree, in Africa; Jane, Frances, Mary, and Charlotte. He married fecondly, in 1752, Sarah, daughter and heir of Thomas Inwen, Efq; late member for Southwark, deceafed, and widow of Henry Earl of Suffolk.

Lucius-Henry, the late Vifcount, married firft, Dorothy, daughter of Francis Molineaux, of London, Efq; by whom he had four fons, particularly Lucius Charles, the prefent Vifcount ; and fecondly, Mifs Dillon, daughter of Lord Dillon, a lieutenant-general in the French fervice.

Of the family of Carey, antiently feated at Cockington, in the county of Devon, was Sir John Carey, Knight of the fhire for that county, and chief Baron of the exchequer in 1387. From him defcended Sir William Carey,

Carey, of Cockington, who, fiding with Henry
VI. at the battle of Tewkfbury in 1471, was
beheaded, notwithftanding a promife of pardon. From him defcended Sir Edward Carey
of Berkhamftead, in the county of Hertford,
mafter of the jewel-office to King James VI.
who had a fon Sir Henry, made Knight of the
Bath in 1616, at the creation of Charles Prince
of Wales ; and being the firft who brought the
news into Scotland of the death of Queen Elizabeth, was thereupon made one of the gentlemen of the King's bed-chamber, and comptroller of his houfehold. He was alfo by that
King appointed Lord-Deputy of Ireland, and
created a Peer of Scotland. Lucius, his fon,
who fucceeded, was appointed Secretary of
State, but loft his life at the battle of New-
bury, on Sept. 20, 1643, in the 34th year of
his age. Lord Clarendon, after giving him
one of the greateft characters that any man
can be intitled to, obferves, that if there was
no other brand upon this odious and curfed
civil war, than that one fingle lofs, it muft be
infamous and execrable to all pofterity : and
another hiftorian of thofe times fays, that by
his death, learning fuffered the greateft lofs
in that age ; he being a complete mafter
thereof, and a glorious benefactor to it.

Henry his heir, the third Vifcount, was a
great patron as well as an ornament of poetry,
and was author of a play called the *Marriage
Night*, which was well received. He was
great grandfather of the prefent Vifcount.

Creations.] Baron and Vifcount Falkland, in
the county of Fife, Nov. 10, 1620, by King
James VI.

F. 4. *Arms.*]

Arms.] Quarterly, 1ft and 4th pearl, on a bend diamond, three rofes of the field barbed and feeded proper, for Carey. 2d, pearl, a fefs between fix annulets ruby, for Lucas. 3d, the arms of France and England quarterly, with a border compone pearl and fapphire, as allied to the Plantagenet family, from that of Beaufort.

Creft.] On a wreath a fwan proper.

Supporters.] On the dexter fide, an unicorn pearl, his horns, mane, tufts, and hoofs topaz. On the finifter a lion guardant proper, his ducal crown, and plain collar topaz.

Motto.] *In utroque fidelis.*

VISCOUNT STORMONT.

DAVID MURRAY, Vifcount STORMONT, Baron of Scoon and Balvaird, and heretable keeper of the palace of Scoon, ambaffador extraordinary and plenipotentiary to the court of Vienna, and one of the fixteen Peers for Scotland, fucceeded his father, David, the late Vifcount, in 1748, and married Henrietta-Frederica, daughter of Henry, Count Bunau, by whom he has a daughter, Elizabeth-Mary. Her Ladyfhip died at Vienna, in March 1766.

David the late Vifcount, married the daughter and fole heir of John Stewart, of Innernytie, Efq; by whom he had two fons and two daughters, David the prefent Vifcount, James, Anne, and Margery.

David, his father, fifth Vifcount, married Margery, daughter of David Scot, of Scotftarvit, Efq; by whom he had iffue four fons and eight daughters, of which laft, Margery

wa3

was wife of colonel John Hay, of Cromlix,
who was, by the pretender, created Earl of
Invernefs, and was forfeited, for the rebellion
in 1715. Of the fons, David was his fucceffor,
as above; James was created Earl of Dunbar, by the pretender, at whofe court he
refided; William, the fourth fon, is the prefent Lord Mansfield: which title fee, in my
Englifh Peerage.

This noble family is defcended from that
of the Duke of Athol. Sir William Murray of
Tullibairdin, marrying Mary, daughter of the
Earl-Marfhal, had by her four fons, of whom
Sir Andrew, the youngeft, was progenitor of
the prefent Vifcount Stormont.

Creations.] Baron of Scoon, April 7, 1604:
Vifcount Stormont, being a barony in the
county of Perth, April 26, 1612, both by
James VI. and Lord Balvaird, in Fifefhire, by
Charles I. 1641.

Arms.] Quarterly, 1ft and 4th, fapphire,
three ftars pearl within a double treffure counterflowered with fleurs de lis topaz, for Murray.
2d and 3d, ruby, three croffes pattee pearl,
for Barclay of Balvaird.

Creft.] On a wreath a buck's head couped
proper, with a crofs pattee between his antlers,
as in the arms.

Supporters.] Two lions ruby.

Motto.] *Meliora fpero.*

Chief Seats.] At Cumlingun, in Annandale;
and at Scoon, in Perthfhire.

VISCOUNT ARBUTHNOT.

JOHN ARBUTHNOT, Vifcount and Baron ARBUTHNOT, in the county of Kincardin, fon of John Arbuthnot of Fordun, eldeft fon by the fecond venter, of Robert fecond Vifcount Arbuthnot, fucceeded his coufin, John, the fifth Vifcount, who died without iffue, in May, 1756, and married firft May, daughter of —— Douglas, of Bridgeford, by whom he had no iffue; and fecondly, Jane, daughter of Alexander Arbuthnot, of Firdourie, by whom he has iffue, Robert, mafter of Arbuthnot; John, Hugh, Charlotte and Margaret.

In the year 1160, Hugo, the firft of this family, marrying a daughter of the family of Oliphard, fheriff of the county of Mearns, with her had the lands of Arbuthnot in that county, from whence he took his firname; and was fucceeded by Duncan de Arbuthnot. In 1367, Philip Arbuthnot was a benefactor to the church of Abeideen; and from him defcended Sir Robert Arbuthnot of that Ilk, who, for his loyalty to King Charles I. was, Nov. 16, 1641, dignified with the title of Baron and Vifcount Arbuthnot.

Creations.] *Ut fupra.*

Arms.] Sapphire, a crefcent between three ftars pearl.

Creft.] On a wreath a peacock's head couped proper.

Supporters.] Two wyverns emerald, fpouting fire.

Motto.] *Laus Deo.*

2   *Chief*

Chief Seat.] At Arbuthnot, in Kincardin-
fhire.

VISCOUNT IRVINE.

CHARLES INGRAM, Vifcount IRVINE, and
Baron Ingram, of Irvine, in the county of
Air, fucceeded his father, Charles, the late
Vifcount, in 1748, and married Mifs Shepherd,
a great fortune, by whom he has iffue, particularly, a daughter born in May 1765, and
another, in June 1766.

Charles, the late Vifcount, fucceeded his
brother Henry, fifth Vifcount, in 1736, was a
colonel in the guards, and adjutant-general of
the forces, and reprefented the town of Horfham, from 1737 to his death.

Henry, the fifth Vifcount, reprefented the
town of Horfham, in feveral parliaments, and
was commiffary of ftores at Gibraltar and Mi-
norca, and died without iffue.

This family is derived from Arthur Ingram,
a wealthy citizen of London, who purchafed
the manors of Temple-Newfome, &c. in Yorkfhire, and was high fheriff of that county, in
1619. From him defcended Henry Ingram,
who, for his loyalty to Charles I. and II. was
created a Baron and Vifcount. Arthur, his
eldeft fon, the fecond Vifcount, married Ifabel,
daughter of John Matchell, of Horfham, in
Suffex, Efq; by whom he had iffue feven fons,
Richard, Edward, Arthur, Henry and Charles,
above mentioned, fucceffively Vifcounts Irvine;
George, canon of Windfor, and William, an
eminent merchant, in Holland.

F 6

Crea-

Creations.] Vifcount and Baron, May 3, 1661, by King Charles II.

Arms.] Ermine on a feffe ruby, three efcallop-fhel's topaz.

Crest.] On a wreath a cock proper.

Supporters.] On the dexter fide a griffin, quarterly ruby and pearl. On the finifter, an antelope of the laft horned, maned, tailed, and hoofed topaz, and gorged with a ducal crown ruby.

Chief Seats.] At Hills, in the county of Suffex ; and at Temple-Newfham, in the county of York.

VISCOUNT DUNBLAINE.

For this noble Family, fee the Duke of Leeds, who is Vifcount Dunblaine, in my Englifh Peerage.

BARONS.

BARONS.

LORD BORTHWICK.

THE Right Honourable HENRY BORTH-WICK, Lord BORTHWICK, was fon of captain Henry Borthwick, by h s wife Mary, daughter of Sir Robert. Pringle of Stitchel.; which captain Henry was fon of William, fon of Alexander, fecond fon of William, fon of William, fon of Alexander, fecond fon of William, third Lord Borthwick, and a'ter fome conteft was declared fucceffor of John the ninth Lord, who died without iffue in 1672, and has voted at the elections for the fixteen Peers ever fince 1734.

This antient family have been very numerous in Scotland, and Thomas de Borthwick obtained fome lands near Lauder, in Berwick-fhire, in the reign of David II. who came to the throne of Scotland, in 1329.

Creations.] Lord Borthwick in 1424.

Arms.] Pearl, three cinquefoils, topaz.

Creft.] A negro's head, couped, proper.

Supporters.] Two angels, proper, winged, topaz.

Motto.] *Qui conducit.*

Chief Seat.] Borthwick-caftle in Lothian.

LORD FORBES.

JAMES FORBES, Lord FORBES, fucceeded his father, James, 15th Lord Forbes, in 1761, and

and married Catherine, daughter of Sir Robert Innes, of Orton, Bart. by whom he has issue a daughter. His Lordship is lieutenant-governor of Fort-William, in Scotland.

James, the late Lord, married first, Mary, sister of Alexander Forbes, Lord Pitsligo, by whom he had issue James, the present Lord, and three daughters: Sophia, wife of Charles Cummin, of Kinninmount; Mary, of James Gordon, of Cowbardie; and Anne of Thomas Erskine, of Pittodrie. He had no issue by his second wife Elizabeth, daughter of Sir James Gordon, of Park, bart.

The antiquity of this noble and numerous family is attested by a grant from Alexander II. about 1230, to Fergus, the son of John, of the lands and tenements of Forbes in the county of Aberdeen; and from thence is derived the firname, according to the mode of those days, as it was in South Britain. The first of this name on record was Alexander Fo bes, who, in 1303, resolutely defended his castle of Urquhart, near Elgin, against King Edward I. which being taken by storm, he and the whole garrison were put to the sword; and by that fatal stroke his family had been extinct, if his wife had not preserved it by Alexander, a posthumous son, which Alexander, in compensation of what his father had lost in the service of his country, had a grant from King Robert I. of divers lands; but he, inheriting the principles of his father, and loyally adhering to King David Bruce, against Edward Baliol, was slain at the great battle of Dupplin in 1332.

In the reign of Robert II. Sir John Forbes of that Ilk, the son of the aforesaid Alexander,

acqui-

acquiring from Thomas Earl of Mar, feveral lands in the county of Aberdeen, was therein confirmed by the charter of that King; and in the fifth of Robert III. he was conftituted juftice and coroner of that county. He had four fons, three of whom were knighted; Sir John, the third, was founder of the family of Tolquhon, from whom defcended thofe of Culloden, Waterton, and Foveran. Sir William, the fecond, was anceftor of the Lord Pitfligo. Sir Alexander, the eldeft, had a fon Sir James, who was knighted by King James II. and afterwards created Lord Forbes by that monarch.

Creation.] Lord Forbes, by James II.

Arms.] Sapphire, three bears heads couped, pearl, muzzled, ruby.

Creft.] On a wreath a ftag's head erafed, proper.

Supporters.] Two greyhounds pearl, each having a plain collar ruby.

Motto.] *Grace me guide.*

Chief Seats.] At Caftle Forbes, in Aberdeenfhire; and at Putachie in the fame county.

LORD SALTON.

GEORGE FRASER, Lord SALTON and Abernethy, fucceeded his brother Alexander, the late Lord, and married Helen, daughter of John Gordon, of Kinedder, Efq; by whom he has iffue two fons and two daughters; Alexander, mafter of Salton, John Frafer, Efq; Henrietta and Mary.

His Lordfhip's father, Alexander, third Lord Salton, married Lady Mary, daughter of George

Earl

Earl of Aberdeen; and by her, who died in Feb. 1753, had iſſue Alexander the late Lord, who died without iſſue; William, who alſo died without iſſue; George, the preſent Lord; Anne and Sophia.

About the year of our Lord 807, in the reign of Achaius King of Scotland, Pierre Fraſer, ſeigneur de Troile, was ſent ambaſſador to Scotland from Charlemain, King of France, and married Euphemia, only daughter of Raham, King Achaius's great favourite; and their children, the Fraſers, were ſettled in Tweeddale, or the county of Peebles.

In the reign of Malcolm III. called Canmore, Alexander Fraſer was donator to the abbey of Kelſo, as was alſo Simon, in the reign of Malcolm IV. called the Maiden, about the year 1157. But ſince the year 1214, in the reign of Alexander II. there is a diſtinct account of the Fraſer family from father to ſon, and their ſeveral marriages; that is, of the predeceſſors of Lord Salton, who, when Lairds of Philorth in Buchan, became heirs to the Thanes of Cowie, their anceſtors in Kincardinſhire. For about this time John Fraſer, who was ſheriff of Tweedale, and laird of Oliver-caſtle in that county, had a ſon, Alexander, thane or ſteward of Cowie; who, in the year 1247, by marrying Elizabeth Cumming, daughter of Sir Walter Cumming, with her acquired lands in the counties of Kincardin and Aberdeen. He had three heroic ſons, the famous Sir Simon Fraſer, William, and Gilbert, among whom he divided his lands. Sir Simon was taken and carried priſoner into England by King Edward I. but being ſet at liberty in the year 1297, and

returning

returning into Scotland, he joined Sir William Wallace. In the year 1302, he was a commander in the Scots army, with his cousin Sir John Cumming, and the said Wallace, when they gained a notable victory over the English, commanded by John Segrave. At the battle of Methven, in 1306, Sir Simon, though he thrice saved the life of King Robert Bruce, could not save himself, but being taken prisoner, was carried to London, and there put to death, leaving only two daughters, Mary, who, about the year 1340, married Sir Gilbert Hay, ancestor of the marquis of Tweeddale; and the other to Sir Patrick, the second son of Sir Robert Fleming, ancestor of the Earl of Wigton. William Fraser, the second son, never married, being archbishop of St. Andrews, and, in the reign of Alexander III. chancellor of Scotland; upon whose death, in 1285, he was made governor of Scotland. Gilbert, the third son, had two sons, John and Andrew; John, the eldest, had no male issue, but left a daughter, Honora, who was married to Robert Keith, ancestor of the Earls Marthals. From this marriage c me only a daughter, who was married to Alexander the first Earl of Huntley, who got thereby the mother's estate.

Andrew, his brother, was father of Alexander Fraser, thane of Cowie, who was made Lord Chamberlain of Scotland during life, and was ancestor of the noble family of Lovat.

Creation.] Baron Salton, in Faft-Lothian, by James II. confirmed by King Charles I.

Arms.] Quarterly, 1st, sapphire three cinquefoils, pearl; 2d, topaz, a lion rampant ruby, debruised with a ribband, diamond, for Abernethy;

nethy; 3d, ruby, a lion rampant, pearl, for
Rofs; 4th, as the 1ft.

Creft.] On a wreath an oftrich, with a horfe-
fhoe in its beak.

Supporters.] Two angels.

Motto.] *In God is All.*

Chief Seat.] At Philorth and Fraferfburgh,
in Aberdeenfhire.

LORD GRAY.

JOHN GRAY, Lord GRAY, fucceeded his father John, the late Lord, in 1738, and in 1741
married Mifs Blair, heirefs of Kinfauns, near
Perth, by whom he has iffue four fons, Andrew, mafter of Gray; Charles, William, and
John; and feven daughters, Jane, who marred
Francis Lord Down, fon and heir of the Earl
of Murray; Helen, Margaret, Barbara, Elizabeth, Anne and Mary.

John, the late Lord, married Helen, daughter of Alexander Lord Blantyre, by whom he
had iffue two fons and one daughter; John,
the prefent Lord, and Charles; and Anne, wife
of William Gray, of Balegarno, Efq;

Of this noble, antient, and flourifhing family,
which took their name from the caftle of Croy
in Picardy, was Anfchetil de Croy, who, coming into England with William the Norman,
obtained divers lands in the county of Oxford,
and elfewhere; and from him fprang many
great and illuftrious families in England, as the
Dukes of Suffolk and Kent, the Marquis of Dor-
fet, Earls of Tankerville and Stamford, the
Barons Grey of Codnor, Ruthin, Wilton, Role-
fton,

. ſton, Wark, &c. alſo Chillingham, from which laſt is deſcended the Lords Gray of Scotland.

Creation.] Lord Gray, by James II.

Arms.] Ruby, a lion rampant, within a border ingrailed, pearl.

Creſt.] On a wreath, an anchor in pale, topaz.

Supporters.] Two lions guardant, ruby.

Motto.] *Anchor faſt anchor.*

Chief Seats.] At the caſtle of Gray, and at Foulis, in the carſe of Gowry.

LORD CATHCART.

CHARLES SCHAW CATHCART, Lord CATHCART, lieutenant-general of his Maj.ſty's forces, governor of Dunbarton caſtle, adjutant general for Scotland, firſt commiſſioner of the police, one of the ſixteen Peers for Scotland, and a Knight of the ancient order of the Thiſtle, ſucceeded his father, Charles, the late Lord, in 1740, and on July 4, 1753, married Jane daughter of Lord Archibald Hamilton, and ſiſter of the Counteſs Brooke and of Warwick, by whom he has iſſue William, maſter of Cathcart, Charles-Allan, George, Jane, Mary and Louiſa.

In 1748, his Lordſhip was one of the hoſtages for the re-delivery of Cape Breton to the King of France, by virtue of the peace of Aix-la-Chapelle. In May 1756, he was appointed high commiſſioner to the general aſſembly of the church of Scotland, in which he was continued for ſeveral years.

Charles, the late Lord, was groom and gentleman of the bed-chamber to George II. one of the ſixteen Peers for Scotland in the eighth parlia-

parliament of Great Britain, colonel of a regiment of horse, and governor of Duncannon Fort in Ireland. He commanded, in chief, the land forces designed for an expedition with admiral Vernon in the West Indies; but died before he arrived at Jamaica, at the island of Dominica, in 1740. He married, first, Margaret, daughter of Sir John Schaw of Greenock, Bart. by whom he had issue Charles-Schaw, the present Lord, and two daughters; Eleonora, wife of Sir John Houston, of that ilk, Bart. and Mary-Anne, of the honourable William master of Napier, son and heir of Lord Napier, in Dec. 1754. He married, secondly, in 1739, Mrs. Sabine, widow of Joseph Sabine, of Tring in Hertfordshire, Esq; but by her had no issue; and surviving him, she married, thirdly, lieutenant colonel Hugh Macguire.

Of this antient family, whose sirname is taken from their lands and barony of Kethcart, in the county of Renfrew, where now is the town of Cathcart, was Reynald de Kethcart, who, in 1278, was witness to a charter of Allan the son of Walter Dapifer; and William de Kethcart, his son, was one of those barons who swore allegiance to King Edward I. of England. To him succeeded his son Sir Allan, a faithful adherer to the interest of Robert I. and he marrying the sister and coheir of Sir Duncan Wallace of Sundrum, in Airshire, with her had that barony; and Sir Allan, their great grandchild, was dignified with the title of Lord by King James II.

Creation.] Lord Cathcart in 1442.

Arms.] Quarterly, first and fourth, sapphire; three cross croslets fitchy, issuing out of as many

crefcents, pearl, for Cathcart; fecond and third
ruby, a lion rampant, pearl, for Wallace.

Creft.] On a wreath, a dexter hand couped
above the wrift, and erect, proper, grafping a
crefcent as in the arms.

Supporters.] Two parrots, proper.

Motto.] *I hope to fpeed.*

Chief Seats.] At Sundrum, in Airfhire;
Sawchie, in Sterlingfhire; Dover-ftreet, London.

LORD SOMERVILLE.

JAMES SOMERVILLE, Lord SOMERVILLE, a
Lord of Police, commiffioner of the board of
trade and forfeited eftates, fucceeded his father
James, the late Lord, in 1766, who was fon of
James, fon of James, fon of James, fon of
James, fon of Hugh, fourth fon of Hugh, feventh
Lord Somerville; and after the title had laid
many years dormant, from the death of Hugh,
ninth Lord Somerville, page of the bedchamber
to James VI. put in his claim, which was allowed by the court of feffion. He was chofen
one of the fixteen peers to the ninth parliament
of Great Britain, and married ———, only
daughter of Henry Bayntun Rolt, of Spy Park
in Wiltfhire, Efq; and by her, who died in
May 1755, had iffue two fons, James, mafter
of Somerville. the prefent Lord, and Hugh, an
officer in the army; alfo a daughter, Anne-
Wichnour, wife of George Burgefs, Efq; who
has by her a fon and daughter. He married,
fecondly, in 1736, Frances, daughter and coheir of John Rotherham, Efq; by whom he had
a daughter, who died in her infancy.

The

The firſt of this name on record is Sir Walter de Somerville, Lord of Wichnore in the
county of Stafford, who came into England
with William the Norman, and was anceſtor of
all the Somervilles in Great Britain; his ſecond ſon, William de Somerville, was a fre-
quent witneſs to the grants of King David I. to
religious houſes, and had a grant of the lands
and barony of Carnwath from that prince.
About the beginning of the reign of King
William, in 1170, the Somervilles were pof-
feſſed of a fair eſtate in the county of Lanerk
and elſewhere; and, at the marriage of Alexander II. who began his reign in the year 1214,
William de Somerville, lineally deſcenced from
the ſaid Sir Walter, was one of the barons appointed by that King to exerciſe in a tourna-
ment at the caſtle of Roxburgh.

Creation.] Lord Somerville, by James II.

Arms.] Sapphire, three ſtars, topaz, accompanied with ſeven croſs croſlets fitchy pearl,
three in chief, one in feſs, two in the flanks, and
the laſt in baſe.

Creſt.] On a wreath, a wheel, topaz, ſur-
mounted of a wyvern emerald, ſpouting fire.

Supporters.] Two greyhounds, proper, each
gorged with a plain collar, ruby.

Motto.] *Fear God in life.*

Chief Seat.] At Drum in Mid-Lothian.

LORD MORDINGTON.

George Douglas, the fourth Lord Mor-
dington, married Catherine, daughter of the
Rev. Dr. Robert Lauder, rector of Shanley in
Hertfordſhire, by whom he had iſſue a ſon,

Charles,

Charles, and two daughters, Mary and Cambe-
lina; and dying in 1741, was succeeded by his
said son, Charles, fifth Lord, who being ar-
raigned in 1746, at Carlisle, for being concerned
in the rebellion, pleaded his peerage, which
was at length allowed. He died some years
after, and in him ended the male line of the
family; but the title is in abeyance between his
sisters above-mentioned.

This family is descended from that of the
Dukes of Douglas: for William, the tenth
Earl of Angus, having three sons, the eldest
was created Marquis of Douglas; and the second, Sir James, was created Lord Mordington: he marrying Anne, the only daughter and
heir of Laurence the fifth Lord Oliphant, the
title and designation of Oliphant was by favour
of King Charles I. changed into that of Mordington, with precedence according to the antient Lords of Oliphant, and was so confirmed
by parliament.

Creation.] Lord Mordington, by James IV.
1458.

Arms.] Quarterly, 1st and 4th pearl, a man's
heart, ruby, ensigned with an imperial crown,
proper; on a chief sapphire three stars of the
first: 2d and 3d ruby, three crescents, pearl,
for Oliphant.

Crest.] On a cap of dignity, a salamander in
flames reguardant, emerald.

Supporters.] On the dexter side a savage,
and on the sinister a stag, both proper; the first
armed with a battoon, and wreathed about his
head and middle with laurel; and the second
collared and chained with leaves of the last.

Motto.] *Forward.*

LORD

LORD SEMPLE.

JOHN SEMPLE, Lord SEMPLE, fucceeded his father Hugh, the late Lord, in 1746, and married Janet, daughter and heir of Hugh Dunlap, of Bifhopftoun, by whom he has iffue a fon, Hugh, mafter of Semple, and a daughter.

Hugh, the late, and eleventh Lord Semple, ferved with great gallantry and reputation, both in Flanders and Spain, in Queen Anne's wars. In 1718, he was major of the 26th regiment; in 1740, appointed colonel of the 42d, at the head of which he purchafed great glory, in the year 1743, in Flanders. In 1745, he was removed to the command of the 25th regiment. At the battle of Culloden, in 1746, he commanded the left wing of the royal army, as brigadier-general, when his courage and conduct were remarkably confpicuous. He afterwards commanded at Aberdeen, and there, in Dec. 1746, the tendon of his arm being pricked in letting blood, that unfortunate accident coft him his life. He married Sarah, daughter and coheir of —— Gafkall, Efq; by whom he had iffue five fons, and fix daughters, viz. John, the prefent Lord; George and Hugh, officers in the army; Philip and Ralph, deceafed; Sarah, wife of Patrick Crawford, of Anchinames, who died in 1750; Jane; Betty, who died young; Anne, wife of Dr. Adam Auftin, phyfician of Edinburgh; Marian and Rebecca.

The principal family of this name was Semple of Ellerfton in Renfrew, where they had large poffeffions and offices, as ftewards and bailiffs,

bailiffs, under the feveral families of Stewart, proprietors of that county before they came to the crown. The firft Lord Semple was John, fon and heir to Sir Thomas, who loft his life with King James III. at the battle of Bannockburn, in 1488; which Sir John being much in favour with King James IV. was by him created Lord Semple, in 1488: but attending his Majefty to the battle of Flodden in 1513, he there with his royal mafter loft his life, and was buried in the collegiate church of Semple, which he had founded: he left two fons, William his heir fecond Lord, and Gabriel, anceftor of the Semples of Cathcart.

Creation.] *Ut fupra.*

Arms.] A chevron cheque, ruby, and of the field, between three bugle horns, diamond, garnifhed of the fecond.

Creft.] On a wreath a ftag's head couped, proper, attired pearl.

Supporters.] Two greyhounds, pearl, each having a plain collar, ruby.

Motto.] *Keep Tryfte.*

Chief Seat.] At Semple-houfe, in the fhire of Renfrew.

LORD ELPHINSTONE.

CHARLES ELPHINSTONE, Lord ELPHINSTONE, fucceeded his father, Charles, the late Lord, in February, 1757, and married Lady Clementina, only furviving daughter and heir of John, Earl of Wigton, by Lady Mary, eldeft daughter of William, ninth Earl Marfhal, by whom he had iffue four fons and four daughters, viz. John, mafter of Elphin-

G   ftone,

ftone, an officer in the army, who was wounded at the battle of Quebec; and married Anne, eldeſt daughter of the Lord Ruthven, by whom he has iſſue; Charles, a gallant youth, who loſt his life, in the Prince George, of 90 guns, burnt at ſea, in 1758; William, in the ſervice of the Eaſt-India company; Keith in the navy; Mary, Eleanor, Primroſe and Clementina.

Charles, the late Lord, married Elizabeth, daughter of Sir William Primroſe, of Carrington, Bart. ſiſter of James, firſt Viſcount Primroſe, and had iſſue four ſons; John, who married Marjory, daughter of Sir Gilbert Fleming, of Farm, and died without iſſue; James, who died unmarried; Charles, the preſent Lord, and Archibald, who died on the expedition to Caithagena, in 1741: alſo two daughters, Griſel, wife of captain Woodroofe Gaſcoign, and Primroſe, of Alexander, Earl of Home.

John, father of the late Lord, married Lady Elizabeth, daughter of Charles, Earl of Lauderdale, by whom he had iſſue three ſons and three daughters; Charles, late Lord Elphinſtone; John, who died unmarried; captain William, killed at Preſton, in 1715; Elizabeth, wife of John Campbell of Mammore, ſecond ſon of Archibald ninth Earl of Argyle, and father of John, the preſent Duke; Margaret, of George, Count Leſley, of Balquhain, and afterwards of Sir James Gordon, of Park; and Mary of Mr. Thomas Buchan, advocate.

The family is of great antiquity: John de Elphinſtone, their immediate anceſtor, was poſſeſſed of the lands and barony of Elphinſtone, in the reigns of Alexander I. and II. and dying

in

in 1263, was fucceeded by his fon Alexander, who was fucceeded by his eldeft fon, Sir John, one of thofe great men that fwore fealty to Edward I. of England, in 1296. He had a fon Alexander, whofe fon, Alexander, was fucceeded in 1399, by his eldeft fon Sir William, whofe eldeft fon, Sir Alexander, was flain at the battle of Piperden, 1437, and leaving an only daughter Agnes, wife of Sir Gilbert, fon of Sir Adam Johnfton, of that Ilk, he, in her right, had the lands and barony of Elphinftone, in Lothian; but the eftate in Stirlingfhire, came, by arbitration, in 1471, to Henry Elphinftone, who was brother of the faid Sir Alexander, and from him, the family hath continued in a direct line to the prefent time. Henry died in 1496, and was fucceeded by his grandfon Sir John Elphinftone, who was fucceeded by his fon and heir, Sir Alexander, created Lord Elphinftone, who was flain at the battle of Floddon, with his royal mafter, James IV. in 1513.

Creations.] Baron Elphinftone, in the county of Stirling, in 1509, by James IV.

Arms.] Pearl, a chevron diamond, between three boars heads erafed, ruby.

Creft.] On a wreath, a lady from the girdle richly attired, holding a caftle in her right hand, and in her left a branch of laurel.

Supporters.] Two favages, proper, each wreathed about his head and middle with laurel, and holding in his outer hand a dart, proper.

Motto.] *Caufa caufit*, or *Chance produced it.*

Chief Seat.] At Cumbernauld, in the county of Stirling.

LORD

LORD OLIPHANT.

DAVID OLIPHANT, Lord OLIPHANT, upon the death of William, the late Lord, in 1751, claimed that honour, which was allowed him, and he is the twelfth Lord Oliphant.

Charles, the seventh Lord, was succeeded by his son, Patrick, the eighth Lord, who dying in 1721, without issue, was succeeded by his uncle, William, ninth Lord ; but he also dying without issue, Francis Oliphant, said to be the next heir male, assumed the title, and was tenth Lord. He married Mrs. Linley, of York, but dying without issue, the title was claimed by William, son of Charles Oliphant, Esq; one of the clerks of Session, who became the 11th Lord, and he dying without issue, as above recited, was succeeded by David Oliphant, of Bachilton, Esq; the present Lord.

David de Oliphant, immediate ancestor of this family, was one of those Barons who, in 1142, accompanied King David I. into England, with an army to assist his niece the Empress Matilda against King Stephen : but after raising the siege of Winchester, the said King David was so closely pursued, that had it not been for the singular conduct of this brave person, the King had then remained a prisoner. David his son succeeded him, and was greatly in the favour of King Malcolm IV. and his brother King William. Sir Walter, son of this David, was one of the hostages for the ransom of the last mentioned Prince, who was taken prisoner by the English, in 1173.

Crea-

Creations.] Lord Oliphant, by James IV.

Arms.] Ruby three crefcents, pearl.

Creft.] On a wreath, an unicorn's head, cou‧ped pearl, armed and maned, topaz.

Supporters.] Two elephants, proper.

Motto.] *A tout pouvoir.*

Chief Seats.] At Don, in the county of In‧vernefs; and at Pittindirk, near the town of Elgin.

LORD TORPICHEN.

JAMES SANDILANDS, Lord TORPICHEN, fucceeded his father, Walter, the late Lord, in 1765.

Walter, the late Lord, was fheriff depute of the county of Edinburgh, and married Eliza‧beth, only daughter and heir of Dr. Alexander Sandilands, a cadet of the family. by whom he had iffue, James, the prefent Lord, Alexander and Walter.

James, father of the late Lord, was a lieu‧tenant colonel and ferved bravely in Queen Anne's wars. In 1715, he commanded Ker's regiment, at the battle of Dunblaine. He quitted the army in 1722, and was appointed a Lord of Police, and continued fo till his death, in 1752. He married Lady Jane, daughter of Patrick, Earl of Marchmont, Lord Chancellor of Scotland, by whom he had iffue eight fons and three daughters, Grifel, Chrif‧tiana and Wilhelmina-Carolina. His illuftrious fons were.

1. James, mafter of Torpichen, who, at the battle of Prefton-Pans, in the year 1745, being a captain in the army, received twenty dange-

rous

)ous wounds, which brought on a confumption, of which he died three years' after, unmarried, in the life-time of his father. 2. Walter, the late Lord. 3. Patrick, captain of an Eaft-India fhip, who perifhed-in a ftorm at fea, leaving no iffue. 4. Alexander, who died young. 5. Andrew, major of the Scotch Fuziliers, who was fhot through the thigh, at the battle of Fontenoy, in 1745, which obliged him, upon the conclufion of the peace, to retire from the fervice. 6. George, who died young. 7. Charles, a lieutenant in the army, who loft his life at the fiege of Carthagena, in America. 8. Robert, now an officer in the army.

Of this noble and antient family, who, in the re'gn of Malcolm III. were driven out of England by William the Conqueror, and then fettled in Scotland, was Sir James Sandilands, who, in the reign of David II. was laird of Sandilands and Whifton; and marrying Eleanor fifter of William firft Earl of Douglas, with her had the barony of Weft Calder; and by the fame Lady he had a fon, Sir James, who was knighted by King Robert II. who gave him the Lady Jane, his fecond daughter, in marriage.

Creation.] Lord Torpichen, in 1563, by Queen Mary.

Arms:] Quarterly, 1ft and 4th, party per fefs, fapphire and topaz; on the firft a crown, and on the fecond a thiftle, both proper; being a coat of augmentation; for as Sir James Sandilands was great prior of the 'order of Malta, in England, the crown and thiftle was a badge of that office. 2d and 3d quarters counter-quartered; 1ft and 4th, pearl, a bend,
fap-

fapphire for Sandilands ; the 2d and 3d are the arms of Douglas, borne as arms of patronage.

Creft.] On a wreath, an eagle difplayed, topaz.

Supporters.] Two favages, each wreathed about his head and middle with laurel, and holding in his outer hand a battoon, all proper.

Motto.] *Spero Meliore.*

Chief Seat.] Calder houfe, Mid-lothian, and the caft'e of Torpichen, in Weft-lothian.

LORD LINDORES.

FRANCIS-JAMES LESLEY, Lord LINDORES, fucceeded his father, Alexander, the fifth Lord, in 1766, and is an officer in the army, and unmarried.

Alexander, the late Lord, upon the death of Dav'd, fourth Lord Lindores, without iffue, being lineally defcended of Sir John Lefley of Newton, fecond fon, of the third marriage, of Andrew fifth Earl of Rothes, fucceeded him according to the entail, being fon of David, fon of Andrew, fon of the faid Sir John. He was, at the time of his deceafe, a major-general, and colonel of a regiment of invalids. He marricd Jane, daughter of Colin Campbell, Efq; late a commiffioner of the cuftoms, and brother of Sir James Campbell, of Aberuchil, by whom he had iffue the prefent Lord.

Andrew, the fifth Earl of Rothes, by his firft wife Jane daughter of Sir John Hamilton of Evandale, had two fons, James, his fuc-ceffor, and Sir Patrick, of Pitcairly, who was created a Baron by King James VI.

Crea-

Creation.] Lord Lindores, Dec. 25, 1600, by James VI.

Arms.] Quarterly, 1ft and 4th pearl, on a bend fapphire, three buckles, topaz for Lefly; 2d and 3d topaz, a lion rampant, ruby, debruifed with a ribband, diamond, for Abernethy, and on a furtout an efcutcheon, ruby, charged with a caftle pearl, mafoned diamond for the title of Lindores.

Crest.] On a wreath. a demi-angel winged topaz, holding in his dexter hand a griffon's head erafed, proper.

Supporters.] Two griffons, pearl, winged, topaz.

Motto.] *Stat promiffa fides.*

Chief Seat.] At Lindores-Abbey in Fifefhire.

LORD BLANTYRE.

WILLIAM STEWART, Lord BLANTYRE, fucceeded his brother Walter, the late Lord, in May 1751, being then a colonel in the fervice of the States General.

Robert, the feventh Lord, fucceeded his brother Walter, fixth Lord, in 1713, and married, firft, Lady Helen, daughter of John Earl of Strathmore, by whom he had a fon, Alexander, who died young: and, 2dly, Margaret, daughter of William Hay, of Drumelzier, Efq· by whom he had fix fons and four daughters: Walter, the late Lord; William, the prefent Lord; Alexander, John, James, and Charles; Margaret; Helen, wife of Oliver Colt, of Au'dhame, Efq; and Elizabeth, wife of William Colquhoun, of Garfcaden, Efq; He died in Dec. 1743.

This

This noble family is defcended from that of the Earl of Galloway. Sir William Stewart having three fons, Sir Alexander, Sir Thomas, and Sir Walter, Sir Thomas, the fecond fon, married Ifabel, daughter and coheir of Sir Walter Stewart of Arthurley, and with her had large poff ffions in the fhires of Renfrew and Cliddefdale. From them defcended Sir Walter Stewart, who, being commendator of Blantyre, and from his youth bred up with James VI. under the famous George Buchanan, he, by that King, was made keeper of the privy feal, gentleman of his bedchamber, and treafurer of Scotland, and was created Lord Blantyre.

Creation.] Lord Blantyre, July 20, 1606, by James VI.

Arms.] Topaz, a fefs cheque pearl and fapphire, furmounted of a bend ingrailed, and in chief a rofe ruby.

Creft.] On a wreath, a dove with an oliveleaf in its mouth.

Supporters.] On the dexter fide, a favage wreathed about his head and middle with laurel, and holding over his fhoulder a battoon, all proper. On the finifter a lion ruby.

Motto.] *Sola juvat virtus.*

Chief Seats.] At Erfkine in Renfrewfhire; at Cardonnel-caftle in the fame county; at Leithington in Eaft-Lothian; and at the Craig of Blantyre, in Cliddefdale.

LORD CRANSTON.

JAMES-CRANSTON, Lord CRANSTON, fucceeded his father, William, fifth Lord Cranfton,

fton, in   , and married Sophia, daughter of —— Brown, an English lady, by whom he has iffue four fons ; William, Mafter of Cranfton ; Brown, James, and Charles.

William, the late Lord, was eldeft and only furviving fon of James, fourth Lord, by Anne, daughter of Sir Alexander Don of Newton, Bart. and married Lady Jane, daughter of William, fecond Marquis of Lothian, by whom he had iffue James, the prefent Lord ; William, who died young ; Archibald, Alexander, and William-Henry, an officer in Lord Mark Ker's regiment, who died at Dunkirk in January 1753 ; Charles ; George ; Jane, who died young ; Anne, wife of —— Selby, Efq; Elizabeth, Jane, and Mary.

Of this family, who took their name from the lands and barony of Cranfton in Mid Lothian and Tiviotdale, was Elfric de Cranfton, who was witnefs to a charter of William King of Scots, to the abbey of Holyro-d-houfe ; and in the reign of Alexander III. Andrew de Cranfton was witnefs to a charter of Hugh de Riddel to the abbey of Newbottle. In the reign of David II. 1329, Thomas de Cranfton obtained a charter of the lands of his name ; and from him defcended Sir John Cranfton of that ilk, whofe only daughter and heir was married to Sir William Cranfton of Morifton, a branch of his own family ; which Sir William was, by King James VI. made captain of the guard ; and Nov. 19, 1609, created baron Cranfton in the county of Edinburgh.

Creation.] *Ut fupra.*

Arms.] Ruby, three cranes pearl.

2   *Creft.*

Crest.] On a wreath, a crane sleeping with its head under its wing, and holding up a stone with its right foot.

Supporters.] On the dexter side a lady richly apparelled, holding a branch of strawberries towards a stag proper, on the sinister.

Motto.] *Thou shalt want, ere I want.*

Chief Seat.] At Creling in the county of Roxburgh.

LORD NAPIER.

FRANCIS NAPIER, Lord NAPIER of Merchiston, a Lord of the police, succeeded Elizabeth Lady Napier, his mother, and married Lady Henrietta Hope, daughter of Charles Earl of Hopetoun, and by her, who died in February 1744-5, had issue a son, William, master of Napier, who, in Dec. 1754, married Mary-Anne, daughter of Charles Lord Cathcart; Charles, a captain in the navy in 1754; Francis, a captain of marines; John, a lieutenant in the 25th regiment of foot, who died in Germany, the day after the battle of Minden; Mark, a captain of foot; and Henrietta, who died in her infancy. His Lordship married, 2dly, Mary, daughter of major George Johnston, in April 1750, by whom he had issue, George; James, who died in 1760; Patrick; James-John; Elizabeth, who died in her infancy; Esther and Mary.

Sir William Scot, son and heir of Sir Francis Scot of Thirlestane, married Elizabeth Lady Napier, daughter of Margaret Lady Napier, second daughter of Archibald, second Lord Napier, by whom she had the present Lord, who

is

is great grandfon of the faid fecond Lord ; and the faid Sir William Scot, upon his marriage, took the name of Napier, and died Oct. 13, 1725.

This family is traditionally faid to be defcended from the ancient thanes or ftewards of Lenox ; but took their firname from the following incident : King David II. in his wars with the Englifh, about the year 1344, convocating his fubjects to battle, the Earl of Lennox fent his fecond fon Donald, with fuch forces as his duty obliged him ; and coming to an engagement, where the Scots gave ground, this Donald taking his father's ftandard from the bearer, and valiantly charging the enemy with the Lennox men, the fortune of the battle changed, and they obtained the victory ; whereupon every one advancing, and reporting their acts, as the cuftom was, the King declared they had all behaved valiantly; but that there was one among them who had *na pier*, that is, no equal : upon which the faid Donald took the name of Napier, and had, in reward for his good fervices, the lands of Gosfield, and other eftates in the county of Fife.

Sir Archibald, the reprefentative of this family, was knighted by King James VI. and made mafter of the mint. His fon and heir, Sir John, being inclined to reading and ftudy, arrived to a very great knowledge in feveral ufeful branches of literature, fo that few equalled him in that age ; and his great experience and abilities in mathematical learning, rendered him fo eminent, efpecially his logarithmic tables, thence called Napier's rods, that they will ever be efteemed as the mafterly product of a great genius.

genius. This great man dying in 1622, was succeeded by his son and heir Sir Archibald, who was by King James VI. made one of the privy-council, treasurer-depute, lord-justice-clerk, and one of the judges in the court of session; and by King Charles I. was made one of the extraordinary lords of session; on March 2, 1626, he was created a baronet; and in May following, advanced to the title of Lord Napier.

Creations.] Lord Napier, May 4, 1627, by Charles I. Baronet, Aug. 22, 1660.

Arms.] Quarterly, 1st and 4th pearl, a saltire ingrailed between four roses ruby, for Napier. 2d and 3d, topaz on a bend sapphire, a star between two crescents of the first, within a double tressure counterflory, with fleurs de lis of the second, for Scot of Thirlestan.

Crest.] On a wreath, a right arm couped below the elbow, and erect, grasping a crescent.

Supporters.] On the dexter side, an eagle, proper. On the sinister, a chevalier in a coat of mail, holding a lance with a penon, all proper; and below the shield, by way of compartment, a mural crown pearl, masoned diamond, out of which issue six lances disposed in saltire, as the former.

Motto.] *Ready, ay ready.*

Chief Seats.] At Bellenton in Perthshire; at Thirlestan, in the county of Berwick, and at Merchiston, in Mid-Lothian.

LORD FAIRFAX.

HENRY FAIRFAX, Lord FAIRFAX, of Cameron, succeeded his brother, Thomas, the late Lord, in 1738.

Thomas,

Thomas, fifth Lord Fairfax, was colonel in the guards, a brigadier-general, and several times before the Union, Knight of the shire for the county of York, which on becoming a Peer of Great Britain, he was obliged to give up. He married Catherine, only daughter and heir of Thomas Lord Colepeper, by whom he had issue Thomas, the late Lord; Henry, the present Lord; Robert, a major in the guards, and member for Kent, to the present parliament, and lieutenant-colonel of the western battalion of the militia of that county. He married the daughter of Anthony Collins, of Baddow, in Essex, Esq; by whom he had a son and heir, born in January, 1743, and other issue since: also four daughters, Margaret, wife of Dr. David Wilkins, late archdeacon of Suffolk; Catherine, Frances and Mary, who all died unmarried. His Lordship died in 1709, and was succeeded by Thomas, the late Lord.

Sir Guy, third son of Richard Fairfax, Lord chief-justice of England, in the reign of Henry VI. being bred to the law, was attorney-general, and afterwards justice of the King's-bench in the reigns of Edward IV. Richard III. and Henry VII. He built Streeton-castle in the county of York, which afterwards became the seat of his family. From him lineally descended Sir Thomas Fairfax, who accompanying the Earl of Essex, then general of the English army, sent by Queen Elizabeth to the assistance of Henry IV. of France, against the Spaniards and Popish league, was there knighted by the said general, in the camp before Roan in Normandy, for his bravery in that service, and was created a Baron by Charles I.

Ferdi-

Ferdinando, his eldeſt ſon, ſucceeded. At the beginning of the civil war, he was the parliament's general for the aſſociated county of York. In Dec. 1642, he was attacked by the Earl of Newcaſtle at Tadcaſter, whom he vigorouſly repulſed, and obliged to retreat with loſs. In Jan. 1643, he routed the Lord Byron at Namptwich in Cheſhire. In April 1644, he defeated Lord Bellaſſiſe at Selby, and took him priſoner, with 1600 of his men. In July following, he commanded the main battle, with the Earl of Leven, at Marſton-moor, where the King's army, under Prince Rupert, was defeated, and thereupon took poſſeſſion of York as governor. His eldeſt ſon Sir William, defeated Lord Byron at Montgomery-caſtle, but was unfortunately ſlain in that action in Sept. 1644; whereupon, March 13, 1647, Thomas, the ſecond ſon, ſucceeded his father Ferdinando.

Sir Thomas Fairfax, in his father's lifetime, in 1642, took the town of Leeds from Sir William Savil, and made 500 men priſoners. In July 1644, he commanded the right wing of the parliament-army at Marſton-moor, having, in the preceding April, joined his father in the battle with Lord Bellaſſiſe. In 1645, being in the 34th year of his age, he was made general in chief of the parliament's armies, which he commanded with great ſucceſs: for in that year he fought and totally routed the King at Naſeby, retook Leiceſter, beat colonel Goring, took Bridgwater, Dartmouth, Briſtol; beat the Lord Hopton; forced the Prince of Wales to retire into Scilly, and from thence to France; and then, reducing all the weſt,
drove

drove the King from Oxford in May 1646. At this time he led the prefbyterian party in the houfe, and the next year waited on the King when he was brought to 'he army, which he led to London, and was made governor of the Tower: but the independents now getting uppermoft in the parliament, as well as in the army, he had no fhare in their violent refolutions; and as he had no hand in the death of the King, he had no power to prevent it. In 1649 he was continued general of the army; but being diffatisfied at the parliament's war with Scotland, he refigned his commiffion in 1650, and was fucceeded by Oliver Cromwell. In 1659 he entered into meafures with general Monk, to whom he gave confiderable affiftance in the reftoration of King Charles II. and was one of the commiffioners fent by the parliament to the King upon that great occafion, when, arriving at the Hague, he was received by his Majefty with fingular favour and goodnefs, which continued to the end of his life.

Creation.] Lord Fairfax, of Cameron, May 4, 1627, by Charles I.

Arms.] Topaz, three bars gemel, ruby, furmounted of a lion rampant diamond, pearl, a bend ingrailed, ruby, for Colepeper.

Creft.] On a wreath, a lion paffant guardant of the laft.

Supporters.] On the dexter fide a lion guardant, diamond. On the finifter, a bay horfe.

Motto.] *Fare Fac.*

Chief Seat.] At Leeds-caftle, in Kent.

LORD

LORD REAY.

Donald Mackay, Lord Reay, and Baronet, succeeded his father, George, the late Lord, in 1765, and is married, and had a son and heir born in May, 1766.

George, the late Lord, married first Marian, daughter of colonel Hugh Mackay, of Big-house, by whom he had issue Donald, the present Lord, and secondly, ——, daughter of —— Fairly, of that Ilk, by whom he had one daughter, Jane.

This family is derived from Alexander, a younger son of Ochonacker, who, about the end of the twelfth century, came from Ireland; and the fourth in descent from him was Donald of Strathnaver, whose son was named Y More: and from him began the firname Macjye, Mackie, or Mackay. From him descended Donald, who, by a warrant from King Charles I. in 1625, carried over to Germany a regiment of 1500 men of his own name and followers, to the assistance of the King of Bohemia, and afterwards entered into the service of the Kings of Denmark and Sweden, where he served with great reputation. On March 10, 1626, returning to his native country, he was created a Baronet; and, on June 20, 1628, was created Baron Reay of the county of Caithness, by Charles I. In the civil war, he joined the royal party; was taken prisoner at the surrender of Newcastle to the Scots army, and sent to the castle of Edinburgh, in order to be tried; but being relieved by the Marquis of Montrose, he retired to Denmark, where he he died. He married Barbara Mackenzie, fifter of Colin, the firft Earl of Seaforth, and left John, the fecond Lord Reay, who married Barbara, daughter of Donald Mackay of Scoury, and had a fon Donald, who, marrying Anne, daughter of Sir George Monro of Culcarn, and dying before his father, left George the third Lord.

Creation.] *Ut fupra.*

Arms.] Sapphire, on a chevron topaz, between three bears heads couped pearl, and muzzled ruby, a roebuck's head erafed of the laft, between two hands holding daggers, all proper.

Creft.] On a wreath, a right hand couped and erect, grafping a dagger, as thofe in the arms.

Supporters.] Two men in a military drefs, with mufquets in a centinel's pofture, all proper.

Motto.] *Manu forti.*

Chief Seat.] At Tong in Strathnaver, in the county of Sutherland.

LORD ASTON.

WALTER ASTON, Lord ASTON, of Forfar, in the county of Forfar, fucceeded Philip, 6th Lord Afton, who died April 29, 1755, and in 1767, married Mifs Anne Hutchinfon.

As I cannot deduce the immediate defcent of his Lordfhip, I fhall fomewhat more largely obferve, that,

Walter, third Lord Afton, who died in 1714, left iffue by his wife Eleanor, daughter of Sir Walter Blount, of Soddington, in Worcefterfhire, Bart. and relict of Robert Knightley,

ley, of Offchurch, in the county of Warwick, Esq; one son,

Walter, fourth Lord, who married Lady Mary, sister of Thomas, Duke of Norfolk, and by her who died in 1723, had issue several children (from one of which probably the present Lord descended.) In 1727, one of his daughters married Robert Weld, Esq; whom she sued for insufficiency, but not obtaining a divorce, they were persuaded to cohabit again. His Lordship dying in 1746, was succeeded by his eldest son,

James, fifth Lord, who married Lady Barbara, daughter of George, Earl of Shrewsbury, who died at Paris, in October, 1759 ; and his Lordship dying in August 1751, leaving only two daughters, the title descended to the next heir,

Philip, sixth Lord, who died, April 29, 1755, as above.

Of this antient family, which is of English extraction, was Ralph de Afton, in the county of Stafford, to whose son Roger, in the time of King Henry III. 1260, Roger de Moland, bishop of Litchfield, gave the keeping of the game in Cankwood in that county, which office hath continued to his posterity ever since. The descendants of the said Roger have been Knights for the county of Stafford, in the reigns of Edward III. Henry IV. Henry VI. Edward IV. Henry VII. and Henry VIII. several of whom were Knights of the Bath, and Knights banneret ; and all had served sheriff of Staffordshire from the time of Edward III. until Sir Walter, who, at the coronation of James I. of England, was made a Knight of the

the Bath, and, in 1611, on May 22, created a
Baronet; and going with the Earl of Briftol to
Madrid, to negotiate a marriage between
Prince Charles and the eldeft daughter of
Spain, he, on his return home, was created
a Baron on Nov. 8, 1628.

Walter his fon, the fecond Lord Afton, during the civil wars, continued in garrifons of
the King; and having a command in Litchfield
when that town furrendered, got permiffion to
go home and compound for his eftate, where
he lived retired till the reftoration of King
Charles II. and then fucceeded to the eftate
at Standon; which eftate, with the grant to
him and his heirs for a weekly market, and
two annual fairs, without an account to be
given into the exchequer, was all the reward
for his loyalty, fervices and fufferings.

Creations.] *Ut fupra.*

Arms.] Pearl, a fefs and in chief three lozenges, diamond.

Creft.] On a wreath, a bull's head couped,
of the laft.

Supporters.] Two Roman Knights com-
pletely armed, their faces, hands, and knees,
bare.

Motto.] *Numini & Patriæ Afto.*

Chief Seats.] At Standon, in the county of
Hertford; and at Tixhall, in Staffordfhire.

LORD KIRCUDBRIGHT.

WILLIAM MACLELLAN, Lord KIRCUD-
BRIGHT, is defcended lineally of Sir Gilbert
Maclellan, fecond fon of Sir Thomas, by
Agnes,

Agnes, daughter of Sir James Dunbar, of Mochrum.

William, the 4th Lord Kircudbright, dying unmarried, the dignity, for want of support, lay dormant, till 1722, when James Maclellan, nephew of John, the third Lord, made his claim, and succeeded as 5th Lord, but dying without male issue, the representation devolved on the present Lord, who making his claim and voting, was entered on the parliament rolls, in 1734, as 6th Lord Kircudbright. He married Margaret Murray, by whom he has a son, John, master of Kircudbright, an officer in the army.

Sir Thomas Maclellan, of Bomby, in the reigns of James III. and IV. was a man of great distinction, and married Agnes Dunbar, as above. Sir William, his eldest son and successor, was slain at the battle of Floddon, in 1513, and left issue Sir Thomas, who was killed in a feud, at Edinburgh, and was succeeded by his son Sir Thomas, and he by his son, another Sir Thomas, whose son, Sir Robert, was knighted by James VI. to whom and Charles I. he was gentleman of the bedchamber, and was created Lord Kircudbright, on May 25, 1633, by Charles I.

Creation.] Ut supra.

Arms.] Topaz, two chevrons, diamond.

Crest.] On a wreath, a right arm, erect, the hand grasping a dagger, with a moor's head, on the point thereof, couped, proper.

Supporters.] On the dexter side, a chevalier in armour, holding in his outer hand a battoon ; on the sinister, a horse, pearl, furnished ruby.

Motto.]

Motto.] *Think on.*
Chief Seat.] At Kircudbright, the county town.

LORD BANFF.

ALEXANDER OGILVIE, Lord BANFF, in the county of Banff, fucceeded to that title, on the death of Alexander, the late Lord, who was a captain in the royal navy, but died unmarried, at Lifbon, in 1747; for Sir Alexander Ogilvie, of Forglan, fecond fon of George fecond Lord Banff, by his wife Mary, daughter of Sir John Allardice, of that Ilk, had four fons, and three daughters; George, who died without iffue; Alexander, father of the prefent Lord; John and Peter; Agnes, wife of Sir Alexander Read, of Barra; Mary, of Andrew Hay, of Mountblairie, and Helen, of —— Smollett, fon and heir of Sir James Smollett, of Bonhill. Alexander, the fecond fon, married Jane, daughter of —— Friend, Efq; by whom he had the prefent Lord, and a daughter.

The prefent and feventh Lord, married Jane, daughter of William Nefbit, of Dirleton, Efq; by whom he has iffue three fons and four daughters; Alexander mafter of Banff; William; Archibald deceafed; Jane, Sophia, Janet, and ——.

This family is defcended from that of the Earls of Finlater. Sir Walter Ogilvie, of Finlater and Deflkford, in the reign of James II. had two fons, Sir James and Sir Walter: Sir Walter, the fecond, had alfo two fons, Sir George, and Sir Walter, anceftor of this family, whofe whose great grandson Sir George was created a Baronet, by Charles I. on July 10, 1627, and on August 30, 1642, Lord Banff.

Creation.] *Ut supra.*

Arms.] Quarterly, first and fourth, pearl, a lion passant guardant, ruby, crowned with an imperial crown, proper, for Ogilvie. 2d and 3d, pearl, three parrots emerald, for Hume, of Faftcastle.

Crest.] On a wreath, a lion's head erased, ruby.

Supporters.] On the dexter side a man in armour, with a target in his right hand. On the sinister, a lion, ruby.

Motto.] *Fideliter.*

Chief Seat.] At Insdreur, in Banffshire.

LORD ELIBANK.

PATRICK MURRAY, Lord ELIBANK, succeeded Alexander the fourth Lord, his father, in 1735, and married Maria-Margaretta, Lady dowager North, relict of William Lord North and Grey, and daughter of Mynheer Elmet, receiver-general of the United Provinces, by whom he has issue. His Lordship was a lieutenant-colonel at the expedition to Carthagena, under admiral Vernon and general Wentworth.

Alexander, the late Lord, married Elizabeth, daughter of Mr. George Stirling, of Edinburgh, by whom he had issue five sons and six daughters: Barbara, wife of Sir James Johnston, of Westerhall, Bart. Elizabeth, who died unmarried; Anne, wife of James Ferguson, of Pitflour, advocate; Janet, of major Robert Murray; Mary; and Helen, wife of Sir John Stuart,

art, of Gairntully Bart. The fons were, Patrick, the prefent Lord ; George, a rear-admiral, who married Lady Ifabel, daughter of George late Earl of Cromartie, by whom he had a daughter ; Gideon, a clergyman ; Alexander, an officer in the army, who incurred the refentment of the honourable houfe of commons, for his behaviour at the Weftminfter election in 1750, was committed to Newgate, and clofely confined during the whole feffion of 1751, and now refides at Paris ; James, a major-general, and late governor of Canada.

This noble family fprung from the houfe of Blackbarony, the head or chief of an honourable tribe of the Murrays.

Sir Gideon Murray, knighted by King James VI. by whom he was made treafurer-depute, was third fon of Andrew Murray of Blackbarony, by Grifel his wife, daughter of Sir John Bethune of Creik. His fon Sir Patrick, in refpect of his loyalty to Charles I. was, May 16, 1628, created a Baronet ; and, in 1643, advanced to the title of Lord Elibank.

Creations.] *Ut fupra.*

Arms.] Sapphire, three ftars within a double treffure counterflory, with fleurs de lis, pearl, and in the center a martlet topaz.

Creft.] On a wreath, a lion rampant, ruby, holding between his paws a battle-ax proper.

Supporters.] Two horfes pearl, bridled ruby.

Motto.] *Virtute fideque.*

Chief Seats.] At Ballencrief in Eaft-Lothian, and at Newark-houfe in the county of Selkirk.

LORD

LORD HALKERTON.

WILLIAM FALCONER, Lord HALKERTON, fucceeded his brother, Alexander, the late Lord, in 1762.

David, the fourth Lord Halkerton, married Lady Catherine, daughter of William Earl of Kintore, by whom he had iffue five fons and four daughters; Alexander, the late Lord; William, David, John, and George, a captain in the navy; Catherine, who died unmarried; Jane, wife of James Falconer of Monkton, Efq; Mary, and Marjory, wife of George Norvill, of Boghall, Efq;

Alexander, the late Lord, married Frances, daughter of Herbert Mackworth, of Glamor-ganfhire, Efq; who, 2dly, married, in 1765, the honourable Anthony Brown, fon and heir of the Vifcount Montagu.

The firft of this family on record is Walter de Lenorp, whofe fon Ranulph, being falconer to King William the Lion, obtained a charter of the lands of Luthra and Balbegno, in the county of Kincardin; which, from his office, were named Hawkertoun, or Halkerton, and the family for many years was honoured with knighthood.

Sir Alexander Falconer, being a gentleman of great knowledge in the law, was, by Charles I. made one of the privy-council, and created a peer, July 29, 1647, by the title of Baron Halkerton of Halkerton, in the county of Kincardin.

Creations.] *Ut fupra.*

Arms.]

Arms.] Sapphire, a falcon displayed, pearl, crowned between a ducal crown topaz, and charged on the breast with a man's heart ruby, between three stars of the second. The stars and heart shew his descent from Douglas by the mother's side.

Crest.] On a wreath, an angel in a praying posture, with an orle of laurel.

Supporters.] Two falcons proper.

Motto.] *Vive ut vivas.*

Chief Seats.] At Halkerton and Glenfarquar, in the county of Kincardin.

LORD BELHAVEN.

JAMES HAMILTON, Lord BELHAVEN, one of the commissioners for the encouragement of the fisheries, and high sheriff of the county of Haddington, succeeded his brother, the late Lord, in 1763.

John, the third Lord Belhaven, in 1721, was appointed governor of Barbadoes; but was lost near the Lizard-point, in the Royal Anne Galley, on Nov. 10, the ship having struck on the Stag rocks, only two men and a boy escaping out of 240 persons. He married Mary, daughter of Andrew Bruce, merchant in Edinburgh, by whom he had issue four sons and one daughter: John, the late Lord; Andrew, an officer in the army, who died unmarried; James, advocate, sheriff-depute for Haddingtonshire, now Lord; Robert, a major of foot; and Margaret, wife of Alexander Baird, Esq; son of Sir William Baird, of Newbeath.

The descent of this noble family is the same with that of the Dukes of Hamilton. Sir David Hamilton

Hamilton marrying Janet, daughter of William Keith, marſhal of Scotland, by her had five ſons. From Robert, the third ſon, deſcended the families of Bruntwood and Broomhill. Sir John Hamilton of Broomhill, duı ing the civil war, taking up arms in defence of Charles I. was, in 1648, created a peer. He marriedd Margaret, natural daughter of James Marquis of Hamilton, and had three daughters; of whom, Elizabeth was married to Alexander Seton, Viſcount Kingſton, and Anne, to Sir Robert Hamilton of Silvertounhill; but having no male iſſue, the honour deſcended to John, the ſon of Sir Robert Hamilton of Preſtinanan, who, in 1704, was one of the Lords of the treaſury, and died in June 1708, in the fifty-ſecond year of his age; leaving by Margaret his wife, daughter of Sir Robert Hamilton of Silvertounhill, two ſons, John, the third Lord, and James, who died in 1732.

Creation.] Lord Belhaven, in the county of Haddingtón, *ut ſupra*.

Arms.] Ruby, a ſword erect in pale pro-per, the pommel and hilt topaz, between three cinquefoils pearl.

Creſt.] On a wreath, a nag's head, couped of the laſt, and bridled of the firſt.

Supporters.] Two horſes peaıl, bridled as the creſt.

Motto.] *Ride through.*

Chief Seats.] At the Biel, near Dunbar, in the county of Haddington; and at Preſtmanan in Eaſt-Lothian.

LORD ROLLO.

JOHN ROLLO, Lord ROLLO, fucceeded his brother Andrew, the late Lord, in 1765, who is married as below, and has feveral children, particularly ——, mafter of Rollo, who, in 1766, married ——, daughter of —— Ayton, Efq;

Robert, fourth Lord, by his wife Mary, eldeft daughter of Sir Henry Rollo, of Woodfide, had four fons, Andrew, the late Lord; Harry, an officer in the army, who had no iffue; John, the prefent Lord, who, by Ciceley, daughter of James Johnfton, merchant in Edinburgh, has iffue; and Clement, who married Maria-Emilia, eldeft daughter of John Irvine, of Bonfhaw, Efq; and had iffue: alfo three daughters; Mary, wife of David Drummond, of Pitkellony; Janet, of captain Robert Johnfton, of Wamphrey; and Ifabel, of John Aytoun, of Inchdairny, Efq; who all had iffue.

Andrew, the late Lord, was a colonel, by brevet in the army, behaved with great bravery in the laft war, and took the ifland of Dominica, in conjunction with Sir James Douglas, in June 1761. He married firft, Catherine, daughter and coheir of Lord James Murray, of Dowally, third fon of John, Marquis of Athol, by whom he had iffue a fon, the honourable captain John Rollo, a brave officer, who died at Martinico, in June, 1762. He had alfo other children by this Lady, who all died in their infancy. His Lordfhip married fecondly, Mifs Murray, daughter of —— Murray, of Abercairny, Efq; a few months before
his

his deceafe, which happened in 1765, on his journey to Scotland.

Of this antient family, which hath long been feated in Perthfhire, was John Rollo, who, in the reign of Robert II. had a grant of feveral lands from David Stewart, Earl of Strathern ; and from him defcended William Rollo, who had a charter from James IV. for erecting his lands into the barony of Duncrib. Andrew was knighted by King James VI. and created a Baron by Charles II. Jan. 10, 1650, by the title of Baron Rollo of Duncrib, in the county of Perth. He married Katharine, daughter of James Drummond Lord Maderty, by whom he had four daughters, and five fons, the youngeft whereof, Sir William, was beheaded at Edinburgh for adhering to the caufe of Charles I.

Creation.] *Ut fupra.*

Arms.] Topaz, a chevron between three boars heads erafed, fapphire.

Creft.] On a wreath, a ftag's head couped, proper.

Supporters.] Two ftags of the laft.

Motto.] *La fortune paffe par tout.*

Chief Seat.] At Duncrib, in the county of Perth.

LORD COLVILLE.

ALEXANDER, Lord COLVILLE, rear admiral of the white, fucceeded his father, John, the late Lord, in 1740, and is unmarried.

This family came originally from Normandy, in 1066, with William the conqueror, and from England to Scotland, with King David I. who fucceeded to the throne in 1124.

Robert,

Robert, who was created Lord Colville in
1609, by his wife Elizabeth, or Isabel, daughter
of Patrick Lord Ruthven, had two sons and
one daughter : James who died unmarried, before his father ; Robert, mafter of Colville,
and Jane, wife of Sir James Campbell of
Lawers, by whom she had John, Earl of Loudoun, Lord High Chancellor of Scotland in the
reign of Charles I. He died in 1620, and was
fucceeded by his grandson,

James, the second Lord, son of Robert,
mafter of Colville, who dying without iffue,
in 1722, was fucceeded by

John, third Lord, eldeft son of Alexander,
eldeft son of Dr. Alexander, eldeft son of
John, eldeft son of Alexander, fecond lawful
son of Sir James Colville, of Eafter-Wemyfs,
commendator of Culrofs, brother-german of
the firft Lord. He married Mifs Johnfton, of
the kingdom of Ireland, by whom he had iffue
five sons and two daughters : Alexander, the
prefent Lord ; George, who died in the Weft
Indies, without iffue ; John and Charles, officers in the army ; James, captain in the navy,
who died in the Eaft-Indies ; Margaret, wife
of captain Caftlemain, and Elizabeth who died
unmarried. His Lordfhip died on the expedition to Carthagena, in 1740.

. *Creations.*] Lord Colville, in 1609, confirmed by Charles II. before his reftoration.

Arms.] Quarterly, 1ft and 4th, pearl, a
crofs moline diamond. 2d and 3d, ruby, a fefs
cheque pearl and fapphire.

Creft.] On a wreath, a hind's head proper.

Supporters.] On the dexter fide a rhinoceros
of the latter. On the finifter, a favage covered
with

with a lion's skin, holding on his exterior
shoulder a battoon.

Motto.] *Oublier ne puis.*

LORD RUTHVEN.

JAMES RUTHVEN, Lord RUTHVEN, of Freeland, succeeded his mother, Isabel, Lady Ruthven, in 1732, and married first, Janet, daughter
of William Nesbit, of Dirleton, Esq; by whom
he had two sons, James master of Ruthven, an
officer in the army; and William, who died
unmarried: and secondly, Lady Anne, daughter of James, Earl of Bute, by whom he had
issue two sons and eight daughters: Stewart,
who died young; John, a captain in the navy;
Anne, wife of captain Elphinstone; Isabel of
captain John Mac Dougal; Wortley Montague; Elizabeth, wife of captain Lawrie; Jane,
who died young; Grace, wife of captain Caul-
field; Janet and Crawford, which last died in
her infancy.

William, second Lord Ruthven, the thir-
teenth generation of the illustrious house of
Gourie, in the direct male line. by his wife
Janet, daughter and coheir of Patrick, Lord
Halburton, of Dirleton, had issue two sons,
Patrick, father of William Earl of Gourie, and
Alexander, the progenitor of this family.

Creation.] Lord Ruthven, of Freeland, in
1651, by Charles II.

Arms.] Palee of six, sapphire and ruby.

Crest.] A ram's head, couped.

Supporters.] On the dexter side, a ram; on
the sinister, a goat, both proper.

Motto.]

Metto.] *Deed ſhaw.*
Chief Seat.] At Ruthven houſe, in Perthſhire.

LORD NEWARK.

WILLIAM LESLEY, Lord NEWARK, an officer in the army, ſucceeded his mother, Jane,
the late baroneſs, in 1740, and has voted at
every election of ſixteen peers for Scotland,
ſince 1749.

David, ſecond Lord Newark, who deceaſed
in 1694, left by his wife, Elizabeth, daughter
of Sir Thomas Stewart, of Grantully, five
daughters; Jane; Mary, who died unmarried; Chriſtian, wife of Thomas Graham, of
Balnagowan, Eſq: Griſel, of Thomas Drummond, of Logiealmond, Eſq; and Elizabeth,
who died unmarried.

Jane, his eldeſt daughter, ſucceeded to the
honour, and marrying Sir Alexander Anſtruther of that Ilk, Bart. had three ſons and ſix
daughters: William, the preſent Lord; David; Alexander, who has iſſue; Chriſtian;
Helen, wife of the Rev. John Chalmers; Jane,
Catherine, Margaret and Joanna.

Andrew, the fifth Earl of Rothes, marrying
Jane, daughter of Sir John Hamilton of Evandale, had a ſon Patrick, who was created Lord
Lindores; and he marrying Lady Jane Stewart, daughter of Robert Earl of Orkney, by
her had five ſons.

David the youngeſt was a colonel of horſe
under the King of Sweden in the wars of Germany. In the reign of Charles I. when the
civil war broke out in Britain, he, returning to
his

his native country, entered into the service of the parliament of Scotland, who had taken the covenant, and raised an army, in defence of their liberties and religion. He was made one of their generals, and so continued till the defeat at Worcester. In 1645, the Scots army under the Earl of Leven, being then in the center of England as allies to the parliament, this David Lesley, after the battle of Naseby, was detached with his whole party of horse to oppose the Marquis of Montrose, who, having deserted his old friends, was grown very formidable, and with an army of Irish and Highlanders, was marching into England, to reinforce the King. The general met him at Philiphaw, near Selkirk, where, on Sept. 13, 1645, the Marquis was defeated with very great loss, and forced to make his escape abroad; and when the Marquis returned, in the year 1650, this David was commissioned with a body of forces to reduce him : but colonel Strahan making a quick march, with a few troops of horse, the Marquis was routed before the King's forces could join him, and being soon after taken prisoner, general Lesley sent him to Edinburgh.

In 1650, the independents in England, having got the supreme power, resolved to exclude all the royal family. The Scots parliament, who never joined in the covenant with such intention, immediately declared for the King under certain limitations. Hereupon an army under Oliver Cromwell was ordered to act against Scotland; and being arrived there, the English lost many men by skirmishing, and endeavouring to get the Scots army, who were 27,000 men under general Lesley, from their

intrench-

intrenchments : whereupon Cromwell, retiring towards Dunbar, prepared to imbark his infantry, and return with his horfe to England. General Lefley, perceiving this motion, left his camp, and followed the enemy clofe, not doubting of a fure and eafy victory : but Cromwell making a ftand, attacked the Scots an hour before day, on the third of September, when, after a vigorous difpute, Lefley was utterly defeated, having loft all his cannon, and more than half his army being killed, wounded, or taken prifoners.

The next year, 1651, after King Charles II. was crowned at Scoon, a new army was formed of about 20,000 men, to try the King's fortune in England. The third of September was again favourable to Oliver; for the royal army was intirely varquifhed at Worcefter, and among many other perfons of diftinction, as well Englifh as Scots, general Lefley was taken prifoner, and committed to the Tower, where he was confined till the reftoration, when, as a return for his fidelity and fervice, the King was pleafed to create him a Peer, Aug. 31, 1660, by the title of Baron Newark in the county of Fife, and to allow him a penfion of 500l. a year. He married Jane, daughter of Sir John York, Knt. by whom he had David his heir, fecond Lord before-mentioned, and three daughters ; and by reafon the honour of Lord Newark was limited to the heirs male of his body, he refigned his honour unto his Majefty, in favour of his fon the faid David, and his heirs general, which his Majefty confirmed.

Creation.] Ut fupra.

Arms.] Quarterly, 1ft and 4th pearl, on a bend fapphire, three buckles topaz, for Lefly ;

7   ad,

2d, topaz, a lion rampant ruby, debruifed with
a ribband diamond for Abernetty ; 3d pearl,
three piles iffuing from the chief diamond, for
Anftruther, and by way of furtout, an efcutcheon ruby, charged with a three towered .
caftle pearl, mafoned diamond for Lindores.

Creft.] On a wreath, a demi-angel, winged,
topaz, holding in his right hand a griffon's
head, proper.

Supporters.] Two griffons pearl, beaked,
winged, and armed, topaz.

Motto.] *Periiffem ni Periiffem.*

Chief Seat.] At Newark, in the county of Fife.

LORD RUTHERFOORD.

ALEXANDER RUTHERFOORD, Lord RU-
THERFOORD, of Hunthill, in the county of Roxburgh, fucceeded John his father, the late Lord,
in February 1744, and is a captain of marines.

Andrew Rutherfoord, a cadet, of the family of
Hunthill, fon of William Rutherfoord of Quarri-
holes, near Leith, by his wife Ifabel Stewart, of
the family of Traquair, went young into the
French fervice, where attaining feveral degrees
of military preferment, he came at laft to be a
lieutenant-general in that kingdom. At the Reftoration, he came over to England with a very
honourable teftimony from the French King, and
for his fingular fervice and fidelity to the crown,
King Charles II. was pleafed to create him a peer,
Jan. 19, 1660, and foon after Earl of Tiviote
to him and the heirs male of his body : but being made governor of Tangier, he was unfortunately flain by the Moors, without iffue, in
1664, and the title of Earl died with him ; but
that of Lord Rutherfoord, according to the
grant

grant of patent, defcended to Sir Thomas Rutherfcord of Hunthill, who became 2d Lord:
his brother Archibald fucceeded as third Lord,
and his younger brother Robert, as fourth Lord;
to whom fucceeded John the fifth Lord, father
of the prefent Lord.

Creation.] Lord Rutherfcord, 19 Jan. 1660,
by Charles II.

Arms.] Pearl, an orle ruby, and in chief three
martlets, diamond.

Creft.] On a wreath, a martlet as in the coat.

Supporters.] Two horfes, proper.

Motto.] *Nec forte nec fato.*

Chief Seats.] At Grange, in the county of
Fife.

LORD BALLENDEN.

JOHN BALLENDEN, Lord BALLENDEN, hereditary ufher of the exchequer, fucceeded his
father, Ker, the late Lord, and is a minor.

This family had its rife in the time of James
IV. Thomas Ballenden, of Auchinoul, Efq;
was juftice clerk, and director of chancery to
James V. as alfo his fon Sir John Ballenden, in
the reigns of Queen Mary and her fon King
James VI. From this Sir John Ballenden defcended Sir William, who, having given many
proofs of his loyalty to Charles II. was, in recompence thereof, after the Reftoration, made
treafurer-depute, one of the privy council, and,
June 10, 1661, created Baron Ballenden of
Broughton; but dying unmarried, made a conveyance of his eftate and honour to John Ker,
a younger fon of William the fecond Earl of
Roxburgh, his coufin, who thereupon changed
his name to Ballenden, and took the arms; and
marrying

marrying Mary widow of William Ramſay, the
third Earl of Dalhouſie, by her had fi e ſons
and four daughters, the eldeſt of whom died
unmarried; the ſecond married to Ephraim M l-
ler of Hartingfordbury, Eſq; Mary, the third,
to the honourable John Campbell of Mammore,
now Duke of Argy'l; and the youngeſt, Diana,
to John Bultel of Fleet in Devonſhire, Nov. 6,
1753. Of the ſons, John, the eldeſt, ſucceeded
his father; but dying without iſſue, in 1741,
was ſucceeded by his next brother Ker, the father of the late Lord. The third ſon was Sir
Henry Ballenden, gentleman uſher of the black
rod to the houſe of Lords.

Creation.] *Ut ſupra.*

Arms.] Ruby, a hart's head couped, attired with ten tynes, between three croſs croſlets fitchy, topaz, all within a double treſſure
counterflory, with fleurs de lis of the laſt.

Supporters.] On the dexter ſide, a lady holding in her right hand a ſword erect, and a pair
of ſcales pendent, both proper. On the ſiniſter,
another ſuch lady holding in her left hand a
branch of palm.

Motto.] *Sic itur ad aſtra.*

Chief Seat.] At Broughton-houſe, in Mid-
Lothian.

LORD KINNAIRD.

CHARLES KINNAIRD, Lord KINNAIRD, of
Inchture, being ſon of George, ſon of George,
ſixth ſon of George, the firſt Lord Kinnaird,
upon the deceaſe of his couſin Charles, the late
and fifth Lord, without iſſue in 1758, ſucceeded to his honour and eſtate. He married Barbara, daughter of Sir James Johnſton of Weſter-
hall,

hall, Bart. by whom he has iffue, George mafter of Kinnaird; Patrick; Elizabeth, Helen, and Margaret.

In the reign of King William, in 1170, Randolph Rufus obtaining from that prince the lands of Kinnaird, in the county of Perth, which continued in his family till the time of King Charles I. he from that barony took his firname; and from him defcended Sir Richard Kinnaird of that Ilk, whofe fon Reginald marrying Margery, daughter and heir of Sir John Kirkaldy of Inchture, in the fame county, he with her had thofe lands, in which he was confirmed by the charter of Robert III.

George Kinnaird, Efq; being of great fervice to King Charles II. during the ufurpation of Oliver Cromwell, he was by that King at his reftoration made one of the privy council; and, Dec. 28, 1682, created Lord Kinnaird, of Inchture.

Arms.] Quarterly, 1ft and 4th topaz, a feffe wavey between three ftars, ruby, for Kirkaldy; 2d and 3d ruby, a faltire between four crefcents, topaz, for Kinnaird.

Creft.] On a wreath, a crefcent rifing from a cloud, with a ftar between its horns, all within two branches of palm difplayed orle-wife.

Supporters.] Two favages, each wreathed about his head and middle with oak leaves, and their hands that fupport the fhield in chains hanging down to their feet; their other hands holding each a garland of laurel.

Motto.] *Patitur qui vincit.*

Chief Seat.] At Drimmie, in the Carfe of Gowrie.

SECOND

SECOND TITLES;

Of Dukes, Marquiſſes, and Earls; by which, in Courteſy, their eldeſt Sons are generally diſtinguiſhed.

Berdour lord, eldeſt ſon of the earl of Moreton.
Ancram earl of, eldeſt ſon of the marq. of Lothian.
Angus earl of, eldeſt ſon of the duke of Douglas.
Balgany lord, eldeſt ſon of the earl of Leven.
Berindale lord, eldeſt ſon of the earl of Caithnefs.
Binny lord, eldeſt ſon of the earl of Haddington.
Bowmont marq. of, eldeſt ſon of the duke of Roxburgh.
Boyd lord, eldeſt ſon of the earl of Kilmarnock.
Boyle lord, eldeſt ſon of the earl of Glaſgow.
Bruce lord, eldeſt ſon of the earl of Kincardin.
Cardroſs lord, eldeſt ſon of the earl of Buchan.
Carmichael lord, eldeſt ſon of the earl of Hyndford.
Carnegy lord, eldeſt ſon of the earl of Southeſk.
Cochran lord, eldeſt ſon of the earl of Dundonald.
Clairmont lord, eldeſt ſon of the earl of Middleton.
Clideſdale marq. of, eldeſt ſon of the duke of Hamilton.
Chrichton lord, eldeſt ſon of the earl of Dumfries.
Cummerlard, eldeſt ſon of the earl of Balcarras.
Dair lord, eldeſt ſon of the earl of Selkirk.
Dalkeith earl of, eldeſt ſon of the duke of Buccleugh.
Dalmeny lord, eldeſt ſon of the earl of Roſeberry.
Dalrymple lord, eldeſt ſon of the earl of Stair.
Dalziel lord, eldeſt ſon of the earl of Carnwath.
Darnley earl of, eldeſt ſon of the duke of Lennox.
Deſkford lord, eldeſt ſon of the earl of Finlater.
Down lord, eldeſt ſon of the earl of Murray.
Drumlanrig earl of, eldeſt ſon of the duke of Queenſberry.
Drummond lord, eldeſt ſon of the earl of Perth.
Dunglas lord, eldeſt ſon of the earl of Hume.
Dupplin viſcount, eldeſt ſon of the earl of Kinnoul.

Elcho

Elcho lord, eldeft fon of the earl of Wemys.
Erfkine lord, eldeft fon of the earl of Mar.
Fleming lord, eldeft fon of the earl of Wigton.
Fenton vifcount, eldeft fon of the earl of Kelley.
Garlies lord, eldeft fon of the earl of Galloway.
Garnock vifc. eldeft fon of the earl of Crawford, formerly
    Lindfay.
Glaimes lord, eldeft fon of the earl of Strathmore.
Gordon lord, eldeft fon of the earl of Aboyn.
Glenorchy vifc. eldeft fon of the earl of Breadalbane.
Graham marquis of, eldeft fon of the duke of Montrofe.
Haddo lord, eldeft fon of the earl of Aberdeen.
Hay lord, eldeft fon of the earl of Errol.
Hope lord, eldeft fon of the earl of Hopeton.
Huntingtour lord, eldeft fon of the earl of Dyfart.
Huntley marquis of, eldeft fon of the duke of Gordon.
Johnfton lord, eldeft fon of the marquis of Annandale.
Keith lord, eldeft fon of the earl of Kintore.
Kelburn vifcount, eldeft fon of the earl of Glafgow.
Kennedy lord, eldeft fon of the earl of Caffils.
Kilmaurs lord, eldeft fon of the earl of Glencairn.
Kintail lord, eldeft fon of the earl of Seaforth.
Kirkwall lord, eldeft fon of the earl of Orkney.
Lefley lord, eldeft fon of the earl of Rothes.
Lindfay lord, eldeft fon of the earl of Crawford.
Linton lord, eldeft fon of the earl of Traquair.
Lorn marquis of, eldeft fon of the duke of Argyll.
Mackenzie lord, eldeft fon of the earl of Seaforth.
Macleod lord, eldeft fon of the earl of Cromerty.
Maitland lord, eldeft fon of the earl of Lauderdale.
Mauchlane lord, eldeft fon of the earl of Loudoun.
Maxwell lord, eldeft fon of the earl of Nithfdale.
Milfington vifcount, eldeft fon of the earl of Portmore.
Montgomery lord, eldeft fon of the earl of Eglington.
Mountftuart lord, eldeft fon of the earl of Bute.
Nidpath lord, eldeft fon of the earl of March.
Ogilvy lord, eldeft fon of the earl of Airly.

                                        Paifley

Paifley lord, eldeft fon of the earl of Abercorn.
Polwarth lord, eldeft fon of the earl of Marchmont.
Ramfay lord, eldeft fon of the earl of Dalhoufie.
Rofehill lord, eldeft fon of the earl of Northefk.
Seton lord, eldeft fon of the earl of Winton.
Strathnavern lord, eldeft fon of the earl of Sutherland.
Tullibairden marq. of, eldeft fon of the duke of Athol.
Yefter lord, eldeft fon of the marquis of Tweeddale.

A Lift of thofe SCOTS PEERS who have been fucceffively returned to all the Parliaments of Great Britain fince the Union, which took place May 1, 1707.

Firft Parliament, fummoned to meet the 23d of October, 1707.

JAMES Douglas, duke of Queenfberry.
James Graham, duke of Montrofe.
John Ker, duke of Roxburgh.
John Hay, marquis of Tweeddale.
William Ker, marquis of Lothian.
John Lindfay, earl of Crawford.
John Sutherland, earl of Sutherland.
John Erfkine, earl of Mar.
Hugh Campbell, earl of Loudoun.
David Wemys, earl of Wemys.
David Lefly, earl of Leven and Melvil.
James Ogilvy, earl of Seafield.
John Dalrymple, earl of Stair.
Archibald Primrofe, earl of Rofeberry.
David Boyle, earl of Glafgow.
Archibald Campbell, earl of Ila.

SECOND

SECOND PARLIAMENT.
8 July, 1708.

JAMES Hamilton, duke of Hamilton.
   James Graham, duke of Montrofe.
John Ker, duke of Roxburgh.
William Ker, marquis of Lothian.
John Lindfay, Earl of Crawford.
John Erfkine, earl of Mar.
John Lefley, earl of Rothes.
Hugh Campbell, earl of Loudoun.
David Wemys, earl of Wemys.
David Carnegy, earl of Northefk.
David Lefley, earl of Leven and Melvil.
George Hamilton, earl of Oikney.
James Ogilvy, earl of Seafield.
Archibald Primrofe, earl of Rofeberry.
David Boyle, earl of Glafgow.
Archibald Campbell, earl of Ila.

THIRD PARLIAMENT.
25 November, 1710.

JAMES Hamilton, duke of Hamilton, *killed in a duel.*
   John Murray, duke of Athol.
William Johnfton, marquis of Annandale.
William Keith, earl Marfhal, *died.*
John Efkine, earl of Mar
Alexander Montgomery, earl of Eglington.
Alexander Hume, earl of Hume.
Hugh Campbell, earl of Loudoun.
Thomas Hay, earl of Kinnoul.
David Carnegy, earl of Northefk.
George Hamilton, earl of Orkney.
Archibald Primrofe, earl of Rofeberry.
Archibald Campbell, earl of Ila.
William Levingfton, vifcount Kilfyth.

                                        Joha

John Elphingſton, lord Balmerino.
Walter Stewart, lord Blantyre.

Returned for thoſe deceaſed.

James Livingſton, earl of Linlithgow and Callender.
James Ogilvy, earl of Finlater and Seafield.

FOURTH PARLIAMENT.
12 November, 1713.

JOHN Murray, duke of Athol.
John Erſkine, earl of Mar.
Alexander Montgomery, earl of Eglington.
James Levingſton, Earl of Linlithgow and Callender.
Hugh Campbell, earl of Loudoun.
Thomas Hay, Earl of Kinnoul.
Charles Hamilton, earl of Selkirk.
David Carnegy, earl of Northeſk.
John Cochran, earl of Dundonald.
James Campbell, earl of Breadalbane.
John Murray, earl of Dunmore.
George Hamilton, earl of Orkney.
Archibald Primroſe, earl of Roſeberry.
David Colyear, earl of Portmore.
William Levingſton, viſcount Kilſyth.
John Elphingſton, Lord Balmerino.

FIFTH PARLIAMENT.
17 March, 1714-15.

JAMES Graham, duke of Montroſe.
John Ker, duke of Roxburgh.
Charles Hay, marquis of Tweeddale, *died.*
William Ker, marquis of Lothian, *died, no new election.*
William Johnſton, marquis of Annandale, *died.*
John Sutherland, earl of Sutherland.
John Leſley, earl of Rothes.
David Erſkine, earl of Buchan.
Hugh Campbell, earl of Loudoun.

George

George Hamilton, earl of Orkney.
John Dalrymple, earl of Stair.
James Stewart, earl of Bute.
Henry Scot, earl of Deloraine.
Archibald Campbell, earl of Ila.
William Kofs, lord Rofs.
John Hamilton, lord Belhaven, *drowned.*

Returned for the deceafed Peers.

Thomas Hamilton, earl of Haddington.
William Gordon, earl of Aberdeen.
James Ogilvy, earl of Finlater and Seafield.

SIXTH PARLIAMENT.
10 May, 1722.

JAMES Graham, duke of Montrofe.
John Ker, duke of Roxburgh.
John Hay, marquis of Tweeddale.
John Sutherland, earl of Sutherland.
John Lefley, earl of Rothes, *died.*
David Erfkine, earl of Buchan.
Thomas Hamilton, earl of Haddington.
Hugh Campbell, earl of Loudoun.
Charles Hamilton, earl of Selkirk.
William Gordon, earl of Aberdeen.
George Hamilton, earl of Orkney.
John Dalrymple, earl of Stair.
James Stewart, earl of Bute.
Charles Hope, earl of Hopeton.
Henry Scot, earl of Delorain.
Archibald Campbell, earl of Ila.

Returned for the peer who died.

James Ogilvy, earl of Finlater and Seafield.

SEVENTH

SEVENTH PARLIAMENT.
28 November, 1727.

JAMES Graham, duke of Montrofe.
John Hay, marquis of Tweeddale.
John Sutherland, earl of Sutherland.
John Lefley, earl of Rothes, *died.*
David Erfkine, earl of Buchan.
Thomas Hamilton, earl of Haddington.
Hugh Campbell, earl of Loudoun.
James Ogilvy, earl of Finlater and Seafield.
Charles Hamilton, earl of Selkirk.
John Murray, earl of Dunmore.
George Hamilton, Earl of Oikney.
John Dalrymple, earl of Stair.
Alexander Hume, earl of Marchmont.
Charles Hope, earl of Hopetoun.
Henry Scot, earl of Delorain.
Archibald Campbell, earl of Ila.

Returned for the earl of Rothes.

James Ogilvy, earl of Finlater and Seafield.

EIGHTH PARLIAMENT.
13 June, 1734.

FRANCIS Scot, duke of Buccleugh.
James Murray, duke of Athol.
William Ker, marquis of Lothian.
John Lindfay, earl of Crawford.
William Sutherland, earl of Sutherland.
George Dougl:s, earl of Moreton, *died.*
John Campbell, earl of Loudoun.
James Ogilvy, earl of Finlater and Seafield.
Charles Hamilton, earl of Selkirk, *died.*
Alexander Lindfay, earl of Balcarras, *died.*
John Murray, earl of Dunmore.

George

2

George Hamilton, earl of Orkney, *died.*
Charles Hope, earl of Hopetoun.
Charles Colyear, earl of Portmore.
Archibald Campbell, earl of Ila.
Charles Cathcart, lord Cathcart.

Returned for the peers who died.

John Campbell, earl of Breadalbane.
John Stewart, earl of Bute.
John Carmichael, earl of Hyndford.
James Douglas, earl of Moreton.

NINTH PARLIAMENT.
25 June, 1741.

WILLIAM Ker, marquis of Lothian.
John Lindsay, earl of Crawford.
William Sutherland, earl of Sutherland.
James Douglas, earl of Moreton.
James Stewart, earl of Murray.
William Hume, earl of Hume.
Charles Maitland, earl of Lauderdale, *died* *.
John Campbell, earl of Loudoun.
James Ogilvy, earl of Finlater and Seafield.
John Campbell, earl of Breadalbane.
John Murray, earl of Dunmore.
John Carmichael, earl of Hyndford.
Charles Hope, earl of Hopetoun, *died* †.
Charles Colyear, earl of Portmore.
Archibald Campbell, earl of Ila.
James Somerville, lord Somerville.

In the room of those deceased.

* John Hay, marquis of Tweeddale.
† John Dalrymple, earl of Stair.

TENTH

TENTH PARLIAMENT.
14 Auguſt, 1747.

COSMO George Gordon, duke of Gordon, *died* §,
Archibald Campbell, duke of Argyll.
John Hay, m·rquis of Tweeddale.
William Ker, marquis of Lothian.
John Lindſay, earl of Crawford, *died* †.
John Leſley, earl of Rothes.
James Douglas, earl of Moreton.
James Stewart, earl of Murray.
William Hume, earl of Hume.
James Maitland, earl of Lauderdale.
John Campbell, earl of Loudoun.
James Ogilvy, earl of Finlater and Seafield.
Alexander Leſley, earl of Leven and Melvil.
George Gordon, earl of Aberdeen.
John Murray, earl of Dunmore, *died* ‖.
John Carmichael, earl of Hyndford.

In the room of thoſe who died.

§ Hugh Hume, earl of Marchmont.
† John Campbell, earl of Breadalbane.
‖ Charles Cathcart, lord Cathcart.

ELEVENTH PARLIAMENT.
31 May, 1754.

ARCHIBALD Campbell, duke of Argyll.
John Hay, marquis of Tweeddale.
William Ker, marquis of Lothian.
John Leſley, earl of Rothes.
James Douglas, earl of Moreton.
James Stewart, earl of Murray.
William Hume, earl of Hume.
James Maitland, earl of Lauderdale.
John Campbell, earl of Loudoun.

James

James Ogilvy, earl of Finlater and Seafield.
Alexander Lefley, earl of Leven and Melvil, *died* †.
John Campbell, earl of Breadalbane.
George Gordon, earl of Aberdeen.
Hugh Hume, earl of Marchmont.
John Carmichael, earl of Hyndford.
David Murray, vifcount Stormont.

Returned for the peer who died.

† Charles Cathcart, lord Cathcart.

TWELFTH PARLIAMENT.
5 May, 1761.

JOHN Campbell, duke of Argyll.
John Hay, marquis of Tweeddale, *died* *.
John Lefley, earl of Rothes.
James Douglas, earl of Morton.
Alexander Montgomery, earl of Eglington.
James Stewart, earl of Murray.
William Hume, earl of Hume, *died* †.
James Hamilton, earl of Abercorn.
John Campbell, earl of Loudoun.
John Campbell, earl of Breadalbane.
William Murray, earl of Dunmore.
James Douglas, earl of March.
Hugh Hume, earl of Marchmont.
John Stewart, earl of Bute.
David Murray, vifcount Stormont.
Charles Cathcart, lord Cathcart.

In the room of those who died.

* William Sutherland, earl of Sutherland, who died in
1766, and John Murray, duke of Athol, was elected
in his room.
† John Carmichael, earl of Hyndford.

ATTAINTED

ATTAINTED PEERS
OF SCOTLAND.

E A R L S.

KEITH, Earl MARISHAL.

THIS noble family is one of the moſt ancient and illuſtrious in Scotland; and derive their origin from Robert, one of the chiefs of the Catti (whence it is ſaid Keith) who performed many glorious exploits againſt the Danes, in the reign of Malcolm II. for which he had granted to him and his heirs the lands and barony of Keith in Eaſt-Lothian, from which, more probably, his poſterity took their ſirname. The aboveſaid Prince advanced him to the hereditary dignity of Marſhal of Scotland, and granted him the iſland of Inch-keith in the gulph of Edinburgh.

The

The fucceffors of this Robert continued to
be among the moft eminent men in Scotland.
Robert Keith, in 1292, had a charter from
John Baliol of his lands of Keith, &c. and by
King Robert Bruce, in 1325, was fent ambaffador to France; but was flain at the battle of
Dupplin in 1332, in defence of his country,
and was fucceeded by his fon John, whofe fon
Sir Robert, who fucceeded him, was, for his
wifdom and valour, knighted by King David
II. His fon, Sir Edward, was flain at the battle of Durham, when King David II. was, taken prifoner in 1346, leaving a fon, Sir William, who, in 1369, was one of the commiffioners who concluded a peace between England and Scotland. He was anceftor of Sir
William, who being a favourite of King James
II. was created Lord Keith, and Earl Marfhal,
or Marifhal, of Keith, in the county of Haddington.

George, the fifth Earl Marfhal, was one of
the privy council to King James VI. by whom
he was fent ambaffador to the court of Denmark, where, at his own expence, he efpoufed
the Princefs Anne, a daughter of that crown,
in the name of his Majefty; and, in the year
1593, founded the Marfhal College in the city
of Aberdeen; and in 1609 was high commiffioner to the parliament. His grandfon,

William, the feventh Earl, in the time of
the civil war, levied, at his own charge, a troop
of horfe for the King's fervice: but being taken prifoner, and fent to the Tower of London, remained there ten years, and then, being releafed, was made one of the privy council to King Charles II. and lord privy feal.

The

The faid feventh Earl was fucceeded by his brother, George, eighth Earl, whofe fon William, ninth Earl, was fucceeded by George his fon, tenth Earl, who joining in the rebellion in 1715, with the Earl of Mar, his eftate and honours were forfeited by attainder, in 1716, with thofe of the Earls of Mar, Southefk, Linlithgow, Panmure, and Seaforth.

His Lordfhip has been long in the fervice of the King of Pruffia, and is his governor of Neufchâtel, in Switzerland, and being next of kin to John, Earl of Kintore (fee that title,) who died without iffue, in 1761, his Lordfhip was enabled, by act of parliament, to inherit his eftate, or any other that might devolve to him.

His Lordfhip's brother was the late renowned field-marfhal Keith, who following his brother's fortune, engaged afterwards in the fervice of Peter the Great, Emperor of Ruffia, who gave him the rank of brigadier-general, and in that fervice he was afterwards field-marfhal. He then entered into the fervice of Frederick III. King of Pruffia, who raifed him to the rank of field-marfhal; but, after many fignal fervices, he was unfortunately killed, Oct. 14, 1758, when the right wing of the Pruffian army, where he commanded, was furprized, at Hochkirchen, by the Auftrians, under Marfhal Daun, who, after the action, buried general Keith with great military honours: but the King of Pruffia, who could not fufficiently regret the lofs of fo great a commander, had his corps taken up, and fent to Berlin, where a fuperb monument is erected to his memory.

He

He had alfo two fifters, Lady Mary, wife of John, Farl of Wigton, and Lady Anne, of Alexander, Earl of Galloway. They were the fons and daughters of William, the ninth Earl, abovementioned, by his wife, Lady Mary, daughter of James, Earl of Perth.

Creations.] Earl Marfhal, of Keith, in 1455, by James II.

Arms.] Pearl, on a chief, ruby, three pallets, topaz.

Creft.] On a wreath, a ftag's head erafed, proper, and attired with ten tynes, topaz.

Supporters.] Two ftags, proper, attired as the creft.

Motto.] *Veritas vincit.*

Chief Seats were,] Dunfter-caftle and Fate-reffo, in Kincardinefhire; Inverugy and Newburgh, in Aberdeenfhire.

ERSKINE, Earl of MAR.

In the reign of Alexander II, 1226, lived Henry de Erfkine, who was witnefs to a gift which Amelick, brother of Maldwin, Earl of Lennox, made to the canons of Paifley; and to him fucceeded Sir John Erfkine, the father of another Sir John, the father of a third Sir John, whofe fon Sir William fucceeded him in the barony of Erfkine, and was father of Sir Robert, who was very ftedfaft and loyal to K. David II; for in the year 1346, when his Majefty was taken prifoner at the battle of Dur-ham, the Lord Erfkine (as he is called in the re-

record) was one of the commissioners employed in that honourable negotiation of the King's redemption, and gave his eldest son as one of the hostages for the performance of the treaty. After his Majesty's return he was made justice-general of the North, lord chamberlain to the King, ambassador to France, sheriff of the county of Stirling, and governor of that castle, and the castles of Edinburgh and Dumbarton; and, at the King's death, he declared for Robert II, and contributed much to the bringing him peaceably to the throne.

Sir Thomas, seventh Lord Erskine, who succeeded him, married Janet, daughter of Sir Edward Keith of Sinton, by Christian his wife. daughter and heir of Sir John Menteith and of Helen his wife, daughter of Gratney Earl of Mar, and by her had Robert the eighth Lord Erskine, who, in 1436, upon the death of Alexander Earl of Mar, laid claim to half of that Earldom, and assumed the title on account of the aforesaid marriage; but the Crown interfering, it was not ended in his days: however, his son Thomas, ninth Lord, who succeeded, prosecuting his father's claim to the Earldom of Mar, had a decree of the committee of estates in his favour, in 1457, and was Earl of Mar.

John fourth Earl of Mar, had the care and tuition of the young King James V. in the castle of Stirling, of which he was governor. In the year 1534, when the King came of age, he was sent ambassador to France, to propose a match between his Majesty and the Princess Magdalen, a daughter of King Francis I. which having

per-

performed, he was sent in the same quality to Henry VIII. of England; and, in 1537, was one of those peers who attended his master into France, where he espoused the said Princess. In 1542, upon the death of the King, the young Queen Mary was also committed to his care, in Stirling-castle; and that great trust his lordship discharged with the same fidelity he had done in her father's minority; for, in 1548, notwithstanding the endeavours of King Henry VIII. of England, and the party that was for him in Scotland, to get her out of his hands, he carried her safe to France.

John, fifth Earl, his son, who succeeded him in 1552, was a person of noble and generous qualities, as well as his father; and though he was then very young, the queen regent, in 1553, appointed him governor of Edinburgh-castle, and one of her Majesty's privy council; and when Queen Mary was happily delivered of the young Prince, afterwards King James VI, she committed him to the guardianship of the Earl of Mar, in the castle of Edinburgh, which trust he discharged so well, that when the Earl of Bothwell had married the Queen, they could not prevail with the Lord Mar to deliver up the young Prince to them, till he had solemnly set the crown upon his Majesty's head. Having been elected regent for Scotland in 1571, during the minority of the said King James VI, he, in the time of his sickness, when his son was a minor, appointed the Laird of Tullibairden, and his own brother Alexander Erskine, to be governors of his Majesty, and keepers of Stirling-castle.

John,

John, the fixth Earl of Mar, was alfo in great favour with King James VI, who committed to his care the tuition of his young fon Prince Henry; and, by a letter under his own hand, charged his Lordfhip, in cafe of his Majefty's demife, not to deliver the Prince either to the Queen or Eftates, till he came of age. In 1601 his Lordfhip was fent ambaffador to Queen Elizabeth, where, in his negotiations, he deported himfelf with fuch prudence and conduct, that his Majefty gratefully owned his peaceable acceffion to the crown of England, was, next to the goodnefs of God, to be afcribed to the Earl of Mar; and thereupon made him a knight of the moft noble order of the garter, one of his privy council in England, and lord treafurer of Scotland.

John, the tenth Earl, was by Queen Anne made colonel of a regiment of foot, knight of the thiftle, and fecretary of ftate; he was alfo one of the commiffioners for the treaty of union between England and Scotland, which being concluded, he was elected one of the fixteen peers, as he was alfo in the three fucceeding parliaments of Queen Anne; and was made again fecretary of ftate in 1713. Upon the acceffion of George I. he was deprived of all his offices, and retired to Scotland; but being joined by feveral noblemen and gentlemen, with their followers, to the number of fix hundred, and fetting up his ftandard, and proclaiming the pretender at Kirkmichael, and his forces increafing to fix or feven thoufand men, a battle was fought at Sheriffmuir near Dunblain, Nov. 13, 1715, between John Duke of

I 4   Argyll,

Argyll, commanding the royal troops, and the Earl of Mar, who commanded the rebel army : the Earl, though he was not brought up in the arts of war, behaved like a brave general, and both armies withdrew, leaving the victory undetermined; the one to Stirling, the other to Perth, where they paffed the winter : but fome difcord arifing in the Earl's army, and their friends in England being defeated the fame day, at Prefton, in Lancafhire, he was forced to take refuge in France, with the perfon he had proclaimed, and who had come over and joined him fome time after the battle ; and in the year 1716, was attainted, with the Duke of Ormond, Lord Bolingbroke, &c. and his eftate and honours forfeited to the crown. From France he went to Italy, where he continued fome time, and then returned to Paris : but turning valetudinary, after fo much fatigue of body and mind, he retired to Aix la Chapelle, where he died in 1732, under the care of his moft dutiful daughter, Lady Frances Erfkine, who fupported him during his life, and continued the fame care to the Countefs her mother.

He married firft, Margaret, daughter of Thomas, Earl of Kinnoul, by whom he had Thomas Lord Erfkine, who is now in poffeffion of his father's eftate, which was purchafed from the government by his trufty friends James Erfkine of Grange, his uncle, and David Erfkine of Dun. He married Lady Charlotte, daughter of Charles, Earl of Hoptoun, by whom he has iffue. In 1727 he was elected to parliament for the burgh of Inverkeithing,
&c.

&c. In January, 1746-7, for the fhire of Stirling; and in the fucceeding parliament, in 1747, for the fhire of Clackmannan. The Earl's fecond lady was Lady Frances, fifter of Evelyn, Duke of Kingfton, by whom he had the above-mentioned Lady Frances, who had fettled upon her by King George I. the fame fortune fhe was intitled to by her mother's marriage fettlement, and her mother had a grant of her jointure. She was married to her coufin, James Erfkine, of Grange, Efq; fon of the above Mr. Erfkine, of Grange, and has iffue two fons, John-Francis and James-Francis, both officers in the army.

Creations.] Created or confirmed Earl of Mar, and Lord Erfkine of Alloa, in the county of Clackmannan, in 1436, by James II.

Arms.] Quarterly, 1ft and 4th fapphire, a bend between fix crofs croflets fitchy, topaz, for the title of Mar; 2d and 3d pearl, a pale diamond, for Erfkine.

Creft.] On a wreath, a dexter hand couped above the wrift, holding a dagger erect, proper, the pommel and hilt, topaz.

Supporters.] Two griphons pearl, beaked, winged, and armed, topaz.

Motto.] *Je penfe plus.*

Chief Seats.] At Stirling, Alloa, &c. Stirlingfhire.

MAX-

MAXWELL, Earl of NITHSDALE.

The firft on record, who ufed this firname, was Hubert de Makfwell, in the time of Malcolm IV. 1160, to whom fucceeded John de Makfwell, who was one of the commiffioners fent to England, to treat of a marriage between Alexander II. and a daughter of that crown, which having concluded, he was thereupon made great chamberlain of Scotland. From him defcended Sir Herbert, who, in 1424, was dignified with the title of Lord Maxwell; and Robert, the ninth Lord Maxwell, was created Earl of Nithfdale. He fuffered much by fequeftration and imprifonment for his loyalty to King Charles I.

William, the fifth Earl, engaging in the rebellion againft King George I. in the year 1715, was taken at Prefton, and brought prifoner to London, was tried, and condemned to be beheaded on Feb. 24, following, with the Lords Derwentwater and Kenmure : but the night before execution he made his efcape out of the Tower; and, in the year 1744, died in his exile at Rome. He married Winifred, youngeft daughter of William Herbert, Marquis of Powis ; and by her left William Lord Maxwell, who married his coufin-german Lady Catharine Stewart, daughter of Charles Earl of Traquair ; by whom he had iffue two daughters ; Mary, who died young, and Winifred, wife of William Conftable, of Effringame, efq; by whom fhe has two fons and a

daugh-

daughter: alfo a daughter, Lady Anne, married to John Lord Bellew, of the kingdom of Ireland.

Creations.] Earl of Nithfdale Oct.-29, 1581, 16 James VI.

Arms.] Pearl, an imperial eagle difplayed, diamond, beaked and membered ruby, furmounted of a fhield of the firft, charged with a faltire of a fecond, and thereupon a hedge-hog, topaz.

Creft.] On a wreath, a mount and holly-bufh, and a ftag lodged, or, couchant.

Supporters.] Two ftags proper, attired, pearl.

Motto.] *Revirefco.*

Chief Seats were] At Terregles, and Carla-varock, in Dumfriesfhire.

SEATON, Earl of WINTON.

This family is one of the nobleft in North Britain, from which many illuftrious families, are defcended. The name is derived from their ancient lands of Seton in Eaft-Lothian; the firft whereof was Dowgal Seaton, who lived in the reigns of King Edgar, and Alexander I. who fucceeded to the crown in 1107; and was fucceeded by Secher his fon, who alfo inherited the lands of Winton and Winfburgh, from whom defcended Sir Chriftopher Seton, who, in the time of Robert I. bravely ftood up for the freedom of his country againft the Englifh ufurpation, and was one of thofe wor-thies, who, at the battle of Methven, near Perth, in 1306, refcued the King from the

I 6 Englifh

English party; whereupon, for that singular, piece of service, the King gave him in marriage his sister the Lady Christian Bruce; but at last he had the ill fortune to be taken by the English, and carried to London, where, with his brother John Seton, and Nigel Bruce, the King's brother, he was put to death. His son Sir Alexander made a great figure during the reign of his uncle King Robert, from whom he obtained sundry grants of lands, and a charter for erecting his lands of Seton into a free barony, and on account of his maternal descent, had his three crescents surrounded with the double treffure, which, with the coat of augmentation given to his father; ruby, a sword supporting an imperial crown, has continued to the family ever since.

The first Lord Seton was Sir John, who was one of the hostages for the ransom of King James I. to whom he was afterwards master of the houshold. He attended the Princess Margaret, that King's daughter, into France, in order to her marriage with Lewis the Dauphin, eldest son of Charles VII. King of France.

George, the sixth Lord Seton, being governor of Edinburgh-castle, during the regency of Queen Mary of Lorrain, was, in 1557, commissioned by the estates in Scotland, to treat with the French King about the marriage of Queen Mary with Francis the Dauphin; and his son Robert, the seventh Lord, being much esteemed by King James VI his Majesty raised him to the dignity of Earl of Winton. George, the second Earl, was one of the privy-council to Charles I. whom, with his

whole

whole retinue, in the King's progrefs to Scotland, he entertained at his houfe of Seton, with great fplendor and magnificence, and was very faithful to that prince during the time of the civil wars.

George, the fourth Earl, unhappily engaging in the rebellion in 1715, was brought prifoner from Prefton, in Lancafhire, to London, and committed to the Tower. In March following he was tried by his peers, found guilty, and received fentence of death ; but in Auguft following, by fome fecret management, he made his efcape, and ended his days at Rome, in 1749, without iffue. The reprefentation of the family is now vefted in Sir George Seaton, of Garleton, fon of Sir George, fon of Sir John, third fon of George, fecond Earl of Winton, who refides in France, and is unmarried.

. *Creation.*] Earl of Winton, Nov. 10, 1600, 31 James VI. (I. of England.)

Arms.] Quarterly, 1ft and 4th, topaz, three crefcents within a double treffure, flowered and counterflowered, with fleurs de lys ruby, for Seaton. 2d and 3d, fapphire, three garbs topaz, the arms of Buchan, as having pretenfion to that earldom, and over all, by way of furtout, an efcutcheon party per pale, ruby and fapphire, the firft charged with a fword in pale proper, pommelled and hilted topaz, fupporting an imperial crown with a double treffure of the laft ; and the 2d, charged with a ftar of twelve points pearl, for the title of Winton.,

Creft.]

Creft.] In a ducal coronet topaz, a dragon emerald spouting fire, his wings elevated.

Supporters.] Two foxes proper, collared and chained topaz, each collar charged with three crescents ruby ; and upon a scroll coming behind the shield, and passing over the middle of the supporters, are these words, *Intaminatis fulget honoribus*, relative to the surtout.

Motto.] *Invia virtuti via nulla.*

Chief Seats were] At Seton, in the county of Haddington ; at Winton, in the same county ; and at Edinburgh.

LIVINGSTON, Earl of LINLITHGOW.

The first of this name is said to be one of the gentlemen that accompanied Queen Margaret, wife of King Malcolm Canmore, into Scotland, from Hungary, where in the reign of David I. he got lands in West-Lothian, which he called Livingstone, after his own name, and was succeeded therein by his son Thurstan, the father of Alexander, whose posterity enjoyed the barony of Livingston above four hundred years, which was till the reign of James IV. when Bartholomew Livingston dying without issue, with him that family became extinct. Others, with more reason, suppose Livingston to be rather a modern Scots name, derived from Levin, which is the name of a town, lake, and river in Fifeshire, Perthshire, and Lenos.

In

In the reign of David II. Sir William Livingſton, the immediate anceſtor of this noble family, marrying Chriſtian, daughter and heir of Patrick de Callendar, Lord Callendar, in the county of Stirling, with her had that barony, and afterwards obtained a royal grant of the lands of Kilſyth, lying weſt of Callendar, then in the King's hands. In 1346, he was one of the commanders at the battle of Durham, where he was taken priſoner with the King; but being releaſed, he was commiſſioned to treat with the Engliſh about the redemption of his royal maſter, which being agreed to, he delivered Sir William, his ſon and heir, as one of the hoſtages for the payment of the King's ranſom.

Sir Alexender Livingſton, his grandſon, was one of the hoſtages for the ranſom of King James I when he was relieved from his captivity in England; and upon the deceaſe of his maſter, was made choice of by the three eſtates of Scotland to be governor to the young King James II. till he was fourteen years of age. James, his ſucceſſor, was created Lord Livingſton, and for his great prudence and ability was made captain of Stirling caſtle, where he had the cuſtody of the young King committed to him by his father, when he was the King's governor; which great truſt he faithfully diſcharged, and was afterwards appointed maſter of the houſhold, one of the privy council, and high chamberlain of Scotland.

Alexander, the ſeventh Lord Livingſton, was much eſteemed by James VI, who, in recompence of his care in the education of his daughter, the Princefs Elizabeth, afterward's Queen of Bohemia, created him Earl of Linlithgow. He dying, in 1622, left two fons, Alexander, who fucceeded him, and Sir James, who, having acquired honours and riches in the wars abroad, was, after his return, by Charles I. in 1633, created Lord Almond, and, in 1641, Earl of Callendar, which Earl dying without iffue left his eftate to Alexander, his nephew, fecond fon of his brother Alexander Earl of Linlithgow.

George, the third Earl, firmly adhered to Charles I. in all his fufferings, and was greatly reduced by his loyalty. At the reftoration, however, he was called to the privy-council, was appointed captain of the foot-guards, and juftice-general of Scotland.

James, the fourth Earl of Callendar, and fixth of Linlithgow, married Lady Margaret, daughter of John Hay, twelfth Earl of Errol, by whom he had a fon, James, who died in 1715, and a daughter, Lady Anne, who became his fole heir, and married William, late earl of Kilmarnock. (See the titles, Earl of Errol, and Earl of Kilmarnock.) The faid Earl, for his concern in the rebellion of 1715, was attainted, and his eftates and honours forfeited to the crown.

Creations.] Earl of Lithgow, or Linlithgow, in Weft - Lothian, Nov. 15, 1600, by James VI. Lord Almond, in 1633, and Earl of Callendar in 1641, both in the county of Stirling, by Charles I.

Arms.] Quarterly, firft and fourth pearl, three cinquefoils ruby, within a double trefsure,

fire, flowered and counterflowered, with fleurs
de lys, emerald, for Livingston. Second and
third, diamond, a bend between six billets,
topaz, for Callendar; and over all, by way of
furtout, in an escutcheon, sapphire, an oak
growing out of the base, topaz, within a border pearl, charged with eight juliflowers, ruby,
as a coat of augmentation, for the title of Earl
of Linlithgow.

Creft.] On a wreath a demi-savage, wreathed about the temples and waist with laurel,
proper, holding in his right hand a battoon
erect, and in the left a serpent, which is twist-
ed about his arm.

Supporters.] Two savages proper, wreathed
as the crest, each holding on his exterior
shoulder a battoon topaz.

Motto.] *Si je puis.*

Chief Seats were] At Callendar-castle in Stir-
lingshire; and at Brighouse, in the county of
Linlithgow.

DRUMMOND, Earl of PERTH.

The first of this family who took the name
of Drummond, was Maurice, son of George, a
younger son of Andreas, King of Hungary,
which Maurice quitted England with Edgar
Atheling, the rightful heir to that crown, but
unjustly deprived thereof, first by Harold, and
afterwards by William Duke of Normandy,
who seized the kingdom in 1066. Maurice,
commanding the ship in which Edgar Atheling,
his mother Agatha, and his sisters Margaret
and

and Chriftian were embarked, and meeting with a violent ftorm at fea, which drove them to Scotland, they put into the river Foith, and landed at a place called Queen's Ferry, from Margaret, the faid Edgar's fifter. This Prin- cefs married Malcolm III. King of Scotland, who rewarded Maurice Drummond with a con- fiderable fhare of wealth and honour, particu- larly a large eftate in the county of Dunbritton or Lennox, and the ftewarty thereof, which eftate and office were enjoyed by his fucceffors.

John, the feventh ftewart of Lennox, having loft the lands which he had in that fheriffdom, retired into Perthfhire, and married Mary, the eldeft daughter and coheir of Sir William de Montefex, lord high treafurer of Scotland, with whom he had divers lands in the faid county, befides the baronies of Scrobhal and Cargil, near Perth ; and by his faid wife had four fons and four daughters, Sir Malcolm ; Sir John ; William ; and Dougal, Bifhop of Dunblane. Of the daughters, the beautiful Annabel, the eldeft, was Queen of Robert III. and mother of James I. King of Scotland ; and by that marriage, the houfes of Auftria and Burgundy, and many crowned heads in Europe, who married the King's daughters, are allied to the Drummonds : Margaret was the wife of Sir Colin Campbell, anceftor of the Duke of Argyll ; Jane, of —— Stewart, of Dowallie ; and Mary, of Macdonald, Lord of the Ifles.

Sir Malcolm, fon and heir of the foremen- tioned John Drummond, at the battle of Otter- burn, or Chevy-Chace, in 1388, joining his own men with his brother-in-law James Earl
of

of Douglas, to fight the Englifh, he there took prifoner Sir Ralph Percy, brother of Henry Lord Percy, called Hotfpur, who, in the fame rencounter, had killed Earl Douglas. His fon Sir John was the father of Sir Walter; and his fon Sir Malcolm the father of Sir John, who was made fteward of Strathern, juftice-general of Scotland, and created Lord Drummond by King James III. He did great fervice to King James IV. having routed the Earl of Lennox and the Lord Lifle, as they were upon their march to join the Earl-marfhal and Lord Gordon, in order to feize the King, under pretence of revenging the death of James III. after which, he was fent ambaffador into England, to conclude a peace with Richard III. but after the death of James IV. he forfeited all his offices and eftate, for giving a box on the ear to Lyon king at arms, who was fent to fummon him before the Parliament, to give an account of the Queen's marriage with the Earl of Lennox; but by the Queen's intereft, and the interceffion of fome great men, he was foon afterwards reftored to his honours and eftate. He had iffue William, his heir, who being at open defiance with the family of Murray, among other feuds between them, there were feveral gentlemen of the houfe of Murray barbaroufly burnt in a church, by fome of Drummond's party; for which crime, notwithftanding he pleaded innocence, he was condemned to lofe his head, and the fentence was executed accordingly in 1511. Of the daughters of the faid Lord John, Margaret was privately married to King James IV. by whom

fhe

she had a daughter Jane, who was married to John Lord Gordon, eldest son of Alexander Earl of Huntley; and a son James, who was Earl of Murray.

James, who was the fourth Lord Drummond, being much in favour with James VI. was by him sent with Charles Howard, Earl of Nottingham, ambassador to Spain, and after his return was created Earl of Perth.

James, the fourth Earl of Perth, his descendant, in 1678, was, by King Charles II. made one of the privy-council; in 1682, justice-general; and in 1684, lord-chancellor of Scotland; in which station he was continued by King James VII. till the revolution in 1688; and then, following that Prince into France, was by him made a duke and knight of the garter; but was outlawed in parliament, and died at St. Germains in France, in the year 1716, in the 68th year of his age. He married Lady Jane, daughter of William Marquis of Douglas, by whom he had James Lord Drummond. His second Lady was Lillias, daughter of Sir James Drummond, of Machany, by whom he had two sons, John, who married the heiress of Dalgarno, and Charles. His third wife was Lady Mary, daughter of Lewis Marquis of Huntley, by whom he had a son Edward, and a daughter Lady Teresa. James, his eldest son, died in his life time, and left issue by his wife, Lady Jane, daughter of George Duke of Gordon, two sons, James and John, and two daughters. James, the eldest, would have succeeded his grandfather, were it not for the outlawry. Both these brothers

thers were in the rebellion in 1745; and next
year, at the battle of Culloden, John commanded the center, and James the left wing; but
the latter, being mortally wounded, died in his
paffage to France. John, the youngeft, married a daughter of Charles, now Earl of Traquair, but as neither of them left iffue, the reprefentative of the family was John, eldeft fon
of their grandfather's fecond marriage; but he
dying without iffue, in 1757, Edward, the only
fon of the Chancellor's third marriage became
the reprefentative; but he dying without iffue
in 1760, the chief of the family now is James;
grandfon and heir of John Earl of Melfort,
fecond fon of James, third Earl of Perth. He
married Lady Rachel Bruce, daughter of Thomas, feventh Earl of Kincardin, by whom he
has iffue Thomas, James, and a daughter Rachel.

Creations.] Lord Drummond, by James III,
Earl of Perth, May 14; 1604; 35 James VI.
(I. of England.)

Arms.] Topaz, three clofets wavey, ruby.

Creft.] On a ducal coronet, topaz, a greyhound, pearl, collared and leifhed, proper.

Supporters.] Two favages bound about the
temples and waift with oak leaves, each holding
on the outer fhoulder a battoon, all proper, both
ftanding on a green hill, femee of Caltropes.

Motto.] *Gang warily.*

Chief Seat was.] At Drummond-caftle in
Perthfhire.

M A C.

MACKENZIE, Earl of SEA-FORTH.

The immediate anceftor of this family was Collin Fitzgerald, of the family of Defmond and Kildare, in Ireland, who, with a few volunteers in 1261, came from that kingdom to the affiftance of Alexander III, King of Scotland, againft the Norwegians and Danes; and then behaved fo well at the battle of Largis in Conningham, that the King, by his charter, dated at Kincardin, 1266, gave him the barony of Kintail, in which he was fucceeded by Kenneth his fon, who, having a numerous offspring, each was called Mackennie, after the highland manner, denoting the fon of Kenneth, and afterwards varied into Mackenzie.

Collin Mackenzie, being a firm loyalift to Queen Mary, during her troubles, had a fon Kenneth, who was created Lord Kintail; and his fon Collin was created Earl of Seaforth.

Kenneth, the fourth Earl of Seaforth, and the father of the late Earl, fucceeded his father Kenneth in 1678; and, by King James VII. was made one of the privy-council, and a knight of the thiftle; and following that King into France and Ireland, was created a Marquis, but that honour was not allowed him in England.

William, the fifth Earl, being a party in the rebellion of 1715, he, with many lords and others, was fummoned, by proclamation, to furrender at Edinburgh; but he made his

escape,

escape, and in April 1719, landed in the North-west of Scotland, with the Marquis of Tullibardin, the Earl Marshal, and some Spanish forces: They were soon attacked, however, at Glenshiel, by major-general Wightman, and his Lordship, with the Earls of Mar, Southesk, Linlithgow, Marshal, and Panmure, was attainted, in June 1716; but through the King's clemency he obtained a pardon, and died at home, in quiet retirement, in 1740.

He married Mary, only daughter and heir of Nicholas Kennet, of Coxhow, in Northumberland, Esq; and by her, who died in France in 1739, had three sons and one daughter, viz. 1. Kenneth Lord Fortrose, who was member for the burghs of Fortrose, &c. in 1741, and for the shire of Ross in 1747, 1754, and 1761. He married Lady Mary Stewart, daughter of Alexander Earl of Galloway, by whom he had issue Kenneth, created, in 1766, Viscount Fortrose, of the kingdom of Ireland; Margaret, Mary, Agnes, Catharine, Frances, and Euphemia. He died in 1762, and was succeeded by his son abovementioned: 2. Ronald; 3. Nicol; and 4. Lady Frances, married to John, representative of the family of Kenmure.

Creations.] Lord Mackenzie, of Kintail, Nov. 19, 1609. Earl of Seaforth, Dec. 3, 1623, by James VI.

Arms.] Sapphire, a stag's head cabossed topaz.

Crest.] On a wreath, a mountain inflamed proper.

Supporters.] Two savages wreathed about their temples and middles with laurel, each holding

holding in his exterior hand a battoon erect, with fire iffuing out of the top of it, all proper.

Motto.] *Luceo non uro.*

Chief Seats.] At Brahan-caftle in the county of Rofs; and at Fortrofe, in the fame county.

WEMYSS, Earl of WEMYSS.

This noble family of Wemyfs is faid to be defcended from the great Macduff, Thane of Fife, who was the chief inftrument of fubduing the tyrant Macbeth: for John the fourth defcendant of the faid Thane, being lord of the barony of Wemyfs, from thence his defcendants affumed their firname.

In the year 1290, Sir Michael Wemyfs was fent to Norway by the lords of the regency in Scotland, to bring over their young Queen Margaret, who, to the univerfal misfortune of the nation, died at the Orkneys, and thereupon happened the competition between Baliol and Bruce, about the right of fucceffion. In the time of King Robert I. Sir David Wemyfs was one of thofe great men of the kingdom who wrote a letter to the Pope, afferting the independency of their country.

James, the fourth and late Earl of Wemyfs, married Janet, daughter and heir of Colonel Francis Charteris, of Amisfield, by whom he had iffue three fons and four daughters, viz.
1. David, Lord Elcho, who, being engaged in the rebellion of 1745, was attainted of treafon,

but

but efcaped to France. 2. Francis-Charteris,
who fucceeded to his grandfather's eftate at
Amisfield, &c. and married Lady Catharine,
daughter of Alexander, Duke of Gordon, by
whom he has iffue a fon. 3. James, who now
reprefents the family, and enjoys the paternal
eftate. He is member in the prefent parliament for Fifefhire, and married Lady Elizabeth, daughter of William Earl of Sutherland,
by whom he has iffue three fons, James, William, and David. 4. Lady Frances, wife of
Sir James Stewart, of Goodtrees, Bart. 5. Lady
Walpole, of ———. 6. Lady Anne, of John
Hamilton, of Bargeny, efq; 7. Lady Helen,
of Hugh Dalrymple, of Fordel, efq.

David, Lord Elcho, on account of his attainder, being incapable of fucceeding, his
Lordfhip made a conveyance of his eftate in
favour of his third fon, James, who fucceeded
him therein, in 1756.

Creations.] Baron Elcho, April 1, 1628;
Earl of Wemyfs, in the county of Fife, May
25, 1633, both by King Charles I.

Arms.] Topaz, a lion rampant ruby, armed
and langued fapphire.

Creft.] On a wreath, a fwan proper.

Supporters.] Two fwans, as the creft.

Motto.] *Je penfe.*

Chief Seats.] At Wemyfs, in the county of
Fife; and at Elcho, near Perth.

K.   C A R-

CARNEGIE, Earl of SOUTH-ESK.

This noble family were anciently proprietors of the lands of Carnegie, in the county of Forfar, which were long poffeffed by them.

John de Carnegie, who was flain at the battle of Floddon in Northumberland, in 1513, with James IV. left a fon Sir Robert, who was promoted by the regent James Hamilton, Duke of Chatelherault, firft to be one of the judges in the court of feffion, then ambaffador to England; and, after his return, was knighted: he was alfo fent ambaffador to France by the faid regent: but dying in 1565, he was fucceeded by his fon Sir John, for whom Queen Mary had a great efteem, for his fidelity and prudence; but dying without iffue, the eftate defcended to his brother, Sir David, who, being bred to the law, and a perfon of great reputation, was, by King James VI. made one of the lords of feffion, one of his privy council, and a commiffioner of the treafury. He was fucceeded by his eldeft fon David, who, April 24, 1616, was, by James VI. created Lord Carnegie of Kinnaird, in the county of Forfar; and Earl of Southefk, in the fame county, June 22, 1633, by Charles I.

James, the late and fifth Earl, embarking in the rebellion of the year 1715, was attainted, and his honours and eftate forfeited. He

made

made his efcape to France, where he died in 1729.

His Lordfhip married Lady Margaret, daughter of James, Earl of Galloway, by whom he had a fon and a daughter, who both died young. The reprefentation of the family is now, therefore, in Sir James Carnegie, of Pitarro, Bart. lineally defcended from Sir Alexander, fourth fon of David, firft Earl of Southefk, and brother of James, the fecond Earl, who was member in the laft parliament for the fhire of Kincardin. He married Chriftian, eldeft daughter of David Doig, of Cookfton, by whom he has four fons and two daughters, viz. David, James, John, and George; Mary and Elizabeth.

Creations.] *Ut fupra.*

Arms.] Topaz, an eagle difplayed fapphire, beaked and membered, ruby.

Creft.] On a wreath, a right hand couped at the wrift, and erect, holding a thunderbolt, inflamed at both ends, all proper, fhafted faltire, and winged in fefs, topaz.

Supporters.] Two greyhounds pearl, each gorged with a plain collar, ruby.

Motto.] *Deum timete.*

Chief Seats were,] At Kinnaird, in the county of Angus; and the caftle of Leuchars, in Fifefhire.

OGILVIE, Earl of AIRLY.

This noble family is defcended lineally from Gilbert, brother of Gilchrift, Earl of Angus, who living in the time of K. William the Lion, obtained from him the barony of Ogilvie, in the county of Forfar, and from thence took his firname. In the reign of Robert I. Sir Patrick Ogilvie had a grant from the King of the lands of Caithnefs, and was fucceeded by Walter his fon, who, in the time of Robert III. was fheriff of Angus; and Alexander his fon, marrying the daughter and heir of Sir William Ramfay of Auchterhoufe, with her had that barony, and was flain at the battle of Harlaw. By the faid lady he had Sir Alexander Ogilvie, fheriff of Angus, and Sir Walter, anceftor of the Earls of Finlater and Seafield; and John, the fon of Alexander, had a fon James, who, by King James IV, 1495, was created Lord Ogilvie of Airly, in the county of Forfar.

James, the eighth Lord Ogilvie, was, Apr. 2, 1639, created Earl of Airly by Charles I. He had three fons, the fecond whereof was flain in the civil war, and the eldeft, James, who fucceeded him, being alfo very zealous in the royal caufe, was taken prifoner at the battle of Philiphaugh, in 1645, when Montrofe was defeated, and condemned by the parliament to be executed; but efcaping the night before, in his fifter's habit, he engaged again in the fame fervice.

David

David his fon, third Earl, by his wife Lady
Grifel, daughter of Patrick, Earl of Strathmore, had two fons, James and John: the
eldeft, James Lord Ogilvie, then only twenty
years old, was attainted for his concern in the
rebellion of 1715; but the eftate not being in
his perfon, was faved, and went to his brother
John. Some time after he was pardoned as to
life, came home, and married Anne, daughter of David Erfkine, of Dun, efq; but died
without iffue.

John, his brother, now reprefents the family, and poffeffes the eftate. He married
Margaret, daughter and heir of — Ogilvie, efq;
of Clunie, by whom he had two fons, David
and Walter; and two daughters, Elizabeth, and
Helen, wife of Robert Robertfon, of Ladykirk,
efq. David, the eldeft fon (calling himfelf Lord
Ogilvie) embarked in the rebellion of 1745,
afterwards efcaped, and was attainted in 1746.
He commands a regiment, bearing his own
name, in the French fervice. He married Margaret, daughter of Sir James Johnfton, of Wef-
terhall, Bart. by whom he has one fon, David, commonly called Mafter of Ogilvie; and
two daughters, Margaret and Joanna.

Creations.] *Ut fupra.*

Arms.] Pearl, a lion paffant guardant, ruby,
crowned with an imperial crown, proper, and
gorged with a ducal crown, topaz.

Creft.] In an earl's coronet of the laft, a wo-
man from her waift upwards, holding a port-
cullis.

Supporters.] Two bulls, diamond, each gorged with a garland of flowers.

K 3   *Motto.*]

Motto.] *A fin.*
Chief Seat.] At Airly-caftle, in the county of Forfar.

DALZIEL, Earl of CARNWATH.

This noble family is of great antiquity in the fhire of Lanerk, and intermarried with many worthy families there, before they moved to the county of Dumfries, where they fettled; and Nifbet, the noted herald, gives the following ftory concerning the origin of their firname. In the reign of Kenneth II. a near kinfman and favourite of that King, being hung up by the Piĉts, it fo exceedingly grieved his Majefty, that he offered a great reward to any of his fubjeĉts that would dare to refcue his corpfe; but none would venture to undertake that dangerous enterprize. At laft, a certain gentleman came to the King, and faid, *Dal zell*, which in the Irifh or old Scots language fignifies, *I dare*; and he effectually performing it to the King's fatisfaĉtion, his pofterity took for their firname the word Dalziel, and for their armorial enfign that remarkable bearing, which has continued to the prefent time.

In the year 1365, Sir Robert Dalziel, who faithfully adhered to King David Bruce, during his captivity in England, obtained a grant of the barony of Selkirk, and Sir William, his fucceffor, having a gift from Robert III. of the revenue of St. Leonard's hofpital, within the town of Lanerk, was fucceeded by George his
fon,

fon, from whom, after feveral generations, defcended Sir Robert Dalziel, of that ilk, a firm friend to Queen Mary, in all her troubles. Sir Robert, his fon, was knighted by James VI. and by Charles I. created Earl of Carnwath, and Baron Dalziel.

John, the fifth Earl, dying a bachelor, in 1702, was fucceeded by Sir Robert Dalziel, fon of Sir John Dalziel of Glenay, fecond fon of the firft Earl, who became fixth Earl; but embarking in the rebellion of 1715, was taken prifoner at Prefton, brought to London, tried by his peers, and condemned on Feb. 19, following. He afterwards obtained a pardon for his life.

He married, firft, Lady Grace, daughter of Alexander, Earl of Eglinton, by whom he had a daughter, Lady Margaret; fecondly, Grifel, daughter of Alexander Urquhart, of Newhall, efq; by whom he had a fon, Alexander; his third wife was Margaret, daughter of John Hamilton, of Bangower, efq; by whom he had a daughter, who died young; by his fourth wife, Margaret Vincent, he had a fon, Robert.

His eldeft fon, Alexander, married mifs Elizabeth Jackfon, an Englifh lady, by whom he has iffue.

Creations.] Lord Dalziel, in 1628, and Earl of Carnwath, in the county of Dumfries, 1639, by Charles I.

Arms.] Diamond, a naked man with his arms extended, proper.

Creft.] On a wreath, a dagger erect, the pommel and hilt topaz.

Sup-

Supporters.] Two chevaliers in compleat armour, each having a target on his exterior
arm, proper.

Motto.] *I dare.*

Chief Seat.] At Kirkmichael in Annandale.

MAULE, Earl of PANMURE.

This noble family is originally French, and
derive their firname from the town and lordfhip of Maule, eight leagues from Paris, in
France, upon the borders of Normandy. Gua-
rin de Maule came into England with William
the Conqueror, from whom defcended Serlo de
Maule, who was a Baron of England, in the
reign of King John.

William de Maule, fiding with David I.
King of Scotland, at the battle of the Stand-
ard, in 1138, obtained from him the lordfhip
of Fowlis, in which he was fucceeded by Sir
Richard de Maule, his nephew. Sir Peter, his
fon, obtained the barony of Panmure by mar-
riage of Chriftian, daughter and fole heir of
William de Valoignes, lord of Panmure, and
great-chamberlain of Scotland in 1224, temp.
Alexander II. From him defcended Patrick
Maule, who was gentleman of the chamber to
James VI. and Charles I. and was created lord
Brechin and Navarre, and Earl of Panmure.
His illuftrious defcendants were eminent both
in the cabinet and the field. James, Earl of
Panmure, was of the privy-council to James
VII. but dying without iffue, and having for-
feited

feited his titles and estate, by engaging in the
rebellion of 1715, the representation devolved
upon his younger brother Harie, who married
first, Lady Mary, only daughter of William,
Earl of Wigtoun, by whom he had issue,
James, who died in the life-time of his father;
William, now Earl of Panmure; and a daughter, Jane, wife of George lord Ramsay, eldest
son of William, Earl of Dalhousie: His second
wife was Anne, sister of John, Lord Viscount
Garnock, by whom he had a son, John, and a
daughter, Margaret, who died unmarried;
which John was member in parliament for the
burghs of Aberdeen, &c. in the year 1739,
and in 1748 was appointed one of the barons
of the exchequer, in Scotland.

William, the eldest son, Earl Panmure of
Forth, in the kingdom of Ireland, (so created
April 6, 1743, also Viscount Maule of Whit-
church in that kingdom, to him and his heirs
male, and in default, to his brother John,) is
colonel of the royal North-british fuzileers, a
lieutenant-general, and member in the present
parliament for the shire of Forfar.

Creations.] Baron of Panmure, by tenure,
in the reign of Alexander II.; Baron of Brechin, by claim from female descent, 1437.
Lord Brechin and Navarre, and Earl of Panmure, in the county of Forfar, Aug. 3, 1646,
by Charles I. and Lord Maule by Charles II.

Arms.] Quarterly, first party per pale, pearl
and ruby, on a border, eight escallops, all
counterchanged, for the name of Maule; second, pearl, three pellets, wavey, ruby, for
Valoignes; being married to the heirefs of that

K 5   family,

family ; third quarter, counter quartered, firft and fourth fapphire, a chevron, betwixt three croffes patees, topaz, for Barclay, Lord of Brechin ; fecond and third pearl, three piles iffuing from the chief, conjoined by the points, ruby, for Brechin, Lord Brechin ; fourth quarter, as the firft.

Creft.] On a wreath, a wyvern, emerald, fpouting fire before and behind.

Supporters.] Two greyhounds, proper, each gorged with a collar, ruby, charged with three efcallop fhells, pearl.

Motto.] *Clementia et animis.*

Chief Seats.] At Panmure, in the county of Forfar ; and at the caftle of Brechin, in the fame county.

MIDDLETON, Earl of MIDDLETON.

This family is defcended from Kenneth, who lived in the reign of Malcolm IV. His fucceffor William, was father of Malcolm, anceftor of all the Middletons in Scotland. John Middleton, efq; was a colonel belonging to the royal party ; and, in 1648, attended .Duke Hamilton into England, when he led the army to Prefton. At the battle of Worcefter, 1651, he commanded as lieutenant-general of horfe, when he and moft of the principal officers were made prifoners ; but he had the good fortune, in a fhort time, to efcape out of the Tower. Soon after the Reftoration, he was appointed

the

the King's high-commiffioner in Scotland, and
general of his forces in that kingdom ; and in
1660 created Baron Clairmont and Earl of Middleton.   This Earl had two daughters, Lady
Helen, married to Patrick, Earl of Strathmore,
and Lady Grifel to William, Earl of Morton ;
and a fon, Charles, who fucceeded as fecond
Earl, and was fecretary of ftate for Scotland
from the year 1684 to the Revolution, when
he followed King James into France, and was
attainted by the Scots parliament in 1695. He
married Lady Catharine, daughter of Robert,
Earl of Cardigan, by whom he had two fons,
John Lord Clairmont, and Charles Middleton,
efq; who were both taken at fea by admiral
Byng, in the defcent which the French in-
tended upon Scotland, in 1708 ; but by the
Queen's orders they were foon releafed, and
died in France without iffue. Their father was
alfo aboard in that armament. He had alfo
two daughters, Lady Elizabeth, wife of Edward, fon of James, Earl of Perth ; and Lady
Mary, of Sir John Giffard, knt. I cannot fay
who now reprefents the family.

Creations.] *Ut fupra.*

Arms.] Party per fefs, diamond and ruby, a
lion rampant, within a double treffure, flowered and counterflowered with fleurs-de-lys,
all counterchanged.

Creft.] A tower embattled, ruby, and on the
top a lion rampant.

Supporters.] Two eagles, ruby.

Motto.] *Fortis in arduis.*

Chief Seat was,] At Montrofe, in the county of Forfar.

K. 6.　　　　　R A D-

RADCLIFFE, Earl of NEW-
BURGH.

Sir John Livingston, of Kinnaird, was lineally defcended from Robert, fecond fon of Sir
John Livingston, of Callendar, who lived in
the reigns of James I. and II. His fon and
fucceffor, Sir James Livingston, of Kinnaird,
was in great favour with King Charles I. who,
on Nov. 13, 1647, created him Vifcount Newburgh, and after the Reftoration he was created Earl of Newburgh, Vifcount Kinnaird, and
Lord Livingston, of Flancraig, &c. by patent,
to his heirs whatfoever. His fon, Charles, the
fecond Earl, by his wife Frances, daughter of
Francis, Lord Brudenel, fon and heir of Robert, and brother of George, Earls of Cardigan, had iffue one daughter and fole heir,
    Charlotte, Countefs of Newburgh, who fuc-
ceeded her father, in 1694. By her firft hufband, Thomas, fon and heir of Hugh, Lord
Clifford, of Chudleigh, fhe had two daughters, Ladies Frances and Anne. Her fecond
hufband was the hon. Charles Radcliffe, fecond
fon of Francis, Earl of Derwentwater, by whom
fhe had iffue, James, James-Clement; Ladies
Charlotte, Barbara, and Mary.
    Charles Radcliffe, her hufband, was taken
at fea, in 1745, fent prifoner to the Tower,
and beheaded upon Tower-hill, Dec. 8, 1746,
upon a former fentence, for his concern in the
rebellion of 1715. The Countefs deceafing in
1755,

1755, James, her eldest son, took the title of Earl of Newburgh, as third Earl.

Creations.] *Ut supra.*

Arms.] Pearl, on a bend, between three juliflowers, ruby, an anchor of the first, all within a double tressure, flowered and counterflowered, emerald.

Crest.] A Moor's head couped, proper, bended, ruby and pearl, with pendlets, pearl, at his ears.

Supporters.] On the dexter, a savage, proper, wreathed about the head and middle, emerald; and on the sinister an horse, pearl, furnished, ruby.

Motto.] *Si je puis.*

Chief Seat,] When the family was in Scotland, was at Kinnaird.

BOYD, Earl of KILMARNOCK.

The first of the sirname of Boyd is said to be Robert, the son of Simon third son of Allan, second lord steward of Scotland. The name is derived from Boydh, a Gallic, or Celtic word, *fair,* or *yellow,* the said Robert being so named from his complexion. His son was Sir Robert Boyd, who, in 1263, signalized his valour at the battle of Largis in Coningham, against the Norwegians, & had thereupon a grant of several lands in that district, wherein he was succeeded by another Sir Robert, and he by a third Sir Robert, who, in the second year of King Robert I. for his loyalty and merit, was rewarded with the lands of Kilmarnock.

Robert,

Robert, the firft Lord Boyd, married Mary
Maxwel, daughter of Sir Robert Maxwel of
Calderwood, by whom he had three fons, Thomas, Alexander, and Archibald, and a daughter Elizabeth, married to Archibald Douglas,
Earl of Douglas and Angus, and was, in Oct.
1466, conftituted regent of Scotland in the minority of King James III. and then marrying
his fon Thomas to the Princefs Mary Stewart,
the King's eldeft fifter, the faid Thomas was
thereupon created Earl of Arran, and afterwards fent ambaffador to Denmark, to treat of
a marriage between his brother-in-law, the
young King, and the Princefs Margaret of
that crown : but while he was abfent, his enemies contrived the ruin of his family, by reprefenting their ambition as too dangerous for
the condition of fubjects, and fo far prevailed
with the King, that he called a parliament,
before whom the Lord Boyd, his fon the Earl
of Arran, and his brother, Sir Alexander Boyd,.
being fummoned to give an account of their
aJminiftration, the old man, fearing the power of his enemies, fled into England; but Sir
Alexander was condemned for high treafon,
and executed. The Earl of Arran arriving
with the Queen at Leith, and being informed
of thefe melancholy circumftances, immediately retired into Denmark with his lady, from
thence into France, and dying at Antwerp, in
1471, was honourably interred by Charles,
Duke of Burgundy.

By his faid lady, who in 1470 was arbitra-
rily divorced, and married to James, the fecond Lord Hamilton, he left a fon James, who
was

was the third Lord Boyd, and second Earl of Arran; but dying without issue, the title of Earl of Arran became extinct: but the title of Lord Boyd descended to his uncle Alexander, the second son of Robert Lord Boyd.

William, the ninth Lord Boyd, was created Earl of Kilmarnock in Coningham, of the county of Air, Aug. 27, 1661, by Charles II.

William, the fourth Earl, unfortunately engaging in the rebellion of 1745, was taken prisoner at the battle of Culloden, tried by his peers, condemned, and beheaded on Aug. 18, 1746, and his title and estate were forfeited to the crown.

His Lordship married Lady Anne, daughter and sole heir of James, Earl of Linlithgow and Callendar, by whom he had issue, James, now Earl of Errol, (which see,) Charles, and William.

Creation.] Earl of Kilmarnock, in Coningham of Airshire, Aug. 27, 1761, by Charles II.

Arms.] Sapphire, a fesse, checque, pearl and ruby.

Crest.] On a wreath, a dexter hand couped at the wrist, and erect, pointing with the thumb and the two next fingers, the other turning down.

Supporters.] Two squirrels, proper.

Motto.] Confido.

Chief Seat was] At Kilmarnock, in the county of Air.

DRUM-

DRUMMOND, Earl of MEL-FORT.

John, fecond fon of James, third Earl of Perth, was created Earl of Melfort, Vifcount Forth, Lord Drummond of Riccarton, Caftle-main, and Gilfton, by King James VII. in 1686, whofe fortune he followed at the Revolution, and was, by him, at St. Germain's en laye, in France, created Duke of Melfort. Not returning to Scotland, in the time limited by act of parliament, he was attainted, and his honours forfeited to the crown.

By his fecond wife, Euphemia, daughter of Sir Thomas Wallace, of Craigie, Bart. the iffue of which marriage only fuffered by the attainder, he had fix fons and five daughters, commonly called Lords and Ladies ; viz. John ; Thomas, an officer in the Auftrian fervice, who died unmarried ; William, abbé prioral of Liege, deceafed ; Andrew, colonel of horfe, in the French fervice, whofe iffue are now in being in France ; Bernard, who died young ; Philip, an officer in the French fervice, who died of his wounds : Henrietta, who died unmarried ; Mary, married to Count Caftel-Blanco, a Spanifh nobleman ; Frances, who by a difpenfation from the Pope married the faid Count, after her fifter's death ; Louifa and Therefa. He died in 1714, at St. Germain's.

John, his eldeft fon, had three fons; Thomas; Lewis, major-general, and colonel of the Royal Scots, in the French fervice ; and John, major-

major-general in the Saxon fervice. Thomas, the eldeft, has a confiderable eftate in Langue-doc, and by Marie Berenger, his wife, has four fons and two daughters; James-Lewis; Charles-Edward; Henry-Benedict; Maurice: Maria-Cecilia-Henrietta; and Emilia-Felici-tas.

MACKENZIE, Earl of CRO-MARTIE.

This noble family is defcended from the fa-mily of Seaforth; for Sir Robert Mackenzie, brother of Kenneth, firft Lord Kintail, mar-rying Margaret, daughter and heir of Tor-quil Macleod of the Lewes-Iflands, had four fons, whereof Sir John, the eldeft, was crea-ted a Baronet by King Charles I. and marry-ing Margaret, daughter and coheir of Sir George Erfkine, of Innerdale, brother of Tho-mas, Earl of Kelly, by her had two fons and five daughters, whereof Roderick, the fecond fon, was one of the judges of the court of fef-fion. Of the daughters, Anne was married to Hugh, Lord Lovat, and Ifabel to Kenneth, the third Earl of Seaforth.

Sir George, the eldeft, who, in 1654, fuc-ceeded his father, had a commiffion from K. Charles II, while in exile, to raife what forces he could, in order to promote his reftoration; and for his good fervices, his Majefty, when he came to the crown, made him one of the judges of the court of feffion, clerk regifter, one of the privy-council, and juftice-general; and, April 15, 1685, he was created Baron Macleod,

Macleod, and Vifcount Tarbat, by K. James
VII. In the reign of Queen Anne he was
made fecretary of ftate, one of the privy-council, and, Jan. 1, 1702, created Earl of Cro-
mertie. He died in Aug. 1714, aged 84; and
by his firft wife, Anne, daughter of Sir James
Sinclair, of May, had three fons and four
daughters :

1. John, fecond Earl, who, marrying Anne,
daughter of Alexander Lord Elibank, had
George, the late Earl.

2. Kenneth, created a Baronet in 1704;
but with precedence, according to his grandfather's patent in 1628; one of whofe fons
married Lady Elizabeth, daughter of Charles,
Earl of Aboyne.

3. James, created a Baronet the fame day
with his brother, was made one of the fena-
tors in the college of juftice.

George, the third, and late Earl, fucceeded
his father in 1731, and was fo unadvifed as to
engage in the rebellion of 1745; but was, with
about four hundred of his men, furprized and
defeated by the Earl of Sutherland's militia,
at Dunrobin-caftle, in Sutherland, April 15,
1746, the day before the battle at Culloden.
He and his fon, Lord Macleod, being taken
prifoners, were fent to Invernefs, and thence
to London, where they were committed to the
Tower. In Auguft following he was tried,
condemned, and received fentence of death,
his eftate and honours being forfeited to the
crown, but was pardoned, and permitted to
refide in England. He married Ifabel, daughter of Sir William Gordon, of Invergordon,
Bart. a lady of fingular merit and beauty, to
whofe

whofe indefatigable application, and his Majefty's great clemency, in behalf of her Lord, he owes his life ; by which Lady he had two fons and feven daughters. His eldeft fon, the Lord Macleod, was likewife pardoned ; and, in 1750, had leave to accept of a commiffion in the fervice of Sweden, where he is a major, and aid-de-camp to the King. The other fons and daughters are ; George, an officer in the army ; Lady Elizabeth, wife of Admiral George Murray ; Lady Mary, of Mr. Drayton ; Lady Anne, of Mr. Atkins ; Lady Caroline, of Mr. Drake ; Ladies Jane, Margaret, and Augufta. His Lordfhip died in 1766.

Creations.] *Ut fupra.*

Arms.] Quarterly, firft topaz, a mountain inflamed, proper, for Macleod ; 2d, fapphire, a ftag's head caboffed, topaz, for Mackenzie ; 3d, ruby, three legs of a man armed proper, conjoined in the centre at the upper part of the thigh, flexed in triangle, and the fpurs, topaz, formerly belonging to the Macleods, as poffeffors of the Ifle of Man ; 4th, pearl, on a pale diamond, an imperial crown within a double treffure counterflory, with fleurs de lys, ruby, for Erfkine of Innerdale.

Creft.] On a wreath, the fun in its fplendor.

Supporters.] Two favages, each wreathed about the head and middle with laurel, and holding a battoon over his fhoulder, proper.

Motto.] *Luceo non uro.*

Chief Seats were,] At Macleod-caftle, Caftle-haven, and New Tarbat, all in the fhire of Cromartie.

VISCOUNTS.

GORDON, Vifcount KEN-MURE.

IN the tenth of King Robert I. Sir Adam Gordon, in reward of his good fervices, obtained from that Prince the barony of Stickel, in the county of Roxburgh. Sir Robert, a defcendant of this Sir Adam, was knighted; and his fon Sir John, by Charles I. May 2, 1626, was created a Baronet. He married Lady Elizabeth, daughter of John Earl of Gowrie, by whom he had Sir John his eldeft fon, who, fucceeding his father, was, May 18, 1633, created a Baron and Vifcount, by Charles I.

William, the feventh Vifcount, being engaged in the rebellion in 1715, was taken prifoner at Prefton, in Lancafhire, brought to London, and on the 24th of February 1715-16, was, purfuant to fentence, beheaded on Tower-hill, together with James Radcliffe, Earl of Derwentwater; his remains conveyed to Leith, by fea, and thence to the burial place at Kenmure.

He married Mary, daughter of Sir John Dalziel, of Glenay, Bart. and fifter of Robert, Earl

Earl of Carnwath, (before fpoken of,) and had by her three fons ; Robert, John, and James, and a daughter, wife of John Dalziel, Efq ;

Robert, his eldeft fon, by the King's cle-mency, got poffeffion of the eftate, by the care and management of Lady Kenmure ; but the title was forfeited, and he, dying unmarried, was fucceeded therein by his brother John, who now reprefents the family. He married Lady Frances, daughter of William, Earl of Seaforth, by whom he has iffue four fons and one daughter ; William, John, Adam, Robert, and Frances.

Creations.] Baronet, Vifcount, and Baron Kenmure, *ut fupra.*

Arms.] Sapphire, three boars heads erafed, topaz.

Creft.] On a wreath, a demi-favage proper, wreathed about his temples and middle with laurel.

Supporters.] Two favages wreathed as the creft, each holding in his outer hand a bat-toon erect, proper.

Motto.] *Dread God.*

Chief Seat.] At Kenmure Caftle in the county of Kirkudbright.

LIVINGSTON, Vifcount KIL-SYTH.

Sir William Livingfton, fon of Sir John, of Callendar, a branch of the family of Linlith-gow, was the anceftor of this family; from him defcended Sir William Livingfton of Kil-fyth, who married Margaret, fifter of William Ramfay, the firft Earl of Dalhoufie, by whom he had a fon William, and a daughter Chri-ftian, married firft to James Macgill, the firft Vifcount Oxenford.

William, his fon, dying in his minority, was fucceeded by his grand uncle Sir James, who was created a Vifcount by King Charles II. and married Eupheme, daughter of Sir David Cunningham, of Robertland, by whom he had iffue James, and William, and a daughter, Elizabeth, wife of major-general Robert Mont-gomery, fon of Alexander, Earl of Eglington. James fucceeded, as fecond Vifcount, but, dy-ing unmarried in 1706, was fucceeded by his brother,

William, third Vifcount, who married, firft, Jane, daughter of William, Lord Cochran, and had iffue a fon William, who died in in-fancy; and fecondly Barbara, daughter of — Macdowgal, of Mackerfton, by whom he had a daughter Barbara, who died young. He was elected one of the fixteen peers in the two laft parliaments of Queen Anne; but joining with the Earl of Mar, in the rebellion in 1715, and
refufing

refufing to furrender, was attainted, and his
honours and eftates forfeited.

Creations.] Vifcount Kilfyth, Lord Campfie,
&c. *ut fupra.*

Arms.] Pearl, three gilliflowers flipped, ruby, within a double treffure, flowered and
counter-flowered, with fleurs de lys, emerald.

Creft.] On a wreath, a demi-favage, wreathed about the temples and waift with laurel.

Supporters.] Two lions, proper.

Motto.] *Spe expecto.*

DRUMMOND, Vifcount STRATH-ALLAN.

James Drummond, commendator of Inchaffery, fecond fon of David fecond Lord Drummond, anceftor of the earl of Perth, the Duke
of Roxburgh, and the Lord Bellenden, was
created Lord Maderty in 1607, by King James
VI. and marrying Jane, daughter of Sir James
Chifholm, of Cromlix, by her had John his
heir, Sir James Drummond of Machany, anceftor of the laft Vifcount, and feveral daughters.

John, who fucceeded his father, marrying
Margaret, daughter of Patrick, Lord Lindores;
by her had David Lord Maderty, his fucceffor;
and William Drummond of Cromlix, who being a lieutenant-general in Mufcovy, was upon
his return home, advanced for his merit to
the like rank in Scotland, by Charles I. In
the time of the ufurpation, being taken prifoner

er, at the battle of Worcester, he made his
escape, and went into the service of the King
of Pruslia, under whom he had some high commands. On the Restoration, he was called
home, and made major-general of the forces,
in which character he served the crown many
years; and when King James VII. ascended the
throne, he was made general of all the forces in
Scotland, and created Viscount Strathallan,
August 16, 1686, by that prince. He married
Elizabeth, daughter of Sir Archibald Johnston,
of Warilton; and dying in 1688, left William
his heir, who marrying Lady Elizabeth Drummond, daughter of John Earl of Melfort, by
her had a son James, who dying a youth, in
1711, the honour of Viscount devolved on William Drummond of Machany, son of Sir John,
son of Sir James, son of Sir Thomas, second son
of James, first Lord Maderty, as above.
Which William, fourth Viscount, joining in the
rebellion, in 1715, was taken prisoner at the
battle of Dunblain, but was discharged by the
act of grace in 1717. He afterwards, with his
eldest son, James Drummond, joined in the rebellion of 1745, and were both attainted in 1746;
but as the Viscount was slain in the battle, and
his son was attainted by the name of James
Drummond, eldest son of William, Viscount
Strathallan, perhaps on account of the misno-
mer, the attainder may hereafter be set aside.
The late Viscount, by his wife Margaret, daughter of William, lord Nairn, had issue, beside
the above James; William, Robert, Henry;
Margaret, Anne, Mary, and Emilia.

James,

James, the eldeſt ſon, Maſter of Strathallan, married Eupheme, daughter of Peter Gordon, of Abergeldy, eſq; by whom he had a ſon, James, and many other children.

Creations.] Lord Maderty, Baron and Viſcount Strathallan, *ut ſupra.*

Arms.] Quarterly, firſt and fourth, topaz, three cloſets wavey, ruby, for Drummond; ſecond and third, topaz, a lion's head eraſed, within a double treſſure counterflory, with fleurs de lys, ruby, as a coat of augmentation.

Creſt.] On a wreath, a falcon riſing, proper, his bells topaz.

Supporters.] Two ſavages, each holding a battoon over his ſhoulder, proper, and wreathed about his temples and middle with laurel.

Motto.] *Lord have mercy.*

Chief Seats were,] At Inchaffery and Machany, in the county of Perth.

GRAHAM, Viſcount DUNDEE.

Colonel John Graham, of Claverhouſe, a branch of the Montroſe family, was created Baron Graham and Viſcount Dundee, in the county of Forfar, by James VII. after whoſe abdication, he commanded a body of High-landers, in that Prince's intereſt, but was ſlain in the battle of Killikranky, with general Mackay, on July 27, 1689. He married Lady Jane, daughter of William, firſt Earl of Dundonald, by whom he had a ſon, James, who

L   died

died in his infancy. He was succeeded by his brother,

David, second Viscount, who being with his brother in the aforesaid battle, was outlawed, and his estate and honours, forfeited, in 1696. He died in 1700, in France, and, if the outlawry had not existed, would have been succeeded by William Graham, of Duntroon, whose posterity engaging in the rebellions of 1715 and 1745, when they were called Viscounts Dundee, were attainted.

GRAHAM, Viscount PRESTON.

Sir John Graham, of Kilbride, was the immediate ancestor of this family. He was second son of Malife, Earl of Strathern and Menteith, a branch of the noble house of Montrose. John, his second son, settled, in the reign of James V. in the north of England, where he obtained a good estate, and of him was lineally descended Sir Richard Graham, of Netherby, and Plump, in Cumberland, gentleman of the horse to King Charles I. who created him a Baronet, in 1629, March 29. His grandson, Sir Richard, was created Baron of Esk, and Viscount Preston, in the county of Haddington, on May 12, 1681, by K. Charles II. By James II. after his abdication, he was created Baron Esk, in Cumberland, but the patent was rejected by the house of Lords, In the year 1690 he was tried, and condemned, with Mr. Afhton, for a treafonable confpiracy to reftore King James. Afhton was executed, but his Lordfhip received pardon for his life. He married Lady Anne, daughter of Charles, Earl of Carlifle, and had iffue a fon, Charles, who married Mifs Cox, fifter of the Countefs of Peterborough, and dying in 1738-9, left iffue by her, William Graham, now a clergyman of the church of England.

Creations.] *Ut fupra.*

Arms.] Quarterly, firft and fourth topaz, on a chief diamond, three efcallop fhells of the field; fecond and third topaz, a fefs, pearl and fapphire; on a chief a chevron, ruby, for Stewart.

Creft.] On a wreath, pearl and fapphire, two wings conjoined.

Supporters.] On the dexter fide an eagle, on the finifter a lion, both ermine, and ducally crowned, topaz.

Motto.] *Reafon contents me.*

B A R O N S.

SINCLAIR, Lord SINCLAIR.

THE defcent of this ancient family is the fame with that of the Earl of Caithnefs. William, Earl of Orkney and Caithnefs, marrying to his firft wife Lady Margaret, daughter of Archibald, fourth Earl of Douglas, and Vifcount Turenne in France, by her had a fon and heir, William, from whom defcended the Lords Sinclair; and by his fecond wife, Margery, daughter of Alexander Gordon, fon of the thirteenth Earl of Sutherland, he had another fon, chriftened alfo William, who was created Earl of Caithnefs.

William, by the firft wife, being a profufe man, was called William the wafter, whofe fon Robert forfeited the honours, and thereby loft the countries of Orkney and Shetland. He married Lady Elizabeth Lefley, daughter of George, Earl of Rothes, and by her had a daughter, Mary, married to Patrick, the feventh Lord Grey, and a fon, Henry Sinclair, of Dyfart, who was created Baron Sinclair, in 1489, 1 James IV. To him fucceeded fucceffively, William, fecond Lord, Henry third, James fourth, Patrick fifth, John fixth Lord Sinclair, which laft left an only daughter, Catharine, married to Sir John Sinclair, of Hermanfton,

manſton, by whom ſhe had a ſon, Henry, ſeventh Lord, who ſucceeded her in the honour,
and married Griſel, daughter of Sir James
Cockburn, of that ilk, by whom he had iſſue.
five ſons, and as many daughters, viz. 1. John,
Maſter of Sinclair, who married, firſt, Margaret, Counteſs dowager of Southeſk, and ſecondly Amelia, daughter of Lord George Murray, brother of the Duke of Athol, and died
in 1750. He was attainted for his concern in
the rebellion of 1715. 2. James, late member
for the ſhire of Fife, a lieutenant-general, and
colonel of the firſt regiment of foot, called the
Royal. 3. William, major of the ſaid regiment.
4. Henry. 5 Matthew. 6. Griſel. 7. Catharine, wife of Sir John Erſkine, of Alva. 8. Mary, of Sir William Baird, of Newbyth. 9. Elizabeth, third wife of David, Earl of Wemyſs.
10. Anne.

John, the Maſter, was afterwards pardoned,
and returned home, and his brother the general, with fraternal affection, reſtored to him
the eſtate for his life, which had been ſettled
upon him by his father ; and both of them dying without iſſue, and his other brothers having no iſſue, the general ſettled the eſtate upon John Paterſon, eſq; ſon of his elder ſiſter,
Grizel, by John Paterſon, of Preſtonhall, eſq;
her huſband, who accordingly ſucceeded him
therein, in 1762, and now repreſents the family.

Creation.] *Ut ſupra.*

Armi.] Quarterly; firſt and fourth ſapphire,
a ſhip at anchor, her oars erect in ſaltire, within a double treſſure with fleurs de lys counter-

L 3   flory,

ſory, topaz, for Orkney; ſecond and third
ſapphire, a ſhip under ſail, topaz, for Caithneſs; and over all, by way of ſurtout, an eſcutcheon pearl, charged with a croſs ingrailed,
diamond, for Sinclair.

Creſt.] On a wreath, a ſwan pearl, having a
ducal collar and chain topaz.

Supporters.] Two griffons, proper, armed and
beaked topaz.

Motto.] Fight.

Chief Seat.] At Dyſart in Fifeſhire.

FRASER, Lord LOVAT.

Sir Alexander Fraſer, Thane of Cowie, and
lord chamberlain of Scotland, marrying Lady
Mary Bruce, ſiſter of Robert I. and widow of
Sir Niel Campbell, anceſtor of the Duke of Argyll, by her had five ſons. Sir Simon Fraſer,
the ſecond, was anceſtor of this family; and
William, the third, was anceſtor of the Lords
Salton. Sir Simon marrying the heireſs of the
family of Biſſet, with her had the Barony of
Lovat, and many other poſſeſſions; and in the
reign of K. James I. Hugh Fraſer of Lovat, by
marrying Janet, ſiſter and heir of Hugh Fenton of that ilk, had a ſon Hugh, who ſucceeded him, and married Lady Janet Dunbar,
daughter of Thomas Earl of Murray, and by
her had Thomas, his heir, who, in the reign
James IV. was created a Baron, and made juſ-
tice-general in the North.

Hugh,

Hugh, the eighth Lord Lovat, marrying Lady Amelia Murray, daughter of John, Marquis of Athol, had four daughters, whereof the eldest, Amelia, assumed the title of Baroness of Lovat, and married Alexander Mackenzie, of Fraserdale; but after a long contest between her and Simon Frafer, of Beaufort, son of Thomas, son of Hugh, sixth Lord Lovat, it was at last determined in his favour, whereupon the said

Simon became ninth Lord Lovat. He married, first, Lady Amelia, widow of Hugh, Lord Lovat, and only daughter of John, Marquis of Athol. For this marriage he was condemned and outlawed; it being wickedly obtained, by fraud and violence; but he found out ways to escape the penalties, till at length the said Lady died.

His second Lady was Janet, daughter of Lodowick Grant, of that ilk, by whom he had two sons and two daughters.

1. Simon, Master of Lovat, who was attainted, with many others, in the parliament 1745; but it appearing that he was over-ruled, and compelled by his father, he some time after obtained his Majesty's free pardon; and, Jan. 5, 1757, was appointed lieutenant-colonel of the second battalion of the two new Highland battalions in North-America. He was afterwards advanced to the rank of a colonel and a brigadier-general, and behaved, during the last war, with great bravery and conduct, in America and Portugal. He is member for Invernefsshire.

2. Alexander, who was an officer in the army; and died in August, 1762.

L 4   3. Janet,

3. Janet, married to Macpherson, of Cluny, chief of the Macphersons, who was attainted in 1746: And,

4. Sibylla, who died unmarried.

His third wife was, Primrose, daughter of John Campbell, of Mammore, father of the present Duke of Argyll, by whom he had one son, Archibald, merchant in London.

In the rebellion of 1745, having no command in the pretender's army, he was not at the battle of Culloden, so that he was not taken till June 1746, when he was sent to London. In March following he was tried before the house of Lords in Westminster-hall; and, after seven days trial, was found guilty, received sentence of death, and, on the ninth of April, 1747, was beheaded on Tower-hill, in the eightieth year of his age, and the title and estate were forfeited to the crown.

Creation.] Lord Lovat, by James IV.

Arms.] Quarterly, first and fourth sapphire, three cinquefoils pearl, for Fraser: second and third, ruby, three Eastern crowns, pearl.

Crest.] On a wreath, a stag's head erased, proper.

Supporters.] Two stags of the last.

Motto.] *Je suis prest.*

Chief Seats.] At Castle-Downie, and Beaufort, in the county of Inverness; and at Beauly, in the county of Ross.

ELPHING-

ELPHINGSTON, Lord BAL-MERINO.

Sir James Elphingſton, youngeſt ſon of Ro-bert, the third Lord Elphingſton, having ſtu-died the law, in a ſhort time became ſo highly eſteemed for his abilities, that King James VI. made him one of the ſenators of the college of juſtice, ſecretary of ſtate, a commiſſioner of the treaſury, lord preſident of the ſeſſion, and, Feb. 25, 1603, created him Lord Balmerino, of the county of Fife.

Arthur, the late and ſixth Lord, ſucceeded his half-brother, James, the fifth Lord, in January, 1745-6, and married Margaret, daughter of Capt. Chalmers, by whom he left no iſſue.

This Lord, who was born in 1688, chuſing a military life, had a commiſſion in a regiment of foot, during the reign of Queen Anne. In the rebellion, 1715, diſliking the ſervice of King George, he reſigned his captain's commiſſion to the Duke of Argyll, and immediately joined the Earl of Mar; but that rebellion being ſup-preſſed, he had the good fortune to obtain a pardon; after which he went into the French ſervice, and, in the next rebellion, command-ed a troop of horſe at the battle of Culloden, April 16, 1746, where he was taken priſoner, and brought to the Tower of London, with the Earls of Kilmarnock and Cromartie, in May following. They were tried before the houſe of lords in Weſtminſter-hall, in July; and, on the firſt of Auguſt, received ſentence of death;

and,

and, on the 18th of that month, this Lord and the Earl of Kilmarnock were beheaded on Tower-hill. His Majesty granted his Lady a pension, in compassion to her distress.

Creation] *Ut supra.*

Arms.] Pearl, on a chevron diamond, between three boars heads erased, ruby, as many buckles of the first.

Crest.] On a wreath, a dove pearl, with a serpent, proper, linked about its legs, emerald.

Supporters.] Two griffons, proper, beaked and membered, topaz.

Motto.] *Prudentia fraudis nescia.*

Chief Seat was,] At Balmerino, in Fifeshire.

BALFOUR, Lord BURLEIGH.

Of this family, which originally took its firname from the barony and castle of Burleigh in Fifeshire, was Michael de Balfour in the said county, who, in 1315, was a member of parliament; and in 1353, Michael Balfour of Pittencrief, exchanging his lands with Duncan Earl of Fife, for the lands and barony of Monquany, the same was ratified by the Charter of K. David II. In the reign of Q. Mary, Sir James Balfour of Monquany, then clerk-register, marrying Margaret, daughter and heir of Michael Balfour of Burleigh, by her had Sir Michael, their heir, in whom the two families became united; and the said Sir Michael, being in great favour with King James VI. was

by

by him sent ambassador to the Dukes of Tuscany and Lorrain; and July 16, 1607, was created a baron by the said King, to him and his heirs general.

Robert, fourth Lord Burleigh, married Lady Margaret daughter of George, Earl of Melvil, and by her had issue Robert, Master of Burleigh; Margaret, and Mary, wife of Alexander Bruce, of Kennet, in Clacmannan, and had issue. He died in 1713.

Robert, his son, Master of Burleigh, having been guilty of a cruel murder, was forced to abscond, and afterwards joining in the rebellion of 1715, was attainted; but by the good management of his sisters the estate was recovered. He died in 1757, without issue, and his sister Margaret now represents the family; but if she dies without issue, the representation will devolve on Robert Bruce, of Kennet, esq; son and heir of her sister Mary, now one of the lords of session.

Creation.] Lord Burleigh, *ut supra.*

Arms.] Pearl, on a chevron diamond, an otter's head erazed of the first.

Crest.] On a wreath, a rock, and thereon a lady holding in her right hand the head of an otter, and in her left the head of a swan.

Supporters.] On the dexter side, an otter sejant, proper. On the sinister, a swan of the last.

Motto.] *Omne solum forti.Patria.*

Chief Seat.] At Burleigh-castle in the county of Fife.

FORBES, Lord PITSLIGO.

Sir John Forbes of that ilk, a branch of the family of Lord Forbes, marrying Elizabeth Kennedy, of the family of Dunure, by her had three sons, who were all knights. Sir William, the second, married Agnes, daughter and heir of Sir William Frafer of Philorth, anceftor of the Lord Salton : and with her had the barony of Pitfligo. From Alexander, the heir of that marriage, defcended Sir John Forbes of Pitfligo, who married Chriftian, daughter of Walter Ogilvie of Defkford, an-ceftor of the Earl of Finlater, and had a daughter Anne, married to Alexander, the tenth Lord Forbes, and a fon Alexander, who was created Baron Forbes, of Pitfligo, July 24, 1633, by Charles I.

Alexander, the fourth Lord Pitfligo, mar-ried Rebecca, daughter of John Norton, of London, merchant, by whom he had one fon, John, Mafter of Pitfligo. He took up arms in the rebellion of 1745 ; but efcaped from the rout of Culloden, 1746, and was attainted, and his eftate and honours forfeited to the crown. He died, very old, in Dec. 1762. His fon, the Mafter, married Rebecca Ogilvie, of the family of Auchincrofs, but has no iffue.

Creation.] *Ut fupra.*

Arms.] Quarterly, 1ft and 4th, fapphire; three bears heads couped, pearl, and muzzled, ruby, for Forbes. 2d and 3d, fapphire, three cinquefoils, pearl, for Frafer.

Creft.] On a wreath, a falcon of the laft.

Supporters.]

Supporters.] Two bears proper, muzzled, ruby.

Motto] *Alius ibunt qui ad summa nituntur.*
Chief Seat was,] At Pitsligo, in Aberdeenshire.

SUTHERLAND, Lord DUFFUS.

This noble family is descended from the Earl of Sutherland. Kenneth, the sixth Earl of Sutherland, having lost his life at the battle of Halidon Hill, in 1333, left two sons; from the youngest of which sons, Nicholas, descended the Lord Duffus; for this Nicholas by his brother's grant in 1360, having obtained the lands of Terboll, had the same confirmed by K. David II. and marrying Jane, daughter and heir of Reynald de Cheyne, Lord of Duffus, by her had Henry, his heir, who was father of Alexander, who married the heiress of Chisholm; and having two sons, Alexander the eldest had one daughter Christian, who was married to William Oliphant of Berindale, whereupon the Barony of Duffus, descended to William Sutherland of Quarelwood, near Elgin; from whom, in a direct line, descended Sir Alexander Sutherland, who was created Baron Duffus, Dec. 8, 1650, by King Charles II.

Kenneth, third Lord, succeeded his father James, the second Lord, in 1705; and being engaged in the rebellion, in 1715, he made his escape, and was attainted by act of parliament; after which he was taken at Hamburgh, brought to London, and committed prisoner to the Tower in 1716; but the next year being released by the act of grace, he withdrew into foreign

foreign parts, and ferved as a flag-officer in the Mufcovite fleet. He married Charlotte, daughter of Erick de Siobladé, governor and admiral of Gottenburg in Sweden, by whom he had a fon Erick, who married Mifs Dunbar, daughter of Sir James Dunbar, of Hemprigs, Bart. by whom he has two fons and three daughters; James; Axley; Elizabeth, Charlotte, and Anne.

James, the fecond Lord Duffus, married Lady Margaret Mackenzie, daughter of Kenneth, the third Earl of Seaforth, by whom he had three fons.

1. Kenneth, the late Lord.

2. Sir James Sutherland, who marrying Mary, the daughter and heir of Sir William Dunbar, of Hemprigs, Bart. changed his name to Dunbar.

3. William Sutherland, of Rofcomen, who married Mary, daughter of William, Lord Forbes.

Creation] *Ut fupra.*

Arms.] Quarterly, firft ruby, three ftars, topaz, for Sutherland; fecond, fapphire, three crofs croflets fitchy, pearl, for Cheyne; third, fapphire, a bear's head erafed pearl, for Chifholm; fourth, as the firft.

Creft] On a wreath, a cat fejant, proper.

Supporters.] Two favages proper, each wreathed about his head and middle with laurel, and armed with a battoon.

Motto.] *Without fear.*

Chief Seats.] At Skelbo, in the county of Caithnefs, and at Elgin-houfe, in the county of Elgin.

NAIRN,

The firſt of this name on record is ſaid to be Michael de Nairn, a witneſs to the grant which Robert, Duke of Albany, made to Andrew de Hamilton, of the lands of Galyſton, from whom deſcended Alexander Nairn, who, in the reign of James II. was many years comptroller of his houſhold.

In the reigns of James VI. and Charles I. Robert Nairn of Strathurd raiſed a competent fortune by the practice of the law ; but after the King's death, taking up arms in defence of King Charles II. he was ſurprized by a party of the Engliſh, and committed priſoner to the Tower of London, where he remained ten years ; but living to ſee his maſter reſtored, was, in reward of his merit, Jan. 27, 1681, created Lord Nairn. He married Margaret, daughter of Patrick Graham, of Inſbraky, and had an only daughter, Margaret, Lady Nairn, who married Lord William Murray, brother of John, firſt Duke of Athol, who in her right was Lord Nairn, and by him had iſſue, four ſons, and eight daughters ; John, Maſter of Nairn ; Robert, of Aldie, who married Jane Mercer, which name his ſon aſſumed ; William, a captain in the Swediſh Eaſt India Company's ſervice, who died without iſſue ; James, an officer in the Britiſh army ; Margaret, wife of William, Viſcount Strathallan ; Emilia, of Laurence Oliphant, of Gaſk ; Catharine, of William, Earl of Dunmore ; Marjory, of Duncan

can Robertfon, of Drumaquhan ; Charlotte, of John Robertfon, of Lude; Mary ; Louifa, wife of David Graeme, of Orchil ; and Henrietta. His Lordfhip taking part againft the government, in the year 1715, was taken at Prefton, in Lancafhire, and received fentence of death; but the King, from his great clemency, and compaffion to his numerous family, pardoned him, and gave back the eftate. He died in 1725, and was fucceeded by his eldeft fon,

· John, third Lord, who married lady Catharine, daughter of Charles, Earl of Dunmore, by whom he had iffue, John, Mafter of Nairn, an officer in the army ; Charles, an officer in the Dutch fervice ; Thomas ; Henry ; and a daughter, Clementina.

This Lord, defperately engaging himfelf in the rebellion of 1745, was attainted, and, if living, probably refides in France.

Creation.] *Ut fupra.*

Arms] Quarterly, 1ft and 4th, party per pale, diamond and pearl, a chaplet charged with four cinquefoils, all counter-changed, for Nairn. 2d, fapphire, three ftars pearl, within a double treffure counter-flory, with fleurs de lis, topaz, for Murray. The 3d is counter-quartered. 1ft and 4th, pally of fix, topaz and diamond, for Athol. 2d and 3d, topaz, a fefs checque pearl and fapphire, for Stewart, Earl of Athol.

Chief Seats were,] At Nairn, and Strathurd, in Perthfhire.

INDEX.

INDEX.

C. Caith-

G. Gal-

Lin-

Pitfligo,

T. Tor-

F I N I S.